Hill

'30' Manhattan East

ARROW BOOKS

ARROW BOOKS LTD
3 Fitzroy Square, London W1

AN IMPRINT OF THE 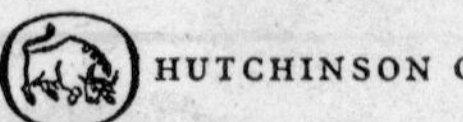 HUTCHINSON GROUP

London Melbourne Sydney Auckland
Wellington Johannesburg Cape Town
and agencies throughout the world

*

First published by
Victor Gollancz Ltd 1969
Arrow edition 1972

Made and printed in Great Britain
by The Anchor Press Ltd,
Tiptree, Essex

ISBN 0 09 906680 7

To:

Lieutenant Francis M. Sullivan
Sergeants Sam Drexler
John Marino
Lou Monaco
Joseph Doyle
Detectives Bill Confrey
Walt Curtayne
Romolo Imundi
Tom Dolan
Andy Dunleavy
Bill Ferris
Ed Kelly
Mike McCarron
Frank Lyons
Pete McPartland
Ray Seiler
Art Connolly
Ray Donnelly
Pete Durdaller
Al Lopez
Bart Mahon
Jim Murphy
Joe Ryan
Bill Seffers
Ray Sullivan
and the memory of John North

[illegible] Lenny M. [illegible]
[illegible]
Tom Martin
Lou Minnes
Joseph [illegible]
[illegible] Bill Coatner
[illegible]
[illegible]
Rod Dolan
Andy [illegible]
Bill [illegible]
Ed Kelly
[illegible]
[illegible]
[illegible]
[illegible]
[illegible]
[illegible]
[illegible]
[illegible]
[illegible]
[illegible]
Bill [illegible]
[illegible]

WEDNESDAY 3:45–9:40 P.M.

Frank Sessions walked through the open door of the twenty-fourth precinct station house at quarter of four, dodged the welter of patrolmen changing shifts, and made it to the elevator at the end of the hall in back. A uniformed sergeant, shrugging into his blue coat, came out of the locker room and called, 'Hey, look at that fashion plate!'

Sessions grinned at him, brushed a loving hand down the sleeve of his dark brown topcoat, and stepped into the car. He pushed the top button, whistled a toneless tune and adjusted the hang of the coat, checking it for stray threads. It was new and expensive and it felt good. It was also tastefully discreet, for though Sessions instinctively favoured the gaudy, he'd been a detective too many years and tailed too many men to wear anything conspicuous.

In addition to clothes, Sessions liked women, food, liquor and books, in that order. Like his clothes, the food and liquor had to be good. Books and women he wasn't so fussy about. And since the wife he'd once had long ago had been remarried the better part of a decade, he was off the hook for alimony and could indulge his tastes.

He got out on the fourth floor and went through the door marked Detective Boro Manhattan North. The room beyond was deep and wide with four twelve-by-twelve offices down the side overlooking 100th Street and two banks of lockers sectioning the rest of it. Charlie Gallagher, the borough patrolman on duty, was at the set of twin desks in front of the first bank, cradling a phone at his ear and taking notes. He nodded as Frank came through the gate and the detective gave him a solemn wink as he went by and into the third of the four offices. HOMICIDE SQUAD, MANHATTAN NORTH was lettered on the glass and three homicide detectives were inside, sitting around in shirt sleeves, talking.

They exchanged greetings with the newcomer, and Ray Ecklin, smoking a cigar behind the desk, said, 'New coat?' when Frank fitted it carefully on a hanger and hooked it on the tree inside the door.

Walt O'Connor, big, grey-haired and florid-faced, turned away from the window and said, 'New jacket too. I can't remember when I bought a new jacket.'

'I bought my kid one,' Ecklin said. 'Last September.'

Frank ignored that. He picked up the phone and started dialling a number. 'Where's the lieutenant?'

John Dunford, the other member of the group, said, 'He went out with Dugan on that fag killing.'

'You mean Baskins? The one with his throat cut?' Frank lighted a cigarette. 'They got anything on it?'

'Not that I know of.'

Frank said into the phone, 'Hello, Sweets. I got the stuff. They did a good job. They fit just right. And the tie you gave me . . . It matches. I'm wearing it now.' He laughed. 'I swear to God I'm wearing it . . .'

Other conversation stopped while Frank talked. Dunford got up and went to the cabinet of small lockers outside the door to take out some papers. O'Connor looked out the windows down at the radio cars and patrolmen in the street. Ecklin grinned at Frank around his cigar and Frank gave him the solemn wink in return. He finished his call and hung up.

'That Lucille?' Ecklin asked.

Sessions snorted. 'Oh, Jesus, don't mention that broad. She's a walking plague.' He went out to the coffee urn by the Youth Division office and drew a cup. It was all there was.

A Negro detective who dwarfed Frank's six feet came to the doorway and said, 'What's the news, Man?'

Sessions said, 'No news is good news. I can do with the rest.' He poured in sugar and milk and put the milk back in the tabletop icebox.

'I hear you got Calvert. Was he a junkie?'

'Yeah. And I lost ten pounds in three weeks chasing him.' Sessions laughed. 'Jesus. What a son of a bitch he was.'

'When's it come to trial?'

'God and the D.A. know, I don't. Anyway, it won't be for a long time.'

'So you're back on the block?'

'Back a week now, Robbie. Back a week.' He returned to the homicide office with his coffee, mashed out his cigarette in a tray on the desk and got out another. Dunford said, 'We're discussing those dart guns there's all that talk about making us use. The ones that're supposed to stun instead of kill. You know, I don't think that's a very good idea.'

Ecklin grinned and took the cigar out of his mouth. 'That depends. Are the criminals going to use them too, or are they going to keep on using the ones that shoot bullets?'

'You're not going to make the criminals use them,' Dunford said. 'What I'm worried about is the department making us use them. What'll we do then?'

O'Connor turned away from the window. 'That's an easy one to answer. We retire. I've got twenty-eight years in. I can quit any time.'

Ecklin puffed sagely. 'Well, now, that's right. All us twenty-year veterans have an easy out. But it's the youngsters I want to hear from. Like Sessions. Kids with only fifteen years in the department. What are your plans, Frank?'

'My plans are very simple. When they issue me that dart gun, I'm going to buy a pair of track shoes. Then any time I come on any trouble, I'm going to run like hell to the station house and hide in a locker.'

Dunford said, 'I don't think it's anything to laugh about.

I think it's very serious. How're we going to protect the citizens with dart guns, I ask you? If that goes through, you watch the crime-rate skyrocket.'

Ecklin grinned. 'You're behind the times, John. Didn't you know? The citizens don't want protection for themselves any more. They want it for the criminals. You've got to get with the society you're living in.'

Sessions clapped him on the back. 'Old worryguts. How's your ulcer, John?'

'It's a wonder I don't have one if you want to know. The Miranda decision, dart guns. Every year our job gets tougher and the criminals get bolder.'

The phone rang and Ecklin sat forward to pick it up. 'Homicide,' he said. 'Manhattan North, Detective Ecklin.' Then he said, 'Yes, Lieutenant,' and listened. Dunford sighed and got up. He and O'Connor started putting on their coats. Sessions moved to the windows where he took deep drags on his cigarette, sipped the brackish coffee and scanned the street. He was a man who seldom sat, seldom stopped smoking and seldom slept.

Ecklin put down the phone and told the assembly that the lieutenant was going to get a bite to eat and might stop in later. If not, he'd be at home. Dunford and O'Connor said their goodnights and went out. Sessions studied the weather and the chill May air. 'This is nothing weather,' he complained. 'Neither friend nor foe. We could have a quiet night or a busy one.'

'What difference does it make? It's Mike's turn to catch, isn't it?'

'I thought it was mine.'

'I don't know, but we ought to give it to him. He was off the chart so long at the beginning of the year we're way ahead of him.'

Mike Connager, the object of their discussion, came in then, hung a topcoat next to Sessions' and went out to check his locker. 'Anything going on?' he asked when he came back.

Frank said, 'Nothing except John's worrying about the dart guns.'

'John's been a worrier as long as I've known him.'

'Age is getting him. He must be over sixty.'

Ecklin shook his head. 'John's fifty-six. He had a birthday in March.'

Connager, who was white-haired but virile, said, 'That's not so old. I'm forty-eight.'

'And I'm forty-two. But it probably looks old to a kid like Sessions. What are you, Frank? Thirty-five?'

'Thirty-seven next month,' Frank said, mashing out his cigarette. 'But it feels like a hundred.'

'You look like a hundred. All lean and wasting away. The women are killing you.'

'Yeah,' he said, draining the rest of his coffee. 'Especially that Lucille. Jesus. Dracula's daughter.' He laughed harshly and went out to the drinking fountain to wash his cup.

The Baskin killing, wherein one Everett Baskin, male, white, known homosexual, was robbed and slain in his apartment by an unidentified Negro he had picked up, and the case of five-year-old Tommy Grove, dead of injuries his mother and her bcyfriend were suspected of inflicting, were the only two homicides undergoing active investigation. Since neither was in the stage of needing extra help, the team of Sessions, Ecklin and Connager had nothing to do but sit and wait for fresh ones to happen.

When homicide sergeant Saul Remick came in at five the waiting was under way. Remick was short, stocky and bald, tough, good-natured and smart, and he found borough headquarters settled in for the night. The Assistant Chief Inspector's office, the Burglary and Youth Division offices were empty and unlighted. Sergeant Gus Laird of the twenty-fifth detective squad had the borough duty at Gallagher's desk and the only other people present were Sessions, who was reading the afternoon *Post* at one of the desks in the section of main room opposite the homicide office, and Ecklin, who was tackling a *Times* crossword puzzle at the homicide desk. Connager, he told the sergeant, was out getting something to eat.

'Eat?' Remick said. 'At five o'clock?'

'He's a growing boy, Sarge.'

'I should grow like him.' Remick took out some papers, spread them on the front of the desk and pulled up a chair. Ecklin got up. 'You want to sit here, Sarge?'

'Naw, it's O.K.'

'Go ahead.' He chucked the paper and Remick moved into his seat. Ecklin went out to his locker and opened it. 'Hey, Frank,' he said. 'Don't you ever take off your jacket?'

'I got holes in my shirt,' Sessions said, turning pages without looking up.

'Lucille must have sharp teeth.' He pulled out a batch of papers, some of them ancient, and started to sort.

Sessions wasn't long going through the *Post* and when he chucked it aside, he went to his locker in the dormitory across the hall for a paperback book. That didn't take him long either, for he was a lightning reader and it went into the wastebasket at quarter of seven.

He joined the others then, where they were talking around Laird's desk about baseball and Mickey Mantle's switch to first base. Then they swapped stories about detectives they knew and collars they'd made until Connager brought out the homicide squad's TV from the dormitory. The others settled down to that, but not Sessions. He paced the room and stared out of windows. The fire sirens of Engine Company 76, housed in the same building, cut loose and he watched the big trucks roll. Then he got another paperback out of his dormitory locker, a thicker one this time, and read it on one of the cots. Again he went through it at a gulp and was finished by half past nine. He chucked it back into his locker and went across the hall to the others. The television was going but he ignored it. He picked up a tomorrow's

News someone had brought in, gleaned what he could from it in five minutes and looked around. 'Jesus, I get bored,' he said. 'Anybody for some coffee?'

Ecklin said, 'You ought to knock wood, Frank. That's the kind of talk that makes the roof fall in.'

Connager, solid and stolid, sitting with his chair tilted back, his arms behind his head, said, 'Watch the TV, Frank. You can find out what police work is all about.'

'Yeah,' Ecklin agreed. 'See how they win for a change.'

Sessions snorted. 'The last television mystery I saw had this private detective breaking into the bad guy's apartment to get evidence. He gets caught in the act, shoots it out with the bad guy and kills him. That's a first-degree homicide rap, right? But does our private detective go to the chair? Like hell. In the last scene he's drinking it up with a cop pal of his down in a Greenwich Village dive. Case solved.' He laughed. 'Television? Jesus.'

The phone rang and Laird answered, punching the phone buttons trying to get the right line. Finally he said, 'Detective Borough, Manhattan North, Sergeant Laird,' and listened. 'It's for you,' he said and held the phone out to Remick. 'Lieutenant Walker in the two-eight.'

Remick hitched his chair closer and took the phone. 'Yes, Lieutenant?' He listened, pulled over a pad of foolscap and picked up a pen. 'Eighth Avenue?' He wrote it down. 'And 118th Street.' He muttered a few 'yeahs' and made more notes. 'All right,' he said and hung up.

'What was that?' Connager asked.

'Two men shot on Eighth Avenue between 118th and 119th. One in the arm, the other in the stomach. They're in Sydenham Hospital.'

'Serious?' Connager asked, getting up.

'The stomach wound might be. We can take a ride over.'

The men started for their coats. Laird wrote it down on his pad. 'Sydenham?'

'That's right. And after that we'll be at the two-eight.'

WEDNESDAY 9:40–10:15 P.M.

The homicide car was an unmarked black Plymouth angled in at the kerb next to the vacant C.O.'s slot. Connager did the driving with Remick beside him. Sessions and Ecklin got in the back. The police radio came on when Connager turned the key and a voice from CB said, 'Twenty-five E, Edward,' and waited for a response.

Connager backed out, squeezing past a standing radio car which nearly blocked them. He cleared and started east. The radio said, 'Twenty-five C, Charlie,' and another voice said, 'Twenty-five Charlie, K?' CB gave an address. 'Report of a disorderly person, K?'

Remick turned down the volume and watched out the side window. 'Who's catching tonight? You, Frank?'

'We ought to let Mike do it. Ray caught the last one and I've had more than my share.'

Traffic was light on Columbus and Connager slipped through the red light. 'The next one's mine,' he said. He went through the light at Manhattan Avenue and turned north.

Sessions lighted a cigarette and held the flame for the stub of Ecklin's cigar. 'I don't know why I do this,' he said. 'Helping you foul up the air with those horse droppings you smoke.'

'It's my secret weapon. I blow smoke in the prisoners' faces and they all confess.'

'So would I. I'd confess to anything! Jesus.'

Remick said, 'That's police brutality, Ray.'

'But it's scientific police brutality.'

It was not quite ten minutes of ten when Connager pulled into the small parking area in back of the hospital and they all got out and went through the emergency entrance to the admitting desk inside. A petite, very black Negro nurse with glasses was behind the counter there and when Connager asked about the shootings, she looked back over the list of entries. 'You don't know the name?'

'Two men,' Connager said. 'Both shot. One in the stomach. Probably half an hour ago.'

Remick said, 'He'd be in ICU. Either that or the O.R.'

She ran a finger up the names, and the detectives, grouped at the counter, looked around. The area was small with a white tiled floor and seats. Men and women, mostly Negro, a few Puerto Rican, sat or stood and watched in solemn, uncurious silence.

'Alfred White,' the nurse said. 'He's in the operating room.'

Connager reached over and lifted a phone from her desk to the top of the counter. 'Who's the doctor?'

'You can't call the doctor. He's operating.'

Sessions saw a familiar figure appear at the end of a short hallway. He nudged Ecklin. 'Hey, that's Trafolo of the two-eight.'

The men left the nurse and went after Trafolo, catching him as he picked up a phone at a small service counter where the corridor turned. They shook hands around and Sessions said, 'Walker with you?'

Trafolo said no, Durkin was. He was on the fourth floor where the operation was taking place.

'What've you got?' Remick asked and took out a notebook. Connager did the same.

Trafolo opened his own notebook. 'The story is supposed to be that this fellow, Alfred White, and a friend, James Johnson . . .'

'Got addresses?'

Trafolo gave their addresses, which the homicide men wrote down. 'White and Johnson,' Trafolo went on. 'The story is they were walking on Eighth Avenue when suddenly they were fired on from ambush. White got it in the stomach, Johnson in the right arm. They didn't see who did it.'

'Crap,' Connager said, scribbling. 'Whose story is it?'

'Johnson's.' Trafolo nodded up the corridor from which he'd appeared. 'That's the man,' he said, indicating a lean, young, very black Negro in pyjamas who sat slumped in a wheelchair, his right arm in a sling, his head bent too low to show his face.

'What about White?'

'We haven't been able to talk to him yet.'

'He a Negro too?'

'No. P.R.'

The homicide men left Trafolo to make his call and went down the corridor to the man in the wheelchair. Connager had his pad ready and stood in front of him. The others moved beyond and away so the youth wouldn't feel overwhelmed. 'Your name Johnson?' Connager asked.

The thin Negro nodded but didn't raise his head.

'Where do you live?'

He muttered the same address he'd given Trafolo.

'What happened?'

'I don't know what happened,' the Negro mumbled.

The other detectives flattened themselves against the wall to let a nurse and a patient on crutches go by. Connager said, 'Jim. Your name's Jim, right? You know you got shot at, don't you? You know that happened, don't you?'

Jim nodded.

'All right, let's have the rest of it.'

Jim's head sank a little lower and his words became harder to understand. Connager had to bend close. 'M'friend and me were walking along Eighth Avenue, not doing nothing, just minding our own business . . .'

'Whereabouts on Eighth Avenue?'

''Tween a hunnert and eighteenth and a hunnert and nineteenth. When I hear some shooting and I feel it in my arm. An' my frien' goes down clutching onto his stomach and twisting. An' that's all I know.'

'Who did the shooting?'

'I didn't see who did the shooting.'

'Of course you saw who did the shooting. He shot you face on, didn't he? Don't tell me you didn't see him.'

'I didn't get no good look at him.'

'Where'd he come from?'

'Outta a doorway somewhere.'

'What doorway?'

'I dunno. All of a sudden, there he is and I see he's got a gun an' I don't see nothing else.'

Connager didn't write anything on his pad. He tucked it in his side pocket. 'How old are you, Johnson?'

'Twenty-two.'

'You a junkie?'

The Negro's head nodded slightly.

Trafolo came back and joined them. Connager said, 'All right, Johnson, we'll talk to you later. Meanwhile, you get busy remembering some things.'

They left him and went on to a circular entrance hall where the front door and elevators were. A tall, thin Puerto Rican lad of fifteen was standing there watching. He was dressed in slacks and a light-coloured jacket, his hair was black and curly, his face sombre. 'This is White's brother,' Trafolo said.

'What happened, kid?' Connager said to him. 'Who shot them?'

The boy shook his head. 'I don't know.'

'Where do you live?'

He gave a 119th Street address that matched the one Connager had.

'How old's your brother?'

'Twenty-five.'

'He ever been busted?'

The boy looked at him questioningly.

'Arrested. Has he ever been arrested?'

'Three times.'

'What for?'

The boy swallowed. 'I don't know.'

Connager turned away from him abruptly and pushed the elevator button. The doors opened and the men went in, leaving the boy behind. Trafolo pressed the fourth-floor button and the car went up. Connager mimicked the boy's 'I don't know' with savage bitterness. 'The son of a bitch,' he said. 'It's his own brother, for Christ's sake.'

Ecklin said, 'Where's the Sarge?'

'He stayed back to sweet-talk Johnson,' Sessions answered. 'Is this your case, Trafolo?'

'Yeah. It's mine.'

They found Durkin in the fourth-floor hall. He was a new detective in the twenty-eighth squad and there were introductions. Ecklin said, 'How's White?'

'White's dead.'

That made it Connager's case too. He took out his notebook. 'Where's the doc?'

A door opened and a short, white-coated Puerto Rican doctor came out into the hall in a businesslike manner. Durkin indicated him and Connager moved over to intercept the little man. 'We're from homicide, Doctor. About the man who was shot—White . . . ?'

'There was nothing we could do for him,' the doctor said. 'The bullet apparently punctured the aorta. There was massive internal haemorrhaging.' The doctor moved to go on.

'May I have your name, Doctor?'

'Segura.'

'How's that?'

'S-E-G-U-R-A.'

Connager wrote it down and the doctor departed, disappearing into another room. Connager said to Durkin, 'Where's the body?'

Durkin led them around a corner and into a ward with a dozen beds in it. One had a light over it and a curtain drawn around. Durkin gestured at it from the doorway while, from other beds, patients stared at them in the dimness.

'We'd better have the kid identify him,' Sessions suggested. 'No sense bringing in the mother.'

Trafolo said he'd get him and started for the elevator. Sessions said, 'And tell Sergeant Remick.'

They waited five minutes and then Trafolo came back with the boy. The boy was paler than before. Sessions said to him gently, 'We have to make an identification, fella. We think it's better if you do it rather than your mother. We'll take you in and show you and if it's your brother you tell us. Just nod if you want. OK?'

The youth inclined his head faintly and they all went in passing between the beds to the one on the far side with the light and the curtain. They moved inside and gathered around the husky, well-built figure that lay there, a pillow under his head, a clean white sheet covering his body, a folded towel over his face. Connager lifted the towel enough for the boy to see. He swallowed and nodded and Connager replaced the towel. They all walked out quietly and quickly.

No one spoke in the elevator but when they got out in the circular vestibule, Connager took the boy aside. 'All right now, kid. What do you want to tell us?'

'I don't know who did it,' the boy said thinly.

'What was he busted for?'

The boy swallowed and said reluctantly, 'Selling junk.'

'Who'd want to shoot him?'

'I don't know.'

'You live in the same house with him, don't you? You're around in the streets. You hear things. You know what's going on.'

'I don't know much.'

'What do you know?'

'I got a friend. I think he might know something.'

'What's your friend's name?'

'Ken.'

Connager wrote that in his notebook. 'Ken who?'

'I don't know his last name.'

'Where's he live?'

'I don't know.'

Connager pointed his pen angrily at the ceiling. 'For Christ's sake, that's your brother who's dead up there!'

The boy swallowed. 'I think he lives between a hundred and seventeenth and a hundred and eighteenth.'

'On Eighth Avenue?'

There was a sudden, sobbing wail down the corridor and the boy went whiter. It came again and Connager said to him, 'You'd better go to your mother.'

The boy left quickly and Connager tucked his notebook away. 'He opened up a little after he found his brother was dead. Not much, but a little.'

Sessions, lighting a cigarette, said, 'Seeing his mother might soften him up some more.'

Connager said, 'Christ, trying to get information . . . !'

Remick appeared and joined them. 'Johnson's co-operating a little more,' he said. 'Finding out his friend died shook him up some. Also he's hoping for a fix.'

Ecklin, chewing an unlighted cigar, said, 'They'll give him one anyway.'

'Yeah, but he doesn't know that.'

Connager said he'd go get a statement and Remick told him Johnson was in a bed now, room opposite the wheelchair.

They watched Mike leave and Sessions said, 'I hope it's a better statement than the kid brother's.'

Remick said, 'Give him a night to think about it and it might be even better in the morning.'

Ecklin grinned. 'All these junkies who get knifed and shot. They're always walking down the street minding their own business when somebody they never saw before jumps them for no reason. That story gets monotonous.'

Sessions laughed. 'They know we don't believe it, but what the hell? What else are they going to tell us? The truth?'

Remick said, 'The truth probably is either they're pushers who sold bad junk, or they robbed a pusher.'

'Either one's a killing offence. What did Johnson tell you?'

'They were walking north on Eighth between 118th and 119th when a man came out of a bar there called the Green Glove, shot them both and fled around the corner of 119th going east.'

Sessions laughed. 'For no reason, huh, Sarge?'

'He can't think of any reason.'

'He describe the perpetrator?'

Remick opened his notebook. 'The perpetrator was about six feet tall, weight a hundred and forty-five. Green turtle-neck sweater, dark pants, no hat.'

'And he doesn't know the man.'

'He claims he doesn't. But he does admit one other thing. He says a man he knows by sight, name of Trench, was a witness.'

'What's Trench's first name?'

'He says he doesn't know. Doesn't know the man, has only seen him a few times and has heard him called by that name. He thinks he lives in the area.'

Sessions said, 'I wonder if Trench is the perpetrator.'

WEDNESDAY 10:15–11:15 P.M.

Trafolo and Durkin called Lt. Walker and then went on ahead to see what they could learn at the Green Glove. Remick, Sessions and Ecklin stayed behind to wait for Connager. He rejoined them at ten twenty-five with a statement that contained what Remick had learned, no more, no less. When they got into the car and started for the bar, the radio was telling 19 Boy to proceed to 154 East 72nd Street, second floor, and investigate a possible DOA. That made Ecklin laugh. 'I had a "possible" once. Possible? The guy'd been dead in the bathtub for ten days. You needed a gas mask to go in there. I said to the people downstairs, "But didn't you smell anything?" And they said, "Sure, but we thought he was cooking corned beef and cabbage."' The men all laughed and Ecklin said, 'And I told them, "Yes, but for a week?"'

The Green Glove was on the avenue, two doors from the corner of 119th Street on the righthand side. It was a small bar, brightly glowing with neon outside, dimly lighted within, and it looked as peaceful and innocent as a baby's bedroom. Trafolo and Durkin were talking together on the sidewalk, deliberately ignored by the passing Negro strollers. It was after half past ten but the streets of Harlem looked like Fifth Avenue at noon.

'The bartender claims he doesn't know a thing,' Trafolo told the homicide men when they parked and got out. 'Didn't see the guy, didn't hear the shooting.'

'That's to be expected,' Remick said. 'Nobody ever sees or hears anything.'

Connager asked if they'd tried the bar on the corner. They hadn't and he went over. A Negro couple, arm in arm, went by, then two youths with their arms around a third. Sessions nodded and muttered, 'There's a kid who's going to be taken and doesn't know it.'

The others agreed, watching the trio go down the street. Trafolo said, 'The perpetrator came out of the door there. White and Johnson fell about here.' He moved away to mark a spot with his toe. 'Then the perpetrator ran around the corner there.'

Sessions said, 'And probably ditched the gun.'

Connager came out of the bar at the corner and returned. 'Nothing there. Let's go,' he said.

They drove in two cars to the twenty-eighth station house on West 123rd Street, parked in front and went inside, up the stairs to the headquarters of the twenty-eighth detective squad. The squad room was empty but Lt. Walker was in his office off a short hall to the right inside the gate. The furnishings were a couple of desks, chairs, a table and file cabinets. It was all there was room for. Walker, smoking a pipe, was behind one of the desks. He said, 'White died, I understand.'

Remick said, 'He's dead,' and got into the chair behind the second desk.

'There's some coffee over there. Help yourself.' He indicated an electric pot on one of the cabinets. 'Have you got anything yet?'

Trafolo said, 'I talked to the bartender at the Green Glove, where it happened. He claims he knows from nothing. He's lying through his teeth.'

Walker relighted his pipe. 'I expect he'll come in here later and give us something. You know how it is. He can't tell you anything in front of the customers. It'd ruin his reputation. But he's going to be worried about losing his licence. He should show up after the place closes.'

Sessions poured himself a paper cup full of coffee and lighted a cigarette. Walker asked about the other fellow, Johnson.

'He's a junkie,' Remick said. 'I think we can soften him up. He's worried. I told him it could've been him on the slab instead of his friend. He may give us something tomorrow.'

Connager said, 'There's also a kid brother of the deceased. A real clam. I can tell you where I'd like to stuff him!'

Walker said, 'Well, we'll check BCI on White and Johnson. That might turn up something. I understand there was a witness?'

'Somebody named Trench—supposed to live in the area. Johnson doesn't know him by any other name.'

'Trench?' Walker tilted his chair back and mused over the name. 'I wonder if he'd be in the fifty-two file.' He got up and went to a small file drawer on top of the cabinet and started through the cards of known criminals residing in the area. 'Here's a Jack Trench. Negro male. Lives on 115th

Street. That's the only one here.' He took a small packet of arrest cards out of another drawer and tried those.

'Narcotics might have a make,' Sessions said. 'It's going to do with junk.'

'We can check.' Walker found nothing in the arrest file and tried parole, also with no success. 'There's just this one,' he said and gave the card to Connager.

Connager looked at the picture of the man and read the data. 'I'll show it to Johnson,' he said and went out. Trafolo and Durkin went with him.

'Don't take our car,' Remick called after them.

'You expecting business?' Ecklin asked.

Sessions said, 'He's thinking about that possible DOA in the one-nine.'

'I'm a Boy Scout,' Remick said. 'Be prepared.'

Walker returned to his seat. 'I called Emergency Service,' he said. 'Just in case the perpetrator ditched the weapon. And photo. We'll want some pictures.'

'There's no blood on the sidewalk,' Remick told him, pouring coffee. 'Nothing to show the spot.'

'Well, we can get pictures of the Green Glove bar and the corner.' He picked up the phone and put in a call to the Bureau of Criminal Identification, requesting information on White and Johnson. He made some notes and hung up. 'White's had thirteen arrests,' he told the homicide men. 'Johnson's been on parole since 1965.'

'Thirteen?' Sessions said. 'The damned kid.'

'What kid?'

Ecklin blew out cigar smoke. 'His kid brother claimed he'd only been dropped three times.'

Sessions said, 'That punk'll be giving us trouble on his own in a couple of years.'

Two uniformed men wearing black leather, fur-lined caps, came breezily through the door. Both were young, dark-haired, lean and Irish. 'Hi, Lieu,' the first one said. 'Or is it "Captain" now?'

Walker said, 'It's still "lieutenant". You Emergency?'

'That's right. I'm Shea, he's O'Toole. He's my straight man. I hear you got a job.'

'Yes, we have.' The lieutenant wrote down their names and pushed the pad aside. 'We're looking for a gun. The perpetrator shot two men on Eighth Avenue in front of the Green Glove bar between 118th and 119th Streets. He ran around the corner on 119th. He might have got rid of the gun somewhere in that block.'

'Which way did he run, east or west?'

'East.' He turned to Remick. 'What do you think, Sarge? From Eighth to St. Nicholas?'

'I think so.'

'Both sides of the street?'

Remick agreed. 'And not just the street and the cars. I'd try areaways and front halls.'

'Gotcha.' They disappeared, dodging around a tall, coffee-coloured Negro coming in. The Negro said, 'Busy, busy, huh?'

'Are you back?' Walker asked and made introductions. The newcomer was Ed Polin, an off-duty detective in the squad. 'Why don't you go home?' Walker asked him.

'I just like to watch the rest of you guys work,' Polin chuckled and helped himself to coffee. 'What's up?'

Ecklin lighted another cigar and told him. Polin chuckled again. 'I'm glad it's not me that's working tonight. Who's got it?'

'Trafolo.'

'Who from your squad?'

'Mike Connager.'

'Yeah. I think I know him. Tall, well-built man with grey hair?'

'We've all got grey hair, or getting that way.'

'Or bald,' Remick put in.

'Only sergeants get bald. The rest of us get grey. All except Frank Sessions here. But he's only a child.'

Remick said, 'And hell with the women.'

'Yeah,' Ecklin agreed, 'but he can't last much longer.'

Sessions said, 'Jesus. The marriage brigade talking. All the grandfathers.'

The phone rang and Walker answered. He held it out to Remick. 'For you, Sarge. It's Boxton in the nineteenth.'

Remick said, 'Yes, Lieutenant,' into it, grunted a few times and made some notes. Sessions said to Ecklin, 'What do you want to bet that "possible DOA" on East 72nd Street has just turned into a probable homicide?'

Ecklin grinned. 'That's a pretty fancy address, Frank. If you're going to catch one it's a good thing you're wearing those new clothes.'

On the phone Remick was saying, 'The M.E.'s been called, but not the homicide M.E.?' He made a couple more notes, said, 'All right,' and hung up. He picked up the phone again and dialled.

Sessions said, 'What is it? The 72nd Street one?'

Remick said, 'You know Monica Glazzard?'

'The columnist?'

Remick nodded.

Ecklin said, 'You mean she's the DOA?'

Remick identified himself into the phone and asked if Dr. Ballou was the homicide M.E. on duty tonight. Then he said to cancel the regular M.E., hung up and pulled a slip of paper out of his wallet. 'It's Monica Glazzard,' he said. 'It's apparent suicide but there are a couple of things about it that seem a little funny.' He dialled a Long Island number from the slip of paper.

'Boxton thinks everything's a little funny,' Sessions said. 'A guy can't jump off a building without Boxton thinking somebody pushed him.'

'He's a worrier,' Ecklin agreed. 'But you'd worry too, Frank, if you had the nineteenth. The homicides are fewer but the DOAs are bigger.'

Polin said, 'Man, Monica Glazzard, that's going to be hot

stuff. A newspaper columnist like her? She's going to be front page all right.'

Ecklin said, 'Frankie, if she's a homicide, you're going to get your name in the paper. You're going to be famous.'

'Yeah,' Sessions answered. 'With a bunch of reporters and all the brass from downtown on my neck. You can have those celebrity homicides.'

Remick got Dr. Ballou on the phone and gave him the essentials: DOA at 154 East 72nd Street, apartment 2A. Question as to cause of death. 'It'll take him about an hour,' he said, hanging up and lifting the phone again. 'Meanwhile, we'd better get on over as soon as I call Laird. Connager left two ninety-nine for us, I hope.'

WEDNESDAY 11:35–11:45 P.M.

When Sessions, Remick and Ecklin arrived at 154 East 72nd, it was eleven thirty-five and four police cars were double-parked out front. Two were radio cars and two were unmarked sedans belonging to the nineteenth detective squad. Number 154 was a nine-storey duplex with a canopy over the walk, located a few doors east of Lexington. The lobby inside was elegant rather than modern. There were no vast walls of glass, piped music, or changing fountains under spotlights. Here the marble was real, the furnishings leather, the mirrors ornate. Here, also, were seven people, two patrolmen, a uniformed sergeant and his chauffeur, Lieutenant Boxton, chief of the nineteenth detective squad, the doorman and the superintendent.

Boxton detached himself from the others to greet Remick and the homicide men as they entered. 'This can be a son of a bitch,' he said, 'if it turns out to be a homicide. I hope to hell it isn't, but you'd better be ready.'

Remick asked what the story was and he said he didn't know much, he'd only just got here himself. 'I'd better let you get the story from them.'

'Who's here from your squad?'

'Devlin and D'Amato. They're checking out the other people in the building. Devlin's catching. He's new. He's only been in the bureau ten months. But he's a good man and I don't want to take it away from him if it can be helped. Which one of your men's got it?'

'Frank. Assuming it's a homicide.'

'And that's the way we're going to play it until we learn different. And listen, Frank, you kind of point the way for Con Devlin, will you? He can pick up a lot from you. I don't mean you have to hold him by the hand. He's not stupid and he's willing to learn.'

Sessions said, 'Sure, Lieutenant.'

'Anything you want, just ask.'

They moved on to the waiting men and Remick introduced himself. 'Now what's happened here? Who's the first man on the scene?'

One of the patrolmen said, 'I was, Sergeant. Nick Barrancas. Me and my partner, John McPartland here, were in radio car nineteen B and we got a call.' He took out his notebook. 'About ten twenty-five to ten-thirty. About a possible DOA on the second floor at this address.'

'We heard it,' Remick said.

'Well, we got here five minutes later and asked the elevatorman about it.'

'What's your name?' Remick asked the elevatorman.

The man, wearing a uniform a size too large, said nervously, 'Harry Berkman.'

'Where do you live, Harry?'

He gave an 86th Street address and Barrancas went on. 'He said he didn't know anything about any DOA so we went up to the second floor with him. There're two apartments there. 2A and 2B and the call didn't say which. It just said second floor. So McPartland and I rang both bells and a man named Krick answered at 2B and he didn't know anything about any DOA. But nobody answered 2A and Berkman here said the newspaper columnist Monica Glazzard lived there but she was never in in the evening. She's out every night at parties and the theatre and nightclubs and things getting material for her column. He said he didn't see her go out but he comes on at five o'clock and she's usually gone by then.'

Remick said, 'When did you last see her, Harry?'

The elevatorman thought about it. 'Sunday evening,' he said. 'She came in about seven o'clock.'

'What hours do you work?'

'I'm on from five in the afternoon till one in the morning this week.'

'You didn't see her yesterday or Monday?'

'No, sir.'

'Where was she?'

'I don't know. Probably out. She usually goes out in the afternoon sometime. And she usually doesn't get in until after one. Sometimes it's earlier but most of the time she's out till two or three.'

'How do you know that?'

'When I work the other shifts. The eight to five, or the one to ten in the morning.'

'So when was it you last saw her?'

Berkman wet his lips. 'Sunday,' he said. 'Sunday evening.'

'And you haven't laid eyes on her since then?'

'No, sir.'

'How was she when you last saw her?'

Berkman shrugged. 'Fine. Like usual. She had a bag. Paper bag. She said, "Hello, Harry"—like that. I said, "Hello, Mrs. Glazzard." '

'What'd she have in the bag?'

'I think she'd been to a delicatessen. Probably something to eat.'

'Did anybody go up to see her that night?'

'No, sir.'

'How about Monday night and last night—while you were on duty?'

'No, sir. Well, just Mr. Motley.'

'Who's Mr. Motley?'

'He's a friend of Mrs. Glazzard's. I think he works for her.'

'Where does he live?'

'I don't know, sir.'

'When did you see him?'

'I think it was Monday night. He came in about half past eleven and went up to her apartment.'

'I thought you said she was out Monday night.'

'He'd come in sometimes when she wasn't there.'

'How does he get in? Does he have a key to her apartment?'

'I believe he does, sir.'

'You're sure he didn't go up to her apartment last night?'

'Yes, sir. It was Monday night, I'm sure.'

'Maybe it was Sunday night?'

'No, it was Monday.'

'Why are you sure it was Monday and not Sunday?'

'Because I had the feeling Mrs. Glazzard was out. She was in Sunday night.'

Remick turned to Barrancas. 'O.K., you rang her apartment and got no answer. Go ahead.'

'So we tried the super. Mr. Hogarth here.'

Hogarth stepped forward. 'I thought it was a gag of some kind. I thought somebody was trying to play some kind of a joke. I told the officers that.'

'We persisted,' Barrancas said. 'Finally Mr. Hogarth got the keys and we went in.'

'It's not that I'm not co-operative with the police,' Hogarth said. 'I don't believe in opening up the apartments without good reason. And I really thought it was a gag. I don't mean the police—I meant somebody phoning in.'

'Just a minute,' Remick said. 'Just a minute. You didn't know about it; Berkman didn't know about it. Who reported the DOA?'

Boxton said, 'That's one of the funny things. It was an anonymous phone call. Devlin checked with CB. That was the first thing he did. And they said it was anonymous. And with the apartment locked, that raises the question who knew she was dead in there?'

'Who indeed.' Remick made a note. 'All right, Barrancas, you wouldn't let the super talk you out of it. You made him open up, right?'

'Yes, sir.'

'You used your head.'

'All I was thinking, Sarge, was if I reported it as a false alarm without going in there and it turned out it wasn't . . . ! Anyway, we went in and we found her. So I called CB and I called the desk and I said it looked like suicide. Then I questioned Berkman and Mr. Hogarth and then Sergeant Kelly arrived.'

Sessions said, 'Where was she found?'

'In the bedroom. In bed.'

'You touch anything?'

'No, sir. I went close enough to see she was dead and then we left everything as we found it and locked the place up again.'

'You get a doctor?'

'Yes, sir. A Dr. Grove came at 11:05, just a couple of minutes after the detectives arrived. He pronounced her dead.'

Two men came through the front door and one, viewing the collection of uniformed men and detectives, said, 'Looks like we've got something.' He was Paget of the *News*, he said. They'd picked up the call on their police radio. 'Anybody we should know about?'

Lt. Boxton said the dead woman was supposedly Monica Glazzard.

'Not our Monica! The newspaper columnist?'

'That's what we understand. We don't have a positive identification yet. We're only just going up to view the scene.'

The reporters wanted to go along but Boxton said no unauthorised personnel could enter the apartment, but he'd do everything he could for them as soon as possible. He said to the super, 'You've got the key? Let's go.'

Seven of them went around to a corridor on the right where the elevator and the stairs were—Boxton, the super, the homicide men, Patrolman Barrancas and Sergeant Kelly.

They boarded the elevator and rode up one floor, getting out into a similar hall. The door to 2A was on the right, toward the front of the building, and was closed. The door to 2B was wide open but no one was in sight.

'Mr. and Mrs. Krick live here,' the super said.

Boxton grunted. He said to Remick, 'I called the district commander. He's coming over. I don't know about Chief Nyborg.'

The super fitted the key in the lock and opened the door. There was a green carpeted hallway through to a large living room, a staircase on the right with a door to the kitchen adjacent. 'She's upstairs in the first bedroom,' the super said.

They went up with Boxton leading the way and he opened the first door on the left. Directly in front of them was a large double bed and Monica Glazzard lay in it peacefully. She was on her back, her head on the pillow, the covers drawn up just below her breasts, her arms lying exposed along her sides. Her hair was dark and curled, her pink and white nylon nightgown not quite sheer, her attractive face turned slightly toward the viewers. She was a slender woman who had worked at keeping herself youthful and she had the figure and appearance of someone much younger than her close to fifty years.

The room was spacious and uncluttered. There was a chaise longue in the far corner, a dressing table, easy chair, a cabinet bar in another corner, a bureau around by the dressing room entrance, low bookcases under the middle window. A pair of small tables with large lamps flanked the bed and on the nearest, close by the body, a small empty bottle and glass stood beside the phone.

Boxton and the homicide men went in and Sessions told Barrancas and the super to wait outside. Remick and Ecklin bent close over the body. Remick said, 'No bruises on the face and neck, Frank. Fleck of blood on the lips.' He stepped aside to give Sessions a chance. Ecklin said, 'She looks kind of "laid out".'

'Yeah, she does,' Sessions agreed and studied her critically. Her skin was remarkably young-looking, but wrinkles and a slight sagging of the flesh under the chin and around the throat showed the woman was older than she appeared.

Ecklin stooped to read the label on the bottle and Sessions went back to the super. 'What's your first name?'

'Claude.'

'You live here?'

'Yes. I have an apartment on the first floor rear.'

Sessions had his notebook out. 'What about Mrs. Glazzard, Claude? Who knows her? Who works with her? She have a secretary?'

'Yes, a Miss Butelle. Stocky sort of woman. Comes in daily.'

'Know her first name? Know where she lives?'

Hogarth didn't.

'Relatives? Next of kin?'

'I believe she has a daughter. I don't know her name. I don't know where she lives.'

'Married or single?'

'I don't know that either.'

'O.K. When did you last see this Mrs. Glazzard alive?'

'I'm not really sure. Last week sometime. I fixed a leaky

faucet for her around Wednesday or Thursday. Miss Butelle called me about it and I went in about two in the afternoon. Mrs. Glazzard came into the kitchen in a dressing gown when I finished to give me a dollar. I didn't see her after that until —tonight.'

'How was she? How did she behave?'

'Very normally. You know, quick. She was very quick the way she moved and talked.'

'She didn't sound depressed?'

'Oh no, sir.'

'How many other people work in this building?'

Hogarth counted them off on his fingers. 'On the elevators and door there's Berkman. He's on now till one. There's Norman Caligliaro. He relieves tonight and will be on till ten tomorrow morning. Lester Fritz will come on at eight—no, that was today. He's off now till Friday at five. Phil Lowe comes on at eight tomorrow morning. Eight till five. And Carl Mancini is on ten to seven.'

'Anybody else employed here?'

'Well yes, two men on the service elevators. George Layman and Pete Tuckman. And there's Joe Moriarty, the janitor. He and his family have an apartment in the basement.'

'You have the addresses of all these people?'

'In my office.'

'You want to get me those addresses?'

Ecklin came up then. 'You got a phone in that office, Claude?'

'Yes, sir.'

'All right, I'll go with you and get the addresses. And I'll check out that prescription.' He said to Sessions, 'It's the Macon Drug Store on Lexington. Sleeping pills, a full bottle a week ago. A Dr. Stevens wrote the prescription.'

Frank nodded and they went out. He wandered over to the windows and pushed the curtains aside. 'All locked,' he said.

Remick, touring the room, paused to study the items on the dressing table. 'And no suicide note so far.'

'No suicide note. Just a handy pill bottle to take its place. You want to bet that isn't supposed to tell us a story?' He went through the dressing room and into the large bathroom beyond. A pair of nylons were hung over the shower curtain, a slip lay soaking in one of twin washbasins, a soapy bra and pair of underpants lay in the other, from which the water had leaked. Sessions looked in the laundry hamper beside a sensitive set of bathroom scales, but it was empty. He opened the door of the medicine cabinet and read the labels on some of the bottles without touching them. There was a space on one of the shelves that the pill bottle would fit. He closed the mirrored door and came back. 'She's a pill-lady,' he said. 'Thyroid extract, three kinds of headache remedies, vitamin capsules, benzedrine.'

Remick said, 'And cosmetics! You see what she's got on that table?'

'She doesn't stint herself on booze either.' Sessions looked over at the curtains. 'I wonder if she always slept with the windows closed.'

Boxton was at the foot of the bed, still staring at the body. 'You don't think it's suicide?'

'It's up to the M.E. to call it so I won't guess, but she washed out her clothes; and all those pills she takes . . . You ever read her column, Lieutenant?'

'Sometimes.'

'She sound to you like the suicide type?'

'Not really.'

'Kind of a brittle, tangy flavour in her writing. And she could do a job on people. She took a new playwright apart in her column today. She's the kind who could make enemies.'

Detectives Cornelius Devlin and Ralph D'Amato came in then. Devlin said, 'We checked out the building, Lieutenant. One family's away on vacation, according to the super. Two others are out for the evening. We talked to the other three—

four, counting the Kricks. They didn't see anything or hear anything. They can't tell us anything. They hardly knew the woman. Only saw her at meetings sometimes. You know, about running the building. It's a co-op.'

'What about people in the apartment above this? Their living room would be right over this bedroom.'

'Their name's Paige. They're not home yet.'

'O.K., keep a check on when they and the other family get in.' Boxton introduced the detectives around. 'Con Devlin is in charge of the investigation,' he said. 'Con, you'll be working with Frank Sessions. We're assuming this is a homicide.'

'Yes, sir.' They shook hands.

'Tell them what CB told you. About the anonymous call.'

'Well, the first thing I did was call CB to find out who made the report and CB said it was an anonymous phone call. The person just said there was a body on the second floor at 154 East 72nd Street and hung up when they asked for the name.'

Sessions said, 'Was it a man or a woman who made the call?'

'CI wasn't sure. They said it sounded like a man but it could have been a woman. It sounded like there was an attempt to disguise the voice.'

'Anything else?'

'Not much. That made me wonder, of course, and then the scene here . . .' He indicated the room. 'I thought it looked kind of suspicious. I mean the bottle on the table. I didn't think she'd leave the bottle there. And there's no note, at least that we can find. I took a look downstairs. She's got an office on the other side of the dining room but there's no note there either.'

Sessions said, 'What about the daughter? You got a make on her?'

'Yeah. The daughter's name is Linda Glazzard and she lives at 302 East 57th, apartment 9D. We put in a call but there's no answer.'

'She's got a secretary . . .'

'Mildred Butelle. We called her. She's the one who told us about the daughter. She's coming over. There's also a cleaning woman, Nettie Sandhurst. Coloured. Works Mondays and Thursdays. Don't have a phone number for her yet but it may be in the deceased's address file downstairs.'

'What about this man Motley?'

'I don't have anything on him yet. The secretary doesn't know his address and he's not in the phone book.'

Sessions made notes. 'All right, what else has been done? Who's been notified?'

Boxton said, 'Photo's been called. And you got hold of the M.E.'

Sessions looked at his watch. It was quarter of twelve. 'How long ago was photo called?'

'Half an hour.'

'How about a policewoman to search the body? How about the police lab?'

They hadn't been called. Sessions said, 'I'll call them. How about it, Lieutenant? Shall we seal off this room now?'

Captain Otto Conklin, Fourth District Commander, a big, red-faced man with crewcut grey hair came into the room. Those present greeted him respectfully and he nodded in acknowledgment and viewed the body. He asked a few questions and was given a briefing. 'I want this to get the full treatment,' he said. 'Assume it's a homicide unless or until you learn different. Get moving on it. Where's that daughter you say she's got, and that secretary? You ought to have them here by now.'

The men said, 'Yes, sir.'

'This woman's a big name. If it's a homicide, I want you working around the clock on it. Boxton, give them all the men they need.'

'Yes, sir.'

Conklin turned to go. 'There're six reporters downstairs in the lobby. Give them everything you can. I want a good press on this. All right, I'll get out of your way. Things are moving slow enough as it is.'

When he got to the door, Boxton said, 'Has the chief been informed?'

Conklin turned. 'I called him. He's not coming over but he's going to want a full briefing first thing tomorrow morning. They're going to be asking him questions about it downtown.'

When he was gone, Boxton said, 'All right, let's empty this room. We're not getting anything done standing around here.'

They trooped out and Devlin caught Sessions in the crowded hall. 'Listen, Frank, I'm kind of new at this and it looks big. You know your way around so you give me any ideas you have or tell me what you want done.'

Sessions said, 'I'll tell you what you can do. Check all the windows and doors for signs of breaking and entering.'

'What're you going to be doing?'

'I'm going to see if the Kricks will let me tie up their phone.'

WEDNESDAY 11:45 P.M.–THURSDAY 12:25 A.M.

The Kricks were eager to co-operate with the police. 'Be our guest,' Mr. Krick said, showing Sessions the living room phone. 'It's a murder?'

'We don't know yet what it is.'

'I thought you said you were from homicide. You wouldn't be called in . . .'

'We're called when there's any suspicion or when an attack might result in death. What's your occupation, Mr. Krick?'

'I'm a corporation attorney. We really hardly knew Mrs. Glazzard.'

'You know any of the people who visit her?'

'No. Our hours don't jibe. She's out most of the night. We're in.'

Sessions laid his notebook on the table beside the phone and made three quick calls; one to photo to find out what the delay was, one to the police lab and one for a policewoman. Then he looked up Linda Glazzard in the phone book, tried her number and got no answer.

'I'd appreciate your not letting anyone else use this phone,' he said to the Kricks. 'I don't want reporters and a lot of other people tying it up.'

'You can count on us, sir.'

Sessions went out and down the stairs to the lobby. Berkman, the elevatorman, was still there along with McPartland, six newsmen and Sergeant Kelly's chauffeur. The newsmen wanted Sessions' name and a story. 'It's Monica Glazzard?' they asked.

'That's what we understand. Any of you know her?'

Three had worked with her some years back, in the days before she had her own column. They were not in touch with her now.

Two men came in, one carrying a big box camera and tripod on his shoulder. 'Photo?' Sessions said.

'That's right. My name's Kuhn. This is MacAllister. Where do we go?'

Sessions took them up in the elevator, through the open apartment door and up the stairs. Remick and Boxton joined them. They went into the bedroom and Kuhn set down the camera. Remick said, 'You're going to want colour, Frank?'

'I'm going to want colour shots of the DOA. Black and white will do for the rest.'

Kuhn said, 'You'll want the room here. Anything else?'

'I'm going to want the whole damned apartment. Every room.'

'Connecting shots too,' Remick told Kuhn. 'So you can get the layout from the pictures.'

'I got you.'

Sessions took Kuhn by the arm. 'Come on in here. This dressing room. Get the sliding doors to these closets. I want a record of how far open they are. Now in here, this bathroom. I want a picture of the medicine cabinet the way it is with the door closed to show that's the way it was found. Then open it and take a picture of the contents.' He brought Kuhn out again. 'And all the windows and doors. The way the locks are. And, of course, this bottle and glass on the table.'

Kuhn said, 'You're the boss,' and started to set up the camera. Ecklin came in and paused for a moment to watch. 'Where'd you get that box?' he said. 'Off Mathew Brady?'

Kuhn patted it. 'You can't beat this camera. These wood ones get you pictures you just can't take with metal ones. Something about wood. It breathes.'

Ecklin said to Sessions, 'I checked out the prescription and the doctor. The prescription is once refillable and was refilled on the third. The doctor says the deceased suffered from hypertension and has been an insomniac since he's known her. It's been getting worse and it's pretty strong stuff he's been feeding her. One pill half an hour before retiring and if that doesn't work, she can't have another for two full hours. Outside of the insomnia and nervous energy, she's O.K. No history of emotional disturbance, was well balanced, well adjusted. The last time he saw her was March thirteenth at three in the afternoon when he gave her a yearly checkup. Everything in order.'

'Not a suicide type?'

'He said he can't imagine her taking her own life even though he doesn't know what kind of a life it is. He says she's too tough.'

Sessions accepted that with a nod and started drawing a crude sketch of the murder room in his notebook. He said, 'There's that guy Caligliaro. Elevatorman who relieves Berkman at one. If he saw the deceased last night . . .'

'I called his home but he's already left to come in here.'

'And that cleaning woman, Nettie Sandhurst . . .' He broke off when McPartland appeared in the doorway. 'Yeah, pal? What's the good word?'

'The people who live on the floor above have just come in. I've got them in the lobby.'

Ecklin said, 'I'll talk to them, Frank.'

'Thanks, Ray. I want to get photo straightened out.'

Ecklin went off with McPartland and Sessions watched while Kuhn set the camera in three different locations to get the deceased from varying angles. When her position and the condition of the bedcovers were established, Frank had him take a closeup of her head and shoulders. Then he said to Remick, 'What about it, Sarge? Do we wait for the M.E. or shall we see what's under the covers?'

'Let's take a look.' Remick lifted her arms and Sessions pulled the covers back, exposing the whole of her body. The nightgown was full length with a pink underlayer and a gauzy white mesh outside. The bottom of it came smoothly to her ankles and only her white, slender feet were revealed. 'Talk about being laid out,' Sessions said. 'How do you like that, Sarge? She might be lying in her coffin.'

'All smoothed out. Might have been done by somebody who loved her.'

'No blood, no visible injuries, no signs of a struggle.' Sessions replaced the covers the way they'd been and Remick lowered her arms. Sessions said to Kuhn, 'I'm going to want some more shots when the M.E. moves her. Especially of the pillow.'

'O.K. Meanwhile, if you'll get the hell out of the way, I'll photograph that bottle.'

'Yeah, pal. And do me a favour. Make it so I can read the label.' He went out and down the stairs, encountering Ecklin coming up. The Paiges, Ecklin told him, had little to contribute. 'Their living room may be over the bedroom here but they've never heard anything. They'd be in their own bedroom another floor up by the time Monica ever got into hers and this building's too solid to carry sounds anyway. They've seen this guy Motley a few times in the elevator. Tall, dark, good-looking, early to mid-thirties, friendly and polite. They don't know him by name but he seemed to have access to the apartment here.'

'Young, good-looking, huh? Maybe a lover?'

Three reporters came up the tenants' staircase and in through the front door. Sessions said, 'Hey, hey. Outside. Out.' He moved them back into the hall.

'Nobody's telling us anything,' they complained. 'We want a story.'

'We don't have a story. Monica Glazzard's dead. That's all we know. We'll tell you more when we've got more.' He beckoned McPartland, who was coming up from the lobby. 'Mac, you're on duty at this door. No unauthorised personnel are to come in.'

Dr. Ballou, assistant medical examiner on homicide duty that night, got out of the elevator and stepped between reporters. He was a tall, slender, dark-haired young man wearing glasses and a light topcoat. 'You can let him in, Mac,' Sessions said and went to shake the doctor's hand. 'I'm Frank Sessions. We met down in the autopsy room a couple of months ago when Dr. Grossman was looking for the bullet that killed Lombard. You helped him find it.'

Ballou smiled. 'I remember. A twenty-two. Deep in the back muscles. You ever find the man who fired it?'

'Ten days ago. A junkie named Calvert.' Sessions led him inside to the staircase.

'And this one is Monica Glazzard, the columnist?'

'Yeah. Supposed to be suicide, but we don't think it is.'

'Why?'

Sessions told him as they went up the stairs: the anonymous call, the 'laid out' appearance of the body, the lack of a note, the presence of the too obvious bottle.

Con Devlin caught them at the top. 'Hello, Doc. Listen,

Frank. I checked doors and windows. No signs of tampering. At least obvious signs. Should we get safe and loft down to take the locks apart just in case?'

'Call them in the morning, Con. No sense dragging them out here tonight.'

They went past the people gathered in the hallway and entered the bedroom. Kuhn and MacAllister were just bringing the camera out. 'We got everything.'

'The medicine cabinet?'

'Yes, and the stuff in the sinks. That's pretty swank. Two washbasins in one bathroom. And the john in a little room by itself.'

'Not like some of those Harlem apartments, huh? Jesus.'

'You going to want that shot of the pillow now?'

'When we turn her over.' Sessions went to the bed where Remick and Boxton were explaining to Ballou that this was how they'd found the deceased. Ballou studied the scene briefly, stripped the covers down for a look at the rest of her and flexed one of her arms. He lifted the eyelids, one by one, and leaned close, then got out a pencil flash for a more thorough inspection. He hmmed to himself, looked at her mouth, forced it open and peered inside with the light. He examined the skin of her face and throat and chest, lifted her ringless left hand and looked at her fingernails. Then he worked his fingers through her hair, feeling for head injuries. Finally he said to Sessions, 'Help me turn her over.'

They pushed her onto her side and Remick went around the bed to pull on her arm and hold her steady. The visible part of her back was purple with thin yellow lines showing the creases of the bedsheets and the straps of her nightgown.

Sessions said to Kuhn and MacAllister, 'Set for a picture? I want the sheet and the pillow. Give me a closeup of the pillow.'

Ballou got out of the way and Sessions studied the indentation of the pillow while the camera was being readied. Remick said to Ballou, 'She's drooling something out of her mouth.' Ballou noted the fact, nodded and ignored it.

When Kuhn had taken his pictures, Sessions turned the pillow over. The underside was clean. 'O.K., Sarge.' He replaced the pillow and they let the body roll back. Ballou turned to the bedside table. 'That the barbiturate bottle? Can I touch it?'

'Not yet, Doc. It's got to be fingerprinted.'

'I'm going to want it.' He took out an inquisition sheet from an inside pocket.

'You'll probably get to take it with you if the lab doesn't hang us up.'

'And I want the lab to put bags over her hands.'

'You figure homicide by strangulation then, huh, Doc?'

'I'm not prepared to say what it is until after the autopsy but I'm going to preserve what's under her fingernails just in case. There's enough here that's suspicious . . .'

'Such as?'

'The things you told me—lack of a suicide note, the bottle there. Also, there are a couple of petechial haemorrhages involving the conjunctival tissues of the eyes . . .'

'That ought to make it pretty conclusive, Doc.'

'That occurs in cases of asphyxiation, yes, but it can also occur from pressure of the blood if the body is face down . . .'

'This body wasn't face down. The lividity . . .'

'I know. And there's a fleck of blood on the lips, which is also consistent with asphyxiation. However, there are no bruises or other indication of how such asphyxiation might have been achieved, so even if that's the cause of death that doesn't indicate that it's a homicide. She might have choked on something, for example.'

'If the perpetrator wore gloves . . .'

'Then there might not be bruises. As I say, it's suspicious, but that's all I'll say at this time.'

'How soon can you do the autopsy?'

'First thing in the morning.'

'You know, we could take her right down there tonight . . .'

'It's not that critical, is it? Won't morning do just as well?'

'I suppose,' Sessions conceded. 'Nine o'clock?'

'That would be the time. You plan to be there?'

'I'll be there.'

Ballou indicated the phone on the bedtable. 'O.K. to call the morgue wagon from here?'

'I've got a phone next door.' He took the doctor out and a policewoman was coming up the stairs. She was stocky and broad of beam. 'There's a body to search?'

'Right in there. Lieutenant Boxton's in charge.' Sessions went around the woman and down the stairs, taking Ballou into the Kricks' apartment through the open door. Ballou called for the wagon and started filling out the inquisition sheet while Sessions phoned the police lab again to give them a nudge. He was told they were on their way. The Kricks, watching television, said, 'Can we give you a drink?' but both men refused. Sessions said, 'Not that I couldn't use one.'

They went out again and encountered the policewoman on the staircase coming down. 'Find anything?'

'She's clean. No place to hide anything with nothing but a nightgown.'

'Women have built-in hiding places.'

The policewoman laughed. 'That's the truth. And some of the things you find! But not this one.'

She went out and Sessions paused by the apartment staircase. 'What about time of death, Doc?'

Ballou said, 'That's hard to say. Rigor mortis is disappearing and there's no decomposition, but there isn't any way to tell how warm that room's been. It's facing north so there's no sun, but that doesn't mean it couldn't be pretty warm.'

'You want to guess at a time?'

'It could be twelve hours, it could be twenty-four hours. There's no way to be sure. If we can find out when she was last seen, that would help. Or, if we can find out when she ate last and see what's in her stomach . . .'

'Twelve to twenty-four at the outside . . .'

'Approximately.'

'When's the most likely? Eighteen?'

'That's probable but don't depend on it. From the fact she was in her nightgown, I'd guess death occurred sometime between the time she went to bed and the time she usually would get up.'

Sessions laughed. 'Hell, we can figure that much ourselves.'

Two uniformed policemen came up the stairs from the lobby carrying equipment kits. 'Police lab,' one said. 'This the place?'

'This is the place.' Sessions recorded their names and one of them, looking around, said, 'Some people know how to live.'

'We're going to want bags on the hands of the deceased,' Sessions told them. 'Fingerprint the bottle and glass on the bedtable right away. Up the stairs. You can't miss it.'

'Grand Central Station,' the man said and they started up. Kuhn and MacAllister came down carrying the camera. 'How many rooms have you got here?' Kuhn asked Sessions. 'This is an all-night job.' They went into the living room. Devlin came out of the kitchen. 'Everything's neat and clean, he said. 'Dishes washed, ashtrays empty. Even the typewriter in her office's got a cover on it. This is the only thing I could find.' He showed Sessions a flexible blue plastic dictaphone belt. 'It was in the wastebasket in the office.'

A section of the belt had been etched with the recording needle and Sessions said, 'Did you play it back?'

'I don't know how to work the machine.'

Ballou said the belt looked like the kind they used in the autopsy room and he could set it up to play.

Sessions saw them off. 'Pray that it's a suicide note, Doc,' he said. He went out in the corridor but the reporters had returned to the comfort of the lobby. Ecklin came up from there and said he'd been talking to them and Berkman. 'What did Ballou have to say?'

'Nothing. Suicide, accident, homicide. Take your pick.'

'They never talk.'

'You can name your own time of death too.'

'I know. I had a case last year. A young bride DOA. The husband claimed she was alive and well when he left for work at ten minutes past eight in the morning, DOA when he got home at half past five. Naturally we figured him as the likely perpetrator—especially if the M.E. would say she was dead before ten minutes past eight. So we kept nudging him to give us a time of death. You know what he finally said? "When did the husband last see her alive?"'

Ecklin and Sessions laughed and McPartland, guarding the door, said, 'Did you ever catch the perpetrator?'

'The next afternoon. It was the janitor in the building. That reminds me. I don't think anybody's talked to this janitor yet.'

Sessions said, 'Nor the secretary. What the hell's keeping her?'

'Has anybody got the daughter?'

'There's no answer at her place. I'll give her another try after I check on those guys from the lab and if that doesn't raise anything, we can send a car over.'

THURSDAY 12:25–12:45 A.M.

Linda Glazzard greeted the night doorman as he helped her from the taxi while, behind her, David Allison paid the driver and followed. They went through the revolving doors to the lobby and Linda said, 'Hello, Bill,' to the elevatorman. After that she only had eyes for David, smiling at him maternally on the ride up. He was holding himself with the special care of a man who's had more to drink than he ought.

When they got out on the ninth floor, Linda unlocked the door of apartment D, directly opposite the elevator, and went in, snapping on lights. David followed rockily. 'Sit, sir,' she said, indicating the big living room sofa. 'I'll put some water on for coffee.'

'I don't want to sit,' he said. 'I won't get up again.'

She went first into the large bedroom where she put her purse on the dresser and threw her spring coat on the bed. She touched her hair in front of the mirror more by force of habit than because it demanded care. They'd only held hands in the cab. They hadn't wrestled.

The hair was bottled blonde, not because she particularly preferred that colour but because her mother's hair was dark. She'd started dyeing her own eleven years before, in her first year at college, as one of her points of rebellion, one of her many needed ways of establishing herself as an individual. Now the hair colour was habit and had lost its cachet as a blow for freedom, but her need for the freedom was still there. It was so damnably difficult to be the daughter of a celebrity. No matter where you went it was the same. 'Glazzard? Did you say your name was Glazzard? Are you any relation to Monica Glazzard? . . . You mean you're Monica Glazzard's daughter?!!' Life would have been a damned sight easier if when her mother had taken her one ill-fated venture into matrimony she had picked a man named Jones.

She came out of the bedroom into the narrow kitchen that was squeezed between it and the living room. She put water into the kettle and turned on the gas. David came to the doorway and watched. She didn't see the way he did it but she could feel it. He was contemplating the body under the dress. It was a very well-developed body and she knew it. David knew it too, for there had been occasions in the past when he had seen her without the dress—without, in fact, the benefit of any covering whatever.

This had not been the case for nearly six months, however,

and hadn't been frequent before that. There was a time when her rebellion against Monica had embraced promiscuity and she was everybody's good-time Charlie. But that was a long time ago, before three years of deep analysis had showed her what she was doing and why. After that the need to escape from Monica's shadow and establish her own identity had taken more positive and fruitful directions until now, at twenty-nine, she fancied herself a well-integrated person with a controlled and well-adjusted attitude toward sex. She was no longer rebelling blindly or strongly, for her revolt had largely succeeded. She was an established personality in her own right these days. As an executive in Cowan and Blakeslee Television Productions, she held a position of high responsibility and good pay and if she did not have her mother's fame among the public at large, she had the esteem of her associates and peers in the television industry. And it was a position she had earned herself. That was what counted most. She had turned her back on anything to do with the newspaper field, for Monica's name opened too many doors. She had had to fight Monica over that, too, for her mother was all too eager to pave the way. For Linda, a job in the newspaper world as Monica Glazzard's daughter would have spelled doom.

David came up behind her when she reached for cups and saucers. He put his arms around her waist and kissed the lobe of her ear. 'Where've you been for so long?' he whispered.

'David,' she said, putting the dishes on the counter, 'you're supposed to be drunk.'

'Not really.' He held her tighter and slid his hands up over her breasts.

'David, stop it.' She tried to push his hands away but he squeezed her tighter. 'David!' This time she broke away. 'Behave yourself. It's half past twelve. You're only to have a cup of coffee and then you're to go.'

David's handsome face got sulky. 'What's the matter with you? I don't get it.'

She was aware of a hot flush on her cheeks. 'Nothing's the matter with me. It's late, I have to get up in the morning—and besides, I don't fancy what you have in mind.'

'You used to.'

'That was a long time ago.' She tried to breathe more evenly, to be in control. 'David, I want us to be friends. Not lovers.'

'It wasn't a long time ago. It was six months ago. And since when do you think we suddenly forget the past and become platonic?'

'But things have happened, David. We didn't really mean anything to each other . . .'

'Whose idea is that?'

'Every book you want to read. It's the woman who takes these things seriously, not the man. I wasn't in love with you and you weren't in love with me. We just liked each other and over the course of time we just—well, we just decided, why not? But that's all. It was just for kicks at the time.'

'And why the hell not now?'

'It's different. We've gone separate ways. You've been dating I don't know how many different girls. I've had my dates. And that's fine. And we see each other in the office and kid and have fun and I've come to think of you as a friend. One of my best friends.'

He grabbed her arm. 'Listen, you're putting me on. If I've dated other girls, it's because you turned down dates . . .'

'How many did I turn down? One? Two? David, you weren't pining for me and you know it. Now, please.'

'All right, I wasn't pining. I didn't say I was in love with you. I'm not in love with anybody, if you want to know. So if you start acting reluctant, I can look elsewhere. O.K., I figured maybe you regretted it, or maybe you were afraid you would get involved. So, all right. We'll just be friends and tell jokes to each other in the office. O.K., so then, suddenly, this morning, you invite me to the theatre. You invite me. I didn't invite you. Now what the hell did you expect my reaction to be?'

'But I told you,' she said, freeing her arm and opening the drawer for spoons. 'I had an extra ticket. There'd been a change of plans.'

'If you had an extra ticket, why didn't you invite one of the girls to go with you?'

'I knew you wanted to see the play and—frankly—I'd much rather go with you than with another girl.'

'Only you want me to behave toward you like another girl—say "ta ta" at the door.'

'I thought of us as friends, David. Pals. We could have fun together without having it go any farther than that.'

'You didn't tell me that when you invited me. You let me take you to dinner before the show, take you out for drinks after, and let me come back to the apartment with you, and after all that come-on, now you tell me you're not interested. Have a cup of coffee and run.'

'I wasn't going to let you come up to the apartment except you were so desperate for a cup of coffee to clear your head. All of a sudden, your head doesn't seem to need any clearing at all.'

'All right, I talked about a cup of coffee because I could sense you were bound and determined I wasn't going to come here. I could tell that right through the show, that you were going to do just what you did do—suggest that I just put you in a cab.'

'And that's why you insisted on drinks after? You were trying to soften me up. That's what you were trying to do.'

'What do you think? You got my expectations up. Then when you've got me panting for you, you put on the innocent little girl act. I don't like being used.'

'I wasn't trying to use you. I was offering you a chance to see a show you wanted to see.'

'And buy you a big dinner.'

'I didn't want you to buy me a big dinner.'

'You let me.'

'And now you want to be paid!' she said, hurt and angry. 'All right, I'll go get my purse.' She started past him but he seized her. She struggled but he kissed her and then he whispered against her cheek, 'Let's not fight.'

'I don't want to fight,' she said with a catch in her voice.

'That's right.' He turned off the gas under the steaming kettle and put his hand on her breast again.

'No,' she said, and pushed it away.

'Yes.'

She pulled back. 'I mean it, David. Now let's have coffee.'

For a moment David tensed as if he might strike her. 'Why the hell are you being such a damned bitch all of a sudden? Why the hell this big reformation at my expense?'

'It's not a reformation.'

'Whose ticket did I use tonight?'

'To the show?'

'Some man's, right? Who?'

'No one you know.'

'And he stood you up, so you picked on me as a stand-in.'

'He didn't stand me up. He was called out of town.'

'And if it'd been him here instead of me, you'd be out of all your clothes right now, wouldn't you?'

'No,' she said desperately, but David had read her right and the no was a lie. If it had been Randy, if he hadn't been called out of town, she'd be naked and in his arms right now.

'You're not kidding me,' he said in a voice thick with bitterness. 'You damned cheat. You play pals with me and all the time . . .' He grabbed her arms and pulled her up close. His eyes had a light in them that frightened her. When he got angry like this all his control seemed threatened.

Then the phone rang and its shrill note froze them both. For a moment they stared at each other and the light faded a little in David's eyes. When the phone rang again, she freed herself and pushed past him into the bedroom, shoving the door so it nearly closed. She threw herself across the bed and reached for the receiver on the adjacent table. 'Hello?'

'Linda.'

The voice was a balm. It belonged to the man she dreamed about at night, held hands with in the day, giggled with, slept with, went starry-eyed over, the man she couldn't wait to say 'I do' to.

'Oh, Randy.'

'Sweet, I miss you. I hated having to go.'

'I know. Oh, but I know. How's your aunt?'

'Just about holding her own. But I'm afraid it's only a matter of time.'

'I'm so sorry.'

'These things happen. I only wish it weren't so far away from you, though.'

'If we could only see each other now and then. Where're you calling from?'

'Auntie's home. I just got back from the hospital.'

'Did you make the plane all right this morning?'

'Just made it. But I'm afraid I ruined your evening—our evening.'

'Oh, good heavens, that doesn't matter.'

'And, of course, that dinner with your mother. That will have to be postponed, I'm afraid.'

'That's all right. I'd just as soon put off the evil moment as long as possible.'

'Have you told her yet that she won't be meeting her future son-in-law on Friday after all?'

'Not yet, but don't you worry.'

'I do worry. What if she doesn't approve of me?'

'I'm sure she won't, darling. Monica has a great faculty for not liking anything I like—or anybody. Or anything I do, for that matter. She has her own ideas on what's going to reflect well on her public image. I'm sorry, darling. I guess I sound bitter and I really do think she'll make an exception in your case. But if she doesn't, she's just going to have to get used to the idea.'

'I'd like it to be with her blessing, though.'

'Oh, when she gets used to the thought, I'm sure it will be. In fact, it'll be all we can do to keep her from trying to run the whole wedding.'

'Just a quiet one, darling. Very small.'

'All we need are the two of us. And I guess a witness. They're necessary, I understand.'

'Love me?'

Linda rolled over. David had pushed the bedroom door open and was standing there. 'Yes,' she said. 'Of course.'

The voice in her ear laughed. 'You sound very non-committal.'

Linda waved at David angrily but he didn't back out, he came closer. 'You know I do,' she said into the phone but the words were strained rather than loving.

'Is everything all right? What's the matter, Linda?'

'No, everything's fine. The play was very good.'

'Did you find somebody to give my ticket to?'

'Yes.'

'Who?'

'One of the girls.'

David wouldn't go away. He was at the side of the bed now, glaring at her, knowing the man on the other end of the wire was the one whose ticket he had used.

In her ear, Randy sounded puzzled. 'You seem distraught, darling. Something wrong?'

'No,' she said desperately. 'Nothing's wrong.'

Beside her, David bellowed loudly, 'Like hell nothing's wrong!'

Linda clapped her hand over the mouthpiece but Randy was already saying, 'Who's that? Do you have company, Linda?'

She tried to laugh. 'Oh, just a couple of people back after the theatre.'

She didn't get away with it. David's mean streak was showing and he was vengeance-minded. He grabbed the phone and said loudly into it, 'What do you mean calling up my girl at this hour of night? Get lost!' He slammed down the receiver.

Linda gave a cry that had an animal sound in it. She leaped on him, swinging her fists, pummelling him. 'Beast! Beast!'

The attack caught him off balance. One of her wildly aimed blows struck his nose and he could feel the blood flow. He caught her wrists savagely and flung her away against a chair. 'You wildcat!'

She sank onto its arm and burst into sobs, burying her face in her hands. 'You ruined it,' she cried. 'You ruined it.'

'Trying to make a fool out of me,' David said fiercely. 'Leading me on!' He was breathing heavily, unused to violent exercise.

'Why did you do it?' she sobbed. 'I love him.'

David looked at her, patted a handkerchief to his nose. Already he sensed he had carried things too far. He and his temper. 'Love him?' he said defensively. 'Come off it.'

'Is that so strange?' she said, looking up at him with the tears still streaming. 'Do you think I'm some kind of a freak?'

'Come on, you're too sensible a girl to get tangled up. You always play it cool.'

'A lot you know,' she sobbed.

David sat down on the bed, patted his nose once more and found the bleeding had stopped. 'Come on, Linda,' he said more gently. 'You know you're exaggerating. He's just a guy, whoever he is.'

'He's not just a guy. He's the guy I want.'

'All right, so if it'll fix things up, I'll tell him it was a gag.'

'Oh fine, and what good will that do? Do you think that's going to make him believe it?'

'Well, what the hell if he doesn't? You're twenty-nine years old, Linda. You know damn well he doesn't think you've been living in a cocoon all these years waiting for him to come along. So if he stands you up, it'd serve him right if you did go with somebody else. He's probably with another woman right now.'

Linda said stiffly, 'He's visiting his sick aunt, if you want to know.'

David snorted. 'Oh, now come off it! Good God, don't tell me you believe a story like that! That's as phony as a female's headache. He's with another woman. I'll bet money on it.'

'Stop it,' she shrieked. 'Will you stop it! He's in Pittsburgh. He flew out this morning. His aunt's dying.'

'All right, he's in Pittsburgh. So when he comes back, you'll pick up where you left off, whether he believes you were true to him or not. That's not going to make any difference to him.'

'Oh you think not?'

'Do you think I kidded myself I was the only guy you were seeing when you were going out with me? So I figured, what the hell, we have fun together.'

She said, crying again angrily, 'Will you stop trying to make me out as some sort of slut? Do you think just because you and I—do you think I just did anything with anybody?'

'Are you going to claim nobody else ever touched you all the time we were having our occasional dates?'

'It's different this time. Back then we were just having good times and no strings and I wasn't trying to pretend it was anything else. We were open and honest, you and I. We liked each other but we weren't in love.'

'So this time it's love. All the more reason for him to come back.'

'You don't understand. We were going to get married.'

'Married?' The sound of the word startled him. Such a thought had never crossed his mind.

'Married,' she repeated, her voice breaking. 'And that makes it all different and that means you don't fool around when his back is turned and it means he's seeing his dying aunt in Pittsburgh because that's what he said he was going to do. It means we trust each other and now he's going to think I betrayed him and it's going to be over.' She wept again. 'And I didn't betray him. I wouldn't.'

David found himself at a loss. He really did like Linda and if he had ever dreamed that she was engaged to a guy—unofficially since she wore no ring and it hadn't been announced—he would have understood. He wouldn't have made a single false move. 'Look,' he said, 'call him back. I'll explain the whole thing to him. I'll straighten him out. Believe me I will.'

'I can't call him back,' she said. 'I don't know where he is.'

'Pittsburgh, didn't you say?'

'He's at his aunt's house and it's not *in* Pittsburgh, it's outside of Pittsburgh.'

'What's his name?'

'Benson. Randy Benson.'

'So call the operator . . .'

'But that's not his aunt's name. I don't know her name.'

The phone rang again, its shrill sound jarring them unnervingly. 'Oh God,' Linda said. 'He's calling back. What am I going to say?'

David decided to be manly. 'I'll do the talking.' He grabbed the receiver as she shrieked and tried to seize it from him. 'Hello?'

The voice on the other end said formally, 'Is Miss Glazzard there, please?'

'Yes, but I've got a couple of things to say first . . .'

Linda tried to wrestle the phone away. 'Give it to me. Please.'

'Wait a minute.' He said into the phone, 'Who is this anyway?'

A chilling voice replied, 'This is Detective Frank Sessions of Homicide and I want to talk to Miss Glazzard. What's your name?'

David didn't answer the question. He held the receiver out to Linda numbly and backed off. She was pale and bloodless when she took it. 'Hello?' she said in a faltering voice.

She went whiter as she listened. 'What kind of accident?' she said. 'How bad?' Then she said, 'Please. I'll come, but I want the truth. What am I going to find?' She ended with a whispered, 'All right,' and put the phone down quietly.

'What was that all about?'

She got off the chair and said, 'My mother is dead.' She picked up her purse and went woodenly to the door.

THURSDAY 12:45–1:05 A.M.

When Sessions put down the phone, Mr. Krick came over to him. 'I guess it's kind of tough having to break the news to the daughter.'

Sessions took a last deep drag and mashed out his cigarette. 'Yeah.'

'I'd have a hell of a time trying to do something like that.'

'You get used to it.'

'Do you get many murders?'

'Our squad? Two hundred a year.'

'That many?'

'It's a dirty world.'

Krick laughed self-consciously. 'Oh, ah, before you go. Will you be here all night on this?'

'Here?' Sessions laughed. 'Jesus, I hope not.'

'If we want to go to bed and you want to use the phone—we could leave the door open. You could close it when you're through. I guess with all you policemen around we'd be safe.'

'Anything you want, Mr. Krick. I appreciate the phone.' Sessions went out and into the Glazzard apartment again. Boxton, coming down the stairs, beckoned him.

'Yes, Lieutenant?'

'Frank, I'm leaving now. The lab men are finishing up in the bedroom. Barrancas is starting a search for valuables.

Miss Glazzard's secretary's here.'

'She see the deceased?'

'She identified her. You get hold of the daughter?'

'She's coming over. How did the secretary take it?'

'Calmly. Quite calmly.' Boxton went by to the door and turned. 'Don't let photo forget to print the deceased. And don't forget what Captain Conklin said. The chief's going to want a full briefing at eight o'clock tomorrow morning—I mean this morning.'

'No, sir.'

Boxton departed and Frank started for the study. In the dining room Kuhn and MacAllister were photographing a glass cabinet housing a collection of polished stones and pebbles collected or sent from all parts of the world, each identified by a card noting the site. Sessions paused briefly to look it over. All fifty states seemed represented, and countless foreign countries. None of the stones had monetary value but a few had the element of the exotic. There was a marble shard from the Acropolis and a fragment of fossilised bone from the Olduvai Gorge. Sessions said, 'Jesus, the stuff some people collect.'

Kuhn said, 'I prefer blondes myself. Only my wife objects.'

'That's the trouble with wives. One of the troubles.' He went around the camera and opened the study door. Devlin was in there alone going through the files while a voice from the dictaphone was saying, '. . . but when he tries to be deep he is only pathetic. A slender talent is worse than no talent, at least to a reviewer. A no-talent writer doesn't get produced. Those with slender talents sometimes do and those experiences are very trying to that part of the anatomy upon which a reviewer sits. Period. Thirty.' There was silence and Devlin switched off the machine.

'Sounds like her column,' he said. 'She must have dictated it before she went to bed.'

'That column ran in the late edition of tonight's paper. I read it. The doc go?'

'He just set the thing up for me and took off. I've been playing it over while I looked around here just to get the feel of the woman—sound of her voice, way of talking. You know.'

'The voice doesn't sound like she was knowingly dictating her last column, does it?'

'Not at all. This is no suicide. That's for sure.'

Sessions sorted through the desk's contents, which Devlin had piled on its top. He found the appointment calendar and opened that to the week's doings. It read:

MONDAY MAY 8, 1967

2:30—Interview Don Huxley on Expo 67. Waldorf 1548.
5:15—Cocktails Betty, Biltmore. (Bring samples)
7:00—Perry/dinner for Majznik.

TUESDAY MAY 9, 1967

3:30—Plaza—Henri
5:00—Arch here. Greg party. Parlor T, Biltmore.
8:30—Anka Theatre—'Little Lost Blue'

WEDNESDAY MAY 10, 1967

1:00—Lunch, Sarah Little, Plaza.
4:00—Fashion Show, Barbizon. Interview M. Ducal
6:30—UN interview Surat. His office.
9:30—Madeline party.

Sessions started copying the engagements into his notebook and Devlin pulled an insurance policy from the file. He thumbed through the sheets and said, 'Here's the jewellery she's got insured. Description, serial number, value.'

'I'll want that.'

Devlin handed it to him. 'Her chequebook stuff is there. She writes about forty cheques a month. And the address file. There must be six hundred names in it. How do you like that for bad news?'

Sessions folded the policy carelessly and tucked it in a side pocket. 'I don't know,' he said, resuming his copying. 'Is there a Motley and a Nettie Sandhurst in it?'

Devlin went through it. 'Not Motley. Let's see. Yes, Nettie Sandhurst. Address and phone.'

'Give her a call. See if you can get her.'

Devlin tried the number and let it ring a dozen times. 'No answer,' he finally said, hanging up.

Sessions finished with the appointment book and turned Nettie's card around to copy the data. 'No wonder,' he said. 'It's a pay phone. Probably in a neighbouring store.'

'Yeah? How do you know?'

'The nine right there. That tells you. Well, she's supposed to show up in the morning so we can catch her then.'

He tucked his book away and left the room, going into the kitchen where he opened the service door for a look. The corridor, elevators and staircase were a mirror image of the tenants' side but not as well appointed. He checked that the outside doorknob wouldn't turn, closed the door again and opened the one to the adjacent maid's room. It showed no signs of recent habitation and there was nothing there but the bare tiled floor, an empty bureau and a bed, spread over with newspapers. He went up the back staircase beside it and down the hall to the master bedroom again.

The body, now covered with a bedsheet, lay ignored and forgotten, but the room was still the centre of activity. Barrancas, Sergeant Kelly, the super and a short, stocky woman with greying bobbed hair were going over a collection of jewellery spread out on the dresser. Ray Ecklin and Ralph D'Amato were looking through bureau drawers; the men from the lab were putting away their equipment.

Kelly said, 'This is Miss Mildred Butelle, Frank, Mrs. Glazzard's secretary. This is Detective Sessions.'

She murmured some word of greeting but didn't meet his eye. Her features were stern, her movement energetic and economical. Frank said, 'Thank you for coming, Miss

Butelle.' To Kelly he said, 'That all the valuables?'

'All we could find. Except for a little money in her purse.'

Sessions took out the insurance papers and handed them to Barrancas. 'Here's the master list. See if it's all present and accounted for. How about it, Miss Butelle? You see anything missing? Anything that you can remember?'

She said shortly, 'I can't think of anything.'

One of the lab men picked up his case and said, 'We got some nice prints off the bottle for you. What do you think of that?'

'Take one giant step. You get any prints from anything else?'

'The glass. And here and there around the room. Can't you see where we've dusted?'

'Yeah, but I'm not supposed to. You're getting sloppy.'

They laughed and went out. Frank went over to Ecklin. 'Getting anything?'

'Just routine stuff. Nothing out of the ordinary. Did Boxton leave?'

'Yeah. Full of parting advice. Don't forget to print the deceased. Don't forget to brief the chief. Jesus, what an ulcer he must have.'

Ecklin laughed. 'Maybe he doesn't think you're housebroken, Frank.'

'Yeah, I guess not.' He looked around. 'Where's the Sarge?'

'Interviewing Caligliaro, the night elevatorman, down in the lobby.'

'What about the janitor?'

'He's forty-five, married, fourteen-year-old son with pimples and a ten-year-old daughter with pigtails. He claims he hasn't seen the deceased in six weeks, that she's never around when he is. I've got a blow by blow account of everything he did yesterday from the time he got up until he went to bed, most of it verified by the wife, so we can throw it at him if he tries to change his story later on. You want to hear it?'

'Hell, no. Put it on a DD5 in case it becomes important. What about keys?'

'He says only the super has a master key and he guards it like the crown jewels. He says no one can get that key without going to the super and you'd better have a damned good reason.'

'That's a lot of crap, that business about nobody can get hold of a key. You get it from the super on a legitimate errand, you make a wax impression, you get a duplicate made.'

'That's right, but you have to have a reason for thinking this guy did that and right now I don't have any.'

'That's O.K., so long as they don't try to use that on me as an alibi.' He went over to Miss Butelle. 'You want to answer a few questions, ma'am?'

She said, 'I suppose so,' without enthusiasm.

'What's your address, Mildred?'

'Four nineteen East Fifty-second Street.'

He wrote that down. 'And when did you see Mrs. Glazzard last?'

'The day before this. Tuesday.'

'You want to tell me about it?'

'I came in at eight o'clock—shortly after eight. I did my usual chores through the morning . . .'

'Which are what?'

'First thing I'd do any cleaning up that was necessary. If there were any glasses or dirty ashtrays around, things like that—if she'd had people in the night before. Mondays and Thursdays the cleaning woman would take care of that. Other days I'd tidy up. Then I'd transcribe her column from the dictaphone and leave it down in the lobby for the boy to pick up.'

'What boy?'

'A messenger boy from the News Features Syndicate. I wouldn't know who. I seldom see them and it's not always the same one. But there's a deadline and I make sure the copy's stuffed in the envelope and down there before eleven o'clock.'

'And the column would always be ready for you on the dictaphone?'

'Most of the time. She liked to get it out of the way before she went to bed. Sometimes, of course, she wouldn't. Then I'd use one of the spare columns she's written and keeps on file.'

'But on this day you transcribed the column? Then what?'

'Then I go through the correspondence, handle the routine things, lay aside those matters for Mrs. Glazzard's personal attention, and then type up any letters she's dictated and carry out any other orders she might have left for me.'

'Where's Mrs. Glazzard during all this?'

'Sleeping. Her work kept her up till all hours. She never rose till past twelve o'clock.'

'Then what?'

'Usually I'd get all that out of the way before twelve. Then I'd prepare a breakfast and take it to her between twelve and one. I'd check over her appointments with her, tell her what she had on for that day, and discuss her plans. Then I'd help her dress and see that she got off to her engagements.'

'And then?'

'That was up to her. Sometimes she'd want me to accompany her. Other times there'd be other things to do—make travel arrangements if she were going somewhere, call people she wanted to see, make reservations, shop for her—do whatever she wanted.'

'And then?'

'Then I'd go home. This could be any time—the middle of the afternoon or the middle of the night.'

'And what time was it yesterday—when you last saw her?'

'I last saw her when she left at three in the afternoon to go to the beauty parlour.'

Frank wrote that down and said, 'And what did you do after that?'

'Finished up some odds and ends. Then I left the apartment around quarter of four, went to Grand Central Post Office to mail a package for her and went home.'

'And you never saw her again after three o'clock yesterday afternoon?'

'No.'

'You didn't see her today, for example, when you came to work?'

She said, 'I didn't come to work today.'

'Why was that?'

'She gave me the day off.'

'You ask for it?'

'No, she just gave it to me.'

She didn't elaborate so Frank said, 'Just like that she gives you the day off?'

'That's right.'

'Tell me about it.'

She said curtly, 'There's nothing to tell. All that happened is when she was leaving to go to the hairdresser's she said, "Don't come in tomorrow, Millie. I won't need you." '

Frank scribbled rapidly and said, 'She give you the day off like this often?'

'No.'

'How often has she done this before?'

'I don't know. Never.'

'She's never said, "Don't come in tomorrow, Millie. I won't need you", before?'

'No.'

'Why did she do it this time?'

'I don't know.'

'You didn't ask her?'

'It wasn't any of my business.'

'Come on, Millie. It wasn't any of your business? Why do you think she gave you the day off?'

'I don't know.'

'Why do you *think* she did?'

'I haven't thought about it.'

Sessions waved behind him at the sheeted body. 'Come on, Millie. Mrs. Glazzard is dead. She's dead the day after she suddenly gives you a day off. Don't tell me you haven't even wondered if there might be a connection.'

'If there is any, all I know is I don't know what it is.'

'Who typed up her column today?'

The woman hesitated. Then she said, 'I don't know. Maybe she didn't write one.'

'Her column is in tonight's paper—about the play she saw last night. It was transcribed from a belt that was in her wastebasket in her office. That was done since she got home from the theatre last night.'

'Well, maybe she typed it herself.'

'Then why would she dictate it?'

Millie compressed her lips and didn't answer.

'Who else besides you has a key to this apartment?'

She said quickly, 'The super.'

'The super and . . . ?'

'Nettie the maid. Perhaps Mrs. Glazzard's daughter would have a key. I really wouldn't know.'

'What's Mr. Motley's relationship to Mrs. Glazzard?'

She blinked. 'Oh, ah—him?'

'He has a key, doesn't he?'

'Yes, I think so.'

'Why weren't you going to tell us about him?'

'I forgot about him.'

'Who is he, what is he, where does he live?'

She steadied herself. 'His name is Robert Motley. I don't know where he lives. On East Seventy-fifth Street I think. He does odd jobs and things for Mrs. Glazzard.'

'You're not going to call him an odd-job man, are you? A man with a key to the apartment? What's his relationship to Mrs. Glazzard?'

She chewed a lip. 'I guess you'd call him her protégé.'

'Could you call him her lover?'

'I don't know.'

'But you don't think I'd be making a big mistake if that's what I called him?'

'I do not concern myself with Mrs. Glazzard's private life. I don't know anything about it.'

'You ever call him on the telephone?'

'Occasionally.'

'He's not in the phone book. Why?'

'His number's unlisted.'

'Why?'

'I suppose Mrs. Glazzard preferred it that way.'

'She paid for his phone?'

'Well, I—uh . . .'

'She pay his rent too?'

'I—uh believe she did.'

'What's his phone number?'

She gave it to him reluctantly. 'I don't think you have a right to pry,' she said bitterly. 'Try to smear a good woman's reputation.'

'The dead have no rights to privacy, Millie, especially when there's a question as to how they died.'

She looked startled. 'You mean there's a question how she died?'

'You don't think there is?'

'The bottle, the glass. It's obviously suicide.'

Remick appeared in the doorway and stopped to listen. Sessions said, 'You know a good reason why she might want to commit suicide?'

'Well no, not really.'

'But you'd like us to believe that's what she did?'

'I don't know. I just don't know.'

Remick interrupted then. 'The daughter's just come in, Frank. She wants to see the deceased—make an identification.'

'O.K.'

'I got a lead for you too. Caligliaro, the night man, is in.

He says the deceased came home last night about quarter past one in the company of two men and another woman. The woman and one man left about quarter of three. The other man left about quarter past.'

'No make on any of them?'

'No make but descriptions. The man who left last has been in before but Caligliaro can't recall his name.'

Sessions turned. 'How about it, Millie? Who were the people?'

'I have no idea.'

'You know her plans. She went to the theatre last night and she had some people back for a party after. You know who they are.'

'No I don't. That must have been impromptu. She didn't tell me she was going to have anybody back.'

'If Sergeant Remick gave you their descriptions . . .'

'I don't think . . .'

Sessions said in exasperation, 'Jesus, Millie. You're her secretary. You're closer to her than anyone else. Are you trying to say you don't know who her friends are? Who're you trying to protect?'

'Not anybody.'

'All right, you wait downstairs. We'll talk some more later.'

She turned gladly from Frank's implacable face and Remick guided her out the door. 'Wait for me in the living room,' he said. 'I'll be down in a minute.' He lowered his voice when he got her into the hall. 'And if I were you, Miss Butelle, I'd co-operate with Detective Sessions. He's a very mean and nasty man if he thinks anyone is trying to lie to him.'

He started her down the stairs and called to have Miss Glazzard sent up. When he came back to the bedroom, Sessions said, 'I heard that, Sarge. What do you want to do, start her hollering "police brutality"?'

Remick grinned. 'I thought it might break her down a little. Besides, you *look* mean and nasty.'

'That's because I don't like people giving me a song and dance.'

Ecklin said in mock surprise, 'Why, Frankie, do you mean to say you didn't believe that poor little old woman's story?'

Sessions snorted. 'Oh, Jesus.'

THURSDAY 1:05–1:20 A.M.

Sessions went to the door when Linda Glazzard came up the stairs. He wanted to watch her as much as possible. It was always interesting in a homicide to see how the relatives and friends of the deceased behaved. He noted the blonde hair, the simple but well-cut tan dress, the elegant pin that set it off, the fact that she wore no coat, that her lipstick was just a tiny bit smudged. 'I'm Detective Sessions,' he said, taking her by the arm in the hallway and holding her away from the crowd. 'I'm sorry I had to get you out on a thing like this but we have to ask some questions.'

She looked at the doorway to the room where the activity was concentrated and moistened her lips. 'May I see her?'

'If you'd like.' He guided her past policemen and detectives into the bedroom and up to the bed. He lifted a corner of the sheet far enough to expose the dead woman's face. 'This is your mother?'

Linda swallowed and nodded and kept looking at the composed, still face until the sheet had dropped again. Sessions said, 'Thank you, Miss Glazzard. If you'll come with me . . .'

Linda's features were set, her face bleak. 'How did she die?'

The bottle and glass were gone now. Nothing pointed to any cause. Sessions said frankly, 'We don't know, Miss Glazzard.'

'Did someone kill her?'

'We don't know what happened. Now if you'll . . .'

She didn't want to leave. 'You said you're from homicide. There're all these people around. All my mother's jewellery is out. You wouldn't be doing all this unless somebody killed her. She was murdered, wasn't she?'

'We're doing all this because we don't know *how* she died. But I must ask you some questions. Shall we go into the next room?'

'I'd rather stay here.' She watched with suspicion the policemen checking off the jewellery. 'Who's going to be responsible for my mother's valuables? Who keeps track of them?'

'They're inventoried, Miss Glazzard. The patrolman is being supervised by the sergeant and the superintendent is a witness. So was your mother's secretary.'

McPartland came in. 'The morgue wagon's here—oh, excuse me, ma'am.' He backed out, flushing.

Sessions said firmly, 'We'll go in the next room, Miss Glazzard. We'll be in the way here.' He took her arm and now she followed him without protest into the adjacent library. He closed the door and it was quiet. She sat down and looked through her purse for a cigarette. He said, 'When did you last see your mother?'

'I don't know. About a month ago.'

He sat on the corner of the large table there and leaned forward to light her cigarette. 'A month ago.' He made note and pushed an ashtray over. Something in his voice made her aware of what a span of time that was for someone living less than a mile away. She added, 'I've talked to her on the phone since.'

'You're her nearest relative?'

'I'm her only relative.'

'Does she have a will?'

'I really don't know.'

'When did you last talk to her on the telephone?'

She bit her lip. 'Just a moment. Why are you asking about a will?'

'It's a routine question.'

'You think she's murdered and you think someone might have done it because of her will, don't you? I'm the prime beneficiary so I'm a suspect, isn't that right?'

Sessions was soothing. 'Now, Miss Glazzard, there's no reason to get upset. These are questions we ask in any questionable death. We don't suspect anybody about anything. We merely want to find out as much as we can about the background of the—of your mother. Now you said you're the prime beneficiary but you don't know if your mother has a will. How is it that . . .'

'I assume I'm the prime beneficiary.' She took a quick drag on her cigarette and knocked off ashes. Her face was very pale.

'When did you talk to her last on the phone?'

'Monday afternoon. She phoned me at work. I work for Cowan and Blakeslee and I do very well so I can assure you I have no interest in my mother's will.'

'What's Cowan and Blakeslee?'

'Television Productions. They make up and package television shows.' She acted surprised that Sessions didn't know about it. 'Offices in the Seagram Building.' She added, 'On Park Avenue,' because if the detective were ignorant of Cowan and Blakeslee, he might not know where the Seagram Building was.

Sessions said, 'I see, and you have a job there?'

'I'm Director in Charge of Contestants of the "Guess the Guest" show.'

'How was your mother when you last talked to her? Was she worried about anything, nervous, upset?'

'No, she was the way she usually was. Busy.'

'What's that mean?'

'Fast, in a hurry.'

'Did she call you for any particular reason?'

'She wanted me to come to dinner on Friday.'

'Can you tell me anything about her private life, Miss Glazzard? Does she have any enemies? Does she have close friends, people she's involved with? Is there anybody you know about who might, for some reason, like to see her dead?'

Linda said, 'I don't know of any.'

'Do you know that there weren't any?'

She shook her head. 'That's the trouble, I'm afraid. I really don't know very much about my mother's affairs. We didn't see each other very often. Months would go by.'

'And then last Monday she called you up and wanted you to come to dinner this Friday? Was this her customary behaviour?'

'Pretty much so, yes.'

'Were you going to dinner with her?'

'Yes.'

'Was this dinner for any particular purpose?'

Linda couldn't really see any point in going into all of that. It would mean explaining about Randy Benson and a lot of things that actually had nothing to do with her mother. All that could conceivably come of that would be that this detective would get a lot of wrong ideas that would only confuse whatever it was he wanted to find out and might prove embarrassing to her and to Randy. Stuff might even get into the papers and she wanted none of that. 'No particular purpose,' she said. 'I hadn't seen her in quite a while.'

'And your mother decided it was time to get together?'

Linda didn't quite like the sound of that. It made her appear a little less than a dutiful daughter. But explanations would only sound lame. 'I suppose you could say that.'

'Your mother has a secretary, a Miss Butelle. You know her?'

'Not very well, but I know her.'

'What do you think of her?'

'I guess she's pretty capable and efficient. I guess Mother

liked her or she wouldn't have kept her.'

'Did you like her?'

That was another question Linda wasn't happy about answering. She really didn't like Miss Butelle though she had no ready explanations as to a reason. What was it, a personality difference? A feeling about her? 'I liked her all right,' Linda said. 'I really didn't know her.'

'Who else did your mother employ?'

'No one else to my knowledge.'

'There's a cleaning woman, a Nettie . . .'

'Oh, yes. I forgot about her.' Linda erased her cigarette and stared at the embers. 'She's had Nettie for years—ever since she bought the apartment.'

'When was that?'

'Eleven years ago.'

'Any other employees your mother might have? Any male employees?'

'No.'

'A man perhaps to run errands, drive the car?'

'She doesn't own a car. When she wants one, she feels it's cheaper and more convenient to hire a limousine.'

'How about a man named Robert Motley?'

Linda said, 'Robert Motley? I never heard of him. Is he supposed to be somebody my mother knows?'

'He's apparently a protégé.'

'A protégé?' She frowned. 'You mean—you really mean a lover?'

'That's a better word for it. Do you think it's likely?'

She started to say no and then stopped. After all, her mother wasn't really over the hill. She'd divorced Linda's father better than a quarter of a century before and she'd never married again. Was it not rash, if not downright ridiculous to assume that Monica had lived a life of continence since then? Linda had never thought about her mother from the sex standpoint before. She'd never bothered to wonder what her mother's feelings were on the subject. She herself had learned the facts of life from the girls at school and everything else she had learned on the subject had been from sources other than Monica. But then, most of the information she had picked up in the world had come from sources outside of Monica. Monica could communicate with her readers, she could communicate with her friends and admirers, but she could not communicate with her daughter.

'I just don't know about lovers,' Linda said slowly. 'I just don't know anything about that.'

'Do you think it likely or unlikely?'

She looked up at Sessions with wonder on her face. 'I don't think I've ever given it a thought before.'

'What do you think now?'

Linda flushed. She reached for another cigarette. Well, what about it? What about her own life? As a result of analysis she had given up promiscuity but she hadn't given up sex. She was careful now and it had to mean something in and of itself and that meant that it didn't happen so often any more. But it did happen. She wasn't living a life of celibacy. In fact, Randy would quite laugh at the thought. They'd been at it pretty hot and heavy for some months. So why not her enlightened and anything-but-conventional mother? What else should she really expect?

'I think it would be quite likely,' Linda said in a low voice, wondering if Sessions was reading in her answer her own behaviour.

He lighted her cigarette again. 'You think it's likely that she'd be having a lover right now, but you don't know anything about it? Were there ever any lovers that you did know about?'

'No.' She didn't meet his eye this time either. She had to raise her head to do that and it was easier to look elsewhere. She also didn't feel comfortable in the face of his penetrating stare. She didn't feel easy in his presence. He was on a case and he was all business and everything about him showed it; the way he looked at things and people, reading and soaking up and draining dry; the way he moved, strictly professionally, no wasted motions, no uncertainty. Even the lean face, a little thinner than it should be, a little paler, had a chiselled, scraped look as if it too had been honed for the purposes at hand and, like the rest of him, was homing in on target.

Sessions said, 'Is there anything else you can think of that might have anything to do with your mother's death, either why she might want to kill herself or why someone else might want to kill her? Can you think of *anything*?'

This time she did meet his eyes. 'No, sir. I can't think of a thing. I can't really believe it.'

He got off the table. 'All right, Miss Glazzard. Thank you very much.' He took her elbow and she rose from the chair at the library table and he guided her to the door. 'You'll have to appear at the Medical Examiner's once tomorrow morning. That's part of Bellevue Hospital and is on the corner of First Avenue and 30th Street. Between eight and nine will be best.'

'Between eight and nine. First Avenue and 30th?' She looked at him. 'What for?'

'There has to be a formal identification in front of certain specific witnesses.'

'But I just said that she's my mother.'

'And you'll have to do it again. It's the law.'

'I see.'

'And while you're there, you can make arrangements as to where you'd like your mother sent.'

'Sent?'

'You'll be making funeral arrangements, I presume.'

'Oh.' She said it numbly. 'Of course.'

The thought had never even occurred to her. What a terrible daughter the detective must think she was. But she had been so much out of her mother's life it was only natural to assume—to assume what? That Millie Butelle would take care of the funeral arrangements? That Monica's friends in the newspaper world would, or some of those people who invited her to the parties she graced? But that, of course, wasn't so. Mildred Butelle was now nobody more than a woman out of a job. The men and women who flocked to Monica's side were only interested in a living, breathing, exciting Monica. She had no claim on them in death.

Only upon Linda could Monica lay a claim and it was one that Linda could not escape. The people at the morgue wouldn't bury the body for her. They wouldn't take care of things. She was going to have to do it. And she realised, suddenly, she didn't have the faintest idea what to do. Did Monica have a cemetery plot somewhere? Had she ever made such a purchase? (Not if Linda knew Monica.) Did Monica have any special ideas about what should be done with her remains? Did she favour cremation? Did she oppose it?

Linda went slowly down the stairs, holding onto the railing, being only vaguely aware of the people coming and going in the hall, the sound and bustle of activity. Her mind was caught up in the problem of the funeral. What funeral home should she call? And when they asked about burial, what could she tell them? Could she ask them for suggestions? Could one buy a plot on two days' notice?

And how much would it cost? Good God, for Monica no cheap funeral would do. The mink-coat set, the theatre stars, the high and the mighty from all walks of life would expect only the best. But who was going to pay for it? Had Monica laid aside a fund? Surely not. And where could Linda raise the money? She earned a good salary but she was not a saver. It came in too readily, and she had less than a thousand dollars in ready cash on hand.

Outside, they were wheeling her mother's body around to the back of the morgue truck. It was wrapped in a sheet but her right foot lay inadvertently half-exposed and tied to her toe was an identification tag. It was the tag that did it. Linda felt the tears come and she hurried blindly away, fleeing from the photographers who had snapped her picture, the reporters who had tried to ask questions, the officials and the curious gathered on the sidewalk under the canopy. What would those detectives think of her? How callous she must have appeared to them. How callous she appeared to herself, thinking of the inconvenience her mother's death had posed rather than of the loss it entailed. Now, all at once, the sight of a tag had made her realise how alone she was. The bulwark of her mother's existence, ignored and dismissed as it might have been, had always been there. Always there had existed the subconscious golden cord. There was someone else in the world of the same blood. But no longer. Now there was nothing. If only Randy's aunt . . . If only Randy . . . She needed him desperately but he wasn't there. He might never be there again.

Behind, back in the apartment, the detectives were thinking about her, though not quite in the way she imagined. It wasn't her callousness that concerned them. 'She's another one with something on her mind,' Sessions said to Ecklin. 'She made a big point about how she doesn't have any need for her mother's money. Told me all about the good-paying job she's got—offices in the Seagram Building which, she insisted on mentioning, is on Park Avenue. Just in case I didn't know that. Just to make sure I'm impressed.' Sessions hitched his shoulders. 'She's afraid we're going to suspect her of killing her mother. We don't even know that it's a homicide but she's afraid we're going to suspect her. Why?'

THURSDAY 1:20–1:40 A.M.

Remick was talking to Miss Butelle in the living room when Sessions got down there. 'She thinks she might know the man who was out with Mrs. Glazzard last night,' the sergeant announced. 'Tall, grey-haired, distinguished type. Right, Miss Butelle? Tell Detective Sessions.'

Miss Butelle was no longer the cold, imperious woman who had first identified her employer and catalogued the valuables. She was nervous and scared now. 'Dr. Archibald Patterson,' she said. 'They were close friends. Known each other for years. I think he's retired now from Columbia, but lectures and writes. He might have seen her last night.'

'Where does he live, Mildred?'

'Morningside Heights, but I don't know the address. Mrs. Glazzard would have it.' She looked appealingly at Remick. 'Can I go now?'

Remick grinned at her. He said to Sessions, 'O.K., Frank? You got what you want?'

'All except for the name of Mrs. Glazzard's lawyer.'

The woman said, 'Lawrence Stockton of Stockton, Bates and Pierce.'

'O.K.'

They let her go and watched as she stumbled blindly up the hallway and out the door. Sessions said, 'What did you do to her, Sarge? She acts scared to death.'

'Don't look at me. I've been holding her hand. What shook her up was finding out we think this is a homicide. She's been assuming it was a suicide.'

'She's been assuming it was a suicide? Or she's been assuming *we'd* think it was a suicide?'

Remick laughed. 'Are you asking me what goes on in her little head, Frankie? I couldn't tell you.'

'You can't and she won't. Well, let's check out these names she gave us and see how much of a favour that is.'

'If Patterson was here with her last night, it could be a big favour.'

'Especially if she knew him well enough to get into her nightgown. If not, then we'd better see what her protégé was doing.'

Sessions went back to the office off the dining room for the address file. Devlin was still sorting through papers. 'This dame wrote some interesting cheques,' he said. He thumbed through the most recent set of stubs. 'Listen to this. April 17. R. Motley. One hundred and fifty dollars. April 26. R. Motley. A hundred and ten dollars. May 2. R. Motley. A hundred and twenty-five dollars.'

'No kidding. Good going, pal.' He jotted it down in his notebook.

'And every month there's a cheque for Hamson and Reed Bros.—they're real estate—for $174.98. You got to figure that's the rent for this guy Motley.'

'Sounds like it.' Sessions hunted through the address file for Dr. Patterson's card and pulled it out.

'Anything special you want me to check, Frank?'

'Yeah. I don't think anybody's checked out the service entrance yet.'

'Yeah, right.' Devlin hurried off and Frank picked up the phone. A voice on the extension was saying, '. . . if any of the following have an arrest record. Claude Hogarth. Present address 154 East 72nd Street. Harry Berkman . . .'

Sessions put the phone down again and went into the Kricks' apartment. 'We won't be much longer,' he told Mr. Krick. 'The lab's finished, photo's going. We're about ready to wrap it up.' He dialled the number on Patterson's card, lighted a cigarette and looked at his watch. It was not quite half past one.

Dr. Patterson's 'Hello' was cultivated and fluid and there was no trace of sleep in it. Sessions went through his identification routine and said, 'I understand you're a friend of Monica Glazzard's?'

Patterson's interest instantly quickened. 'Detective? Homicide did you say? Why yes, of course I know Monica. Why?'

'Mrs. Glazzard died late last night or sometime this morning. We understand . . .'

'Monica's dead? You must be joking!'

'This is not a joke, Dr. Patterson.'

'If this is one of her gags . . .' The voice suddenly lost some of its conviction that it was one of her gags. 'You're—this isn't any . . . ? Now look, please don't joke.'

'I am not joking, Doctor. Mrs. Glazzard died early today. We understand that you saw her last evening.'

'Who did you say you were again?'

'Detective Frank Sessions. Homicide Squad. Manhattan North. Shield number three-six-seven-nine. Check it out if you don't believe me.'

'No, no, I do believe you. You sound like a detective. But Monica's dead, you say? I can't believe it. How did it happen?'

'We don't know yet. We understand . . .'

'Murdered? You think Monica was murdered?'

'I said we don't know how she died, Doctor. We're hoping you can throw some light on the matter.'

'I?' He sounded startled. 'But that's an incredible thought. How could I . . .'

'We understand you were with her last night . . .'

'No, no. You're quite mistaken about that. No, I didn't see her last night.'

'You weren't with her at all last night? You didn't see her yesterday at any time?'

'No, no I didn't.'

'But you knew her well.'

'Oh yes. Very well. One of the really great people. Oh this is a terrible shock. This is an awful thing.'

'Doctor, we're hoping you can help us.'

'Yes, of course. Anything I can do. Anything at all.'

'Could you come over here to her apartment right away?'

'Of course, of course. I'll be right over.'

Sessions next tried the number Millie had given him for Robert Motley. A man's voice answered on the third ring, Sessions identified himself and went through it again. 'I'm sorry to bother you this time of night, Mr. Motley. . . . You're a friend of Monica Glazzard, is that right? . . . I'm very sorry to have to tell you this, but Mrs. Glazzard is dead. . . . That's right, she died sometime this morning. . . . We're looking into it because it appears she might have taken her own life and we have to talk to her relatives and close friends. We'd like to talk to you, Mr. Motley. . . . That's right. You're one of her friends, we understand.' Sessions frowned and one corner of his lip curled. He flipped open his notebook and laid it on the telephone table. 'You're a good enough friend,' he said icily, 'for Mrs. Glazzard to write you out a cheque for a hundred and fifty dollars on the seventeenth of April. And on the twenty-sixth, she made you out a cheque for a hundred and ten.' His eyes got their nasty light in them. 'That's right, Mr. Motley. We'd like to ask you some questions about Mrs. Glazzard. We'd like you to come down to the nineteenth precinct house at 153 East 67th Street. Go up the stairs to the detective squad room on the second floor. Ask for Lieutenant Boxton and tell him Frank Sessions asked you to come in.' He listened and raised his eyes to the ceiling. 'Of course I mean right now. . . . Yes, I know what time it is. But there's a question here as to how a close friend of yours came to die. We know you want to help. . . . Thank you, Mr. Motley.'

He hung up and muttered a four-letter word that was much stronger than 'Jesus'.

THURSDAY 1:40–2:15 A.M.

Con Devlin caught Sessions leaving the Kricks. 'Frank, I checked out the service entrance. There's a service door down in the basement to a side alley—down a ramp between the buildings from the sidewalk out front. The service door has no handle on the outside. It only opens from the inside. The door's got a bar lock on it. In addition, there's a gate at the sidewalk. It's kept open all day but they lock it at night. So if it's a homicide, it's someone who came in the front door, huh, Frank?'

Sessions wasn't impressed. 'Who's got keys to the outside gate?'

'The janitor.'

'Who else?'

'I don't know. You mean you think somebody might've had a key and come down the ramp . . . ?'

'I don't know what happened. What I want to know is what couldn't have happened.'

'Well, I think it's highly unlikely . . .'

'If this is a homicide, and there's no robbery, then it's likely the motive is personal, which makes it likely that the perpetrator knows the victim well. Probably, since we can't find signs of breaking and entering, he also has a key—has as many keys to this place as the victim has. The perpetrator would doubtless also be known to the elevatormen on duty. The perpetrator would therefore want to avoid being seen by the elevatormen on duty. The perpetrator might, therefore, use the service entrance as his means of entry. Unlike you, I do not, therefore, regard the use of the service entrance as "highly unlikely". If there is any way for the perpetrator to get a key, or persuade someone to leave that gate unlocked, and rig the bar lock on the service door, or jam the latch or jimmy the door, I'd feel this was a highly likely means of entry—more likely than loitering across the street for a chance to sneak inside when the night man is out hailing a cab.'

Devlin said, 'Jeez, Frank, you're right. I'd better check it out again.'

'What I want,' Sessions said, 'is the name of the man who's willing to swear that that gate was locked last night. And when you get safe and loft in here in the morning, you'll get from them whether those locks were tampered with. The gate and the service door. Not just the locks in this apartment.'

Con said, 'You're right, Frank,' and he hurried off, writing in his notebook as he went. Ecklin and D'Amato came by and Ray said, 'What're you doing, giving lessons on how to be a detective? I hope you're charging professional fees.'

'He's a good kid. He's new, but he's willing.'

'Like the young prince being shown his father's harem?'

'Jesus, Ecklin, does your wife know what kind of a mind you've got?'

Remick approached. 'You get Patterson and Motley, Frank?'

'Yeah. Patterson's meeting us here. Motley's going to the nineteenth.'

'You should have told Patterson to go to the one-nine too. We're ready to call it quits and get over there ourselves.'

'We got to have him come here, Sarge. He claims he wasn't the guy who brought Monica home last night. I want to show him to that elevatorman—Caligliaro—and see if he'll give us a make.'

'All right, we'd better wait for him.'

Ecklin said, 'I've got something for you to read if you want to help pass the time.' He pulled a thin packet of letters bound by a thick elastic from his jacket pocket.

'What's that?'

'Unless there's somebody else named Bobby in her life, Mr. Motley is a letter-writer. Purple prose too. Here, sample his style.' Ecklin distributed a random letter for each to peruse. They all began with a passionate address to 'Monny' and ended with a passionate farewell from 'Bobby'. Between the two names were a number of startling paragraphs describing in intimate and erotic detail the activities attending their most recently shared moments.

Remick read halfway through his letter and said to Ecklin, 'What would you call this—hard-core pornography?'

'I don't know, but I don't think the postmaster general

would approve of it going through his mails. The real question is, is this truth or fiction?'

Sessions stuffed his letter back in the envelope, noting that there was no return address. 'It sounds like the deceased,' he said, 'not only liked it, she liked reading about it. And this guy Motley gets a kick out of writing it. He likes talk as well as action. I'll bet they talked a blue streak all the time they're making love.'

'She's earthier than we've been thinking.'

'Where'd you find the letters, Ray?'

'Down in the basement in her storage cubicle. In the drawer of a cabinet she's got down there.' He handed the packet to Frank. 'Here. It's your pigeon so you can hold the literature. Just make sure some rookie patrolman doesn't catch you with them. He might try to make you his first collar.'

'Thanks. I suppose I can always read them on subways and buses.' He collected the lot and tucked them in his pocket. 'Don't let me forget to make out a receipt.'

Remick said, 'We finished here? Let's close up the place and tell the super nobody gets in.'

They checked the apartment one last time and locked it up. Sessions thanked the Kricks and took the key back to Hogarth. He returned to the lobby and only Remick, Ecklin, D'Amato and Norman Caligliaro were there. The patrolmen, the photographers, the lab men, the reporters—all had gone. The building was a quiet, empty place, tucked in for the night. Remick said to Caligliaro, 'A man's going to come in here pretty soon. You tell me if you know his name or who he is, and when you last saw him. Right?'

Caligliaro touched his cap. 'Sure, Chief.'

Con Devlin came out from the tenants' hallway. He went up to Sessions and flipped open his notebook. 'The service elevator is open from six in the morning till ten at night Mondays, Tuesdays and Wednesdays, Frank, nine to five the other four days. The guy who closes it locks the outside gate when he leaves. So last night, Tuesday night, Pete Tuckman closed and locked the gate about ten o'clock, maybe a few minutes later. He leaves by the service ramp when he goes off duty and locks the gate. The guy in the morning unlocked it when he came on duty.'

'So the gate's open half the night and the service door's probably left open part of the time—for ventilation if nothing else.'

'They say it wasn't, but I know what you mean, Frank. They wouldn't want to admit they might have goofed.'

Remick and Ecklin had gathered around. 'And,' Remick added, 'Caligliaro goes to the john and maybe he takes a smoke in there. Nobody can swear that somebody with a key to the Glazzard apartment didn't get in and out of there without being seen.'

A man got out of a cab out front and paid off the driver. Remick motioned Caligliaro front and centre. The little man, thin and gaunt, hurried forward and stationed himself. 'Good evening, sir,' he said as the man entered.

'Evening.' The man was tall, grey and trim. He wore a light topcoat, a hat cocked at a rakish angle, and he carried an ivory-headed walking stick. He was handsome, urbane, polished and aware of it all.

'Dr. Patterson?' Sessions made introductions all around and took him aside to thank him for coming. He did it so deftly the newcomer never noticed Caligliaro murmuring to Remick.

'Terrible thing,' Patterson said. 'Just terrible. She was so —so vibrant, so full of life, such a good and dear friend. Who could have done such a thing?'

'We don't know what's been done yet, Doctor . . .'

'She didn't take her own life, I can tell you that. And don't call me "Doctor". I'm not a medical man. I'm a sociologist. "Mister" is perfectly all right with me. I always expect people who call me doctor to ask me for a diagnosis.' He chuckled and the detectives smiled without really joining in.

He glanced around with slight uncertainty. 'You know?' he said. 'You are the fellows I really admire. There are those of us who observe life, who sit and watch. And there are those who, having observed life, proceed to pontificate. I suppose I'm one of those. But there are those who get in and act. They don't waste their time watching and listening, they get in and experience. I read about crime. I study crime. I suppose that surprises you. I don't suppose you would have imagined that. But man in crime is man at his most fascinating. When the law fails to hold him and he is totally himself. The criminal is man in reality, as man really is—stripped bare of subterfuge. But as I say, I study crime but you fight crime. You are the men of action. You are the heroes.'

The four detectives listened politely to this and then Sessions said, 'Yes, well, Mr. Patterson, we'd like to ask you a few questions if you don't mind.'

'Mind? Believe me, I want to help. Anything I can do. You know, I was probably closer to her than anyone else. I daresay I know more about her, know more of her friends—I want to work with you on this.'

'Yes, well, we have a few questions but we'll . . .'

'Believe me, this would be no inconvenience for me. It would work to our mutual advantage. If I could feel that I assisted in solving the question of the death of a close friend, this would be ample reward. And, believe me, I welcome the opportunity to be with you men. I'll tell you. Some years ago I tried to get on the inside of the police department, particularly the detective bureau. I might say, particularly homicide. Man the criminal, you know. And Man the hunter. Yes, well, the red tape of being allowed a peek inside—well, I'm afraid I didn't have a very happy experience. Everywhere I went I was given only a minimum of information and then told if I wanted more I'd have to go through channels. And the channels I had to go through didn't seem to fancy giving me access to that further information.' He laughed. 'Maybe the police are suspicious of intellectuals.'

'Yes, now, Mr. Patterson, we're going over to the nineteenth detective squad. Everything's done here and . . .'

'And you'd like to get me on your home ground, so to speak? Certainly. I've never seen a detective squad room.'

Remick caught Frank's eye. Sessions said, 'It's a thing of beauty.'

'Do I ride there with you? I came over by cab.'

'Yes.' They went out and Sessions pointed. 'That black car. Detectives D'Amato and Devlin will ride in this one.'

Patterson opened the door tentatively. 'It looks like an ordinary car. Does it have a siren?'

'It has a siren.' Sessions waited till Patterson ducked into the back seat and muttered to Remick, 'What did the elevatorman say?'

'He makes him. He's it.'

THURSDAY 2:15–2:20 A.M.

Linda Glazzard shut off the shower and listened. At two-fifteen in the morning was that her phone? It rang again and she threw aside the curtains and leaped from the tub, grabbing a towel as she ran into the bedroom.

In the thirty-five minutes since her return from her mother's place, Linda had smoked four cigarettes, sipped four and a half ounces of whiskey, taken off her clothes and got into a shower. The cigarettes and the liquor had been to settle her jangled nerves, give her time to think and at the same time keep her from thinking too much. The shower was to wash away the feel of her mother's place, the clammy room in which her mother lay dead, the coldhearted cops filled with suspicious questions rather than sympathy, the dusty morgue wagon and a bared white foot with a tag tied to the toe.

The smoking and the drinking hadn't done a great deal for her in that half-hour interval. She hadn't untracked herself very much. But now the phone had rung and all would become well. It could only be Randy and he'd fix everything. He might have been suspicious and he might have been angry, but he loved her. He really did love her. And he knew about her too. She had been honest with him.

Of course, the man she intended to marry would hardly come to her believing that, at twenty-nine, she was still a virgin—especially when he had prior experience with her himself. But there's a difference between an affair or two and the lurid kind of past that had been Linda's life before she found herself. But she had told Randy all and he said he didn't care. He wanted her anyway—not just for present fun, but for life. He wanted to marry her, raise a family with her, and do all in the world for her. Poor Randy. He wanted to give her the moon but he couldn't yet afford a ring. He was between jobs and trying to make his meagre savings last till he could relocate.

But that wouldn't be for long and the main problem at the moment was to straighten out the difficulties that David's behaviour had caused. And Randy was calling to do it.

She wasn't sure how long the phone had been ringing when she scrambled wetly across the bed and seized the receiver. 'Hello,' she said, and her heart was beating hard as she tried to straighten the towel out to sit on.

It was Randy's voice that responded but it wasn't the kind of voice he usually used in speaking to her. This was a cold voice with an almost foreign sound to it, as if he were direct dialling from some address in Europe rather than one relatively close at hand. 'Miss Linda Glazzard?'

'Oh, Randy. Oh, I was hoping that was you.'

'Just pining to hear from me, weren't you?'

'Darling, if you ever knew. I've been going out of my mind. That stupid David . . .'

'David who?'

'You know. I've talked about him before. He's at Cowan and Blakeslee. I've known him since I first started working there.'

'Is he one of the ones you sleep with?'

That one stung. 'David?' she said with forced jollity. 'He's just a clown. He heard me on the phone with you and broke in just to make you think the wrong thing. That's his idea of a practical joke.'

'And what's your idea of a practical joke, dear?' Randy said icily. 'Telling me you went to the show with a girlfriend and ending up with a man in your apartment?'

'Randy, don't,' she said desperately. 'If it was the kind of thing you're thinking—I mean if I was the kind of girl who'd do a thing like that—do you think I'd let him say anything into the phone? After all, darling!'

'You didn't sound as if you let him, Linda. You sounded as if you didn't want him to. And what's more, he didn't sound like somebody playing a practical joke.'

Linda hugged her knees for warmth. She was nude and wet and not only Randy's voice but the room was making her shiver. 'Be reasonable, Randy,' she said, trying to be reasonable herself. 'If you'll just let me explain.'

'I've been trying. But you not only hang up on me, you don't answer when I call you back. If you hadn't answered this time, Linda . . .'

'Oh my God,' Linda said, and again it had slipped her mind completely. 'You don't know what's happened. My mother. The police called me up. Monica's dead.'

'What?'

'Monica. She's dead. She died this morning. The police called me right after you did. Something about coming to identify her. Oh, darling, can you come home? I need you. Right now I need you like crazy.'

Randy said carefully, 'I don't suppose that's another practical joke. That couldn't be.'

'No. Honest to God. Randy, it'll be in all the papers. I just got back from her place three-quarters of an hour ago. Honest, it was right after you called. David took me over in a cab and went on home.'

'Well, I'm sorry to hear about your mother, Linda.' The voice sounded sincere about that but it was still cold.

'Randy, I'm at my wits' end. I know your aunt is dying, but I need you. I need somebody to help me get through the next few days. I don't know how I'm going to do it.'

Randy didn't give a fraction of an inch. 'I'm needed here, Linda.'

'But God damn it, I'm the girl you love. I'm in trouble. Please, Randy. It's *my own* mother.'

Randy was still unforgiving. 'You make that sound important, Linda, as if *your own* mother meant something to you. As far as I could make out, your only emotion toward her was fear. *She* had to pass on me before you could marry me.'

'Not pass on you. Do you think I wouldn't have married you no matter what she said or did?' Linda wailed then. 'Oh, Randy. What are we doing? We're squabbling. It's two o'clock in the morning and we're squabbling. And I'm cold. You got me in the shower. So here I'm sitting with nothing on.' She laughed. 'Don't you wish they had phon-o-vision?'

He said, 'Let me ask you a question. Would you have liked it if we'd had phon-o-vision the last time I called?'

Her face hardened. 'Why do you say things like that? Why don't you trust me? How could you even believe I'd look at another man?'

'You have, haven't you?'

'Not since you. Not once, since you. And that's even before we realised we were in love.'

'But how do I know?'

'Because you know me. Just as I know you and I know you're not off with some other woman right now, though the accusation has been made against you tonight!'

'Oh,' Randy said with interest. 'By who?'

'By David. And I told him he didn't know what he was talking about . . .'

'Why would he make such a remark?'

'Oh, damn it, Randy, because he did try to make a pass at me. If you must know, he did try it. And I told him about you—that was after you phoned and I told him what he'd done by trying to show me in a bad light. He said you probably stood me up for another woman and I told him you wouldn't and I knew it because I knew you. And I told him that, for the very same reason, you'd know I wasn't out with another man because you knew me. And you *do* know me.'

'I *do* know you, Linda. Your past as well as your present.'

'My past?' she said in alarm. 'What about my past? I thought you said that had nothing to do with things.'

'The past does not, Linda. That's true. What counts is the present. And that's what's got me concerned right now. I don't blame you, my dear. But after what's happened tonight, I have to ask myself, "Is the past really past?" Have you really changed, Linda, or do you only think you have because you can be faithful to one man?'

'I don't like being put on the spot like that, but since you ask, I should certainly think that being faithful to one man is all that you or anyone should ever want from a girl.'

'Yes, but faithful, I mean, so long as he's available. Then the moment his back is turned . . .'

'Nothing happened!' she shouted. 'I'm telling you nothing happened!'

'I know you're telling me that. And I hope you're telling the truth. But I also realise, dear, that you would tell me nothing happened whether it did or it didn't. And you've told at least one other lie tonight, so, you see, I'm in no way of knowing what's going on—whether you're the same Linda behind my back that you are to my face or whether you revert back to an earlier type. And if we're going to be married, this is something I've got to be sure of. I would hate to find out after marriage that, well, the minute I went out of town . . .'

'I'll save you all that worry, you god-damned, self-righteous prig. Because there isn't going to be any marriage. I wouldn't marry you if you were the last man on earth.'

With that she slammed down the receiver and burst into tears.

THURSDAY 2:25–2:45 A.M.

The squad room of the nineteenth detectives was a large rectangle beyond the fenced and gated area just inside the door. The detention cage was against the right wall, desks were bunched in the middle, the lieutenant's office and a small kitchen were off to the left. It was an old room in an old building, as were the squad rooms in most of the precincts, and though no two such rooms were the same in size, structure or furnishings, they all served the same purposes, were used by men in the same line of work, and all had a certain sameness of look, smell and feel about them. In the nineteenth, the fingerprint desk was against the wall in the far corner and when the homicide men came in with Dr. Patterson, a detective was struggling to fingerprint a staggering Negro who was neither recalcitrant nor co-operative. The Negro, turning to view the newcomers, leaned so far off balance that only the fingerprint man's grip on his wrist kept him from falling on his face. 'Ya got a butt?' the prisoner asked the newcomers.

Lt. Boxton met the men at his office door. They introduced Patterson and asked about Motley. He hadn't shown. D'Amato and Devlin arrived then and the Negro swayed and tried to get a butt from them. The fingerprint man jerked him around impatiently.

Sessions, Devlin and the lieutenant settled themselves in the office with Patterson and the others retired to the kitchen to make coffee and talk. Patterson sat down facing the open door and a view of the wobbling Negro; Sessions took a corner of Boxton's desk. He lighted a cigarette and opened his notebook and Patterson asked what the Negro was being held for. Boxton said, 'Trying to break into a parked car.'

'Poor man.'

Sessions said, 'Lucky car owner you mean. This guy's not a first offender. He knows the inside of a squad room. Now when did you say you last saw Mrs. Glazzard? Just to change the subject.'

Sessions was casual but Patterson came to attention, eyed him carefully and managed a nervous smile. 'The elevator-man said something, didn't he?'

'He said you saw Mrs. Glazzard home last night. Do you want to deny it?'

'No, sir. It's the truth.'

'Earlier you denied you saw her at all.'

Patterson nodded. 'That's right, I did. And I've been asking myself why. I suppose it was fear.'

'What were you afraid of?'

'I don't know. Being accused, perhaps. You said you were from homicide and my first reaction was not to get involved.' Patterson tried to smile disarmingly. 'But on the way over I realised how foolish that was. I want to help you every way I can. Monica was one of my dearest friends. Anything I can do I will.'

'Tell us about last night. Tell us everything you did yesterday.'

Patterson went through a slow, thoughtful account. He'd got up at nine-thirty, his usual time. His housekeeper had breakfast ready for him. He'd eaten and engrossed himself with the newspapers. He subscribed to five: three New York papers, the *Times*, the *News*, the *Post*, plus his hometown daily, plus the *Christian Science Monitor*. After that, he did some work on an article he was doing on Freud. His housekeeper had lunch for him at one. After that he had got a haircut, gone to the Columbia library to work and had spent some time visiting a Professor Edward English there. He returned to his home to bathe and change, then went by cab to Mrs. Glazzard's apartment, arriving about five. They had a drink together, then attended the Gregory Buckingham party for Frederick and Florence Lyle, stars of the off-Broadway show *Little Lost Blue*, which was opening that night. They went to the play, joined the Lyles and others for supper at Lindy's after, and waited there for the morning papers to come out with the reviews. The reviews praised the actors but damned the play, an opinion both Patterson and Mrs. Glazzard shared.

'Then we—the Lyles, Monica and I—came back to Monica's for a nightcap or two. Monica was going to write about them the next day. They left somewhere around half past two, I guess, but Monica wanted me to stay. She wanted me to judge her column after she dictated it. So she went into her office to dictate and I poured myself a drink. She came out in about fifteen minutes and played it back for me so I could hear the way she had made the points we had both thought should be made.' Patterson smiled. 'And, of course, she was brilliant, as usual. We had ourselves quite a chuckle.

'Then I left. Probably about half past three, and the doorman got me a taxi.'

Sessions, writing something in his notebook, said without looking up, 'How was she dressed when you left her?'

'Dressed?'

'What was she wearing? Nightgown, pyjamas, a négligé, which?'

Patterson stared at Sessions. Finally he said, 'I think you've got the wrong idea. She was wearing a black dress. The one she wore to the theatre.'

'She didn't get ready for bed while you were there?'

'No, sir. Certainly not. That's an unheard-of idea.'

Boxton came in with a change of subjects. Had Mr. Patterson sensed in any way that someone else might have been in the apartment? Were there any sounds or smells? Was there, for example, the odour of cigarette smoke when they first came in? How about Mrs. Glazzard? Was there anything about her manner that would indicate she knew someone else was around or was expecting someone to come?

Patterson tried manfully to think of something, to have smelled something, to have noticed something, but ultimately, if he wanted to be honest about it, he could point to nothing. He had no sense of not being alone with Monica in the apartment. 'But of course,' he said, 'that was on the first floor. I don't know what might have been upstairs.'

Sessions went after his background then. How long had he known the deceased? What was their relationship?

Patterson, in résumé, said that he had known Mrs. Glazzard about nineteen years, that he regarded her as a close personal friend, that they frequently ran into each other at social functions but they also sought one another out on other occasions. They would dine together now and then or she might ask him to escort her to some show she was to review. She was always given tickets in pairs if a party wasn't being arranged and she could do what she liked with the extra. Of course, Dr. Patterson hastened to make clear, he wasn't the only man she invited to play escort, he was only one close friend among many, but Monica particularly enjoyed theatre-going with him, for he had insights and understanding that could enhance her column still more.

As for the last previous time he had seen Monica, he'd have to think about that. Was it a week ago Friday or a week ago Thursday? He rather thought it was Thursday but he could check his engagement book. It was a cocktail party Monica had for Robin Weir, the playwright, on the occasion of his twenty-eighth birthday. Weir was the author of the off-

Broadway play *Something of Colour*, which both he and Monica had found most praiseworthy. Monica had, in fact, taken up a crusade in her column to get people to go see it and its present success might in no small degree be due to her efforts.

'How well does she know this Robin Weir?'

'I don't think very well. She took him to lunch, she was so pleased with his play, and she met him that way, and I think the cocktail party is the only other meeting they've had. She wanted him to meet a lot of the theatre people and she wanted them to meet him. It could help him a lot.'

'What was she getting out of all this?'

'My dear fellow, you don't understand the situation at all. She felt his is a remarkable talent and she wanted him to succeed. It's as simple as that. If you want to ascribe a selfish motive, I suppose you could say that Monica could claim, after he became a smash success, to have discovered him, or been the first to see his potential.'

'Then he wasn't what you might call a "protégé" of hers?'

'Oh good heavens no. Certainly not to my knowledge. And I'm sure I'd know.'

'Any other protégés that you do know of?'

'No. Monica doesn't go in for protégés.'

'Know a man named Robert Motley?'

'No. I can't say I do. Is he a friend of Monica's?'

'We were hoping you could tell us.'

'He could well be. I don't begin to know all of her friends. She has thousands of them. All over the world.'

What about boyfriends? the detectives asked. What about men who wanted to marry her, or worship her, or go to bed with her? Patterson found himself remarkably naïve in this field. He started to insist that she didn't have any love-life when he realised that the proper answer was that he didn't know anything about her love-life. He sat back fretting a little, deciding he wasn't quite as close a friend of the glamorous, shrewd, sharp, gifted, brilliant columnist as he had thought. These detectives, who'd never laid eyes on her live, who knew nothing of her as an individual, who couldn't really touch the hem of her skirt when it came to talent and ability, they acted as if they knew more about her than he himself did, the experienced sociologist, the student of mankind, the close personal friend and intimate. The trouble was, these detectives had minds that immediately went to the vulgar. They saw a dead woman and they thought in terms of sex. Sex wasn't what you thought about with Monica—or so Dr. Patterson felt, and yet, those detectives might be the right ones after all and it was Dr. Patterson who had been led astray; the brilliant mind deceived by the nuances and shades and gradations of sound, scene and behaviour that the ordinary mind was not distracted by because it did not even hear, see or note.

Sessions, lighting one cigarette from another, said, 'What about enemies, Mr. Patterson?'

'Enemies? Monica?'

'You don't think she had any?'

'I can't say. It's a matter that I've just never considered.'

'Did you ever read her column? Wouldn't you say that her methods of attack, ridicule, and character assassination might raise some ill-will toward her?'

Had her column really been like that? She was so brilliant and clever, with such a devastating way with words, that what he had admired was her manner of dismissing the trivial, the trite and the dull. What he had not bothered to consider, sociologist though he was, was how those who had created the trivial, the trite and the dull might react to the incisive and humiliating demolition of their creations. As the ugliest child is still loved by its mother, perhaps even the most banal work is admired by its author.

'Well,' Patterson said, 'I suppose there are those who might take offence.'

'But she never spoke to you of enemies?'

'No.'

'Did she ever speak to you of death?'

'Death? No.' So this was another area they were probing and again it was one he had not shared with her.

'Do you know what her views were on suicide? Life after death?'

He didn't. At least not on suicide. As for life after death, he recalled that she had been baptised an Episcopalian.

'Did she practise the faith?'

'She never mentioned religion much. If she ever went to church, she never talked about it. I do recall her talking about Bishop Pike, though.'

'What was her view of Bishop Pike?'

'She liked the idea of his stirring things up. She thought that was very healthy. He was a man she wanted to meet and talk to.'

'That doesn't tell us an awful lot, Mr. Patterson. So you don't really know what her views were on death or life after death?'

'No,' he said in some chagrin. 'I guess not.' They had him again. He was such an intimate friend of Monica's? Now he was beginning to wonder if he knew anything about her at all.

Then, from his chair, Patterson could see a man come into the room and pause at the gate. He was young and dark and very good-looking, he wore good clothes, but he looked around uncertainly and his face was very pale. Unlike the Negro who was at that moment being taken out to the stairs, this was a man who did not know the inside of a detective squad room.

The squat, balding sergeant went to meet him and let him in and Patterson wondered if this man were a complainant come to air a grievance or if he played a role in Monica's death. He suspected the latter, yet the newcomer didn't look like the kind of man Patterson expected Monica Glazzard to know. He wasn't talented like Robin Weir, distinguished like himself, or rich like some of her other intimates. This young man was only pretty.

But now the sergeant was coming to the door and telling the lieutenant and the detectives that Mr. Motley was here.

THURSDAY 2:45–3:10 A.M.

Dr. Patterson rather hoped that he'd have the privilege of listening to the detectives query the newcomer. Obviously the handsome young man was a figure in Monica's life, suggesting to the sociologist new and interesting facets to his late friend. The police, however, were not co-operative and Patterson found himself on the outside, this time with Ecklin and D'Amato, while Remick, Sessions, Devlin and Boxton closeted themselves in the lieutenant's office with Robert Motley.

Patterson could have gone home but he elected to stay. Even if he couldn't hear what Motley knew, crime held a fascination for him and here he was, in the middle of what seemed to be one.

Inside the office, Motley didn't react with the same enthusiasm. He was white-faced and smoked nervously, holding his cigarettes between fingers stained almost as brown as Sessions'.

'How old are you, Bob?' was Sessions' first question. He was perched on the corner of Boxton's desk again with a tin ashtray in front of him.

Motley, in Patterson's chair, said, 'I'm thirty-two.'

'What's your address?'

'331 East 75th Street. That's between First and Second.'

'What's your occupation?'

Motley thought about that for a moment. 'I'm a writer,' he finally answered.

'What do you write?'

'Articles. Essays.'

'You make out pretty well at it?'

'I manage to get by.'

Sessions eyed him sideways, rubbed out his cigarette and got out his notebook. 'How much did you make last year?' he asked. 'Writing articles, I mean.'

'Last year?' Motley managed not to meet his eye. 'Let me try to remember.'

'Come on, Motley, what was it? Fifty dollars? Five hundred dollars? Fifty thousand dollars?'

Motley smiled. 'It wasn't fifty thousand.'

Sessions didn't smile. 'Did you make anything last year? Did you sell one single thing you've written?'

Moley wasn't smiling now either. 'No.'

'Have you *ever* sold anything you've written?'

Motley looked down at the floor. 'No.'

'So what do you want to lie to us for? You want to hide something from us?' Sessions cocked his head deliberately. 'Would you like to call a lawyer, Mr. Motley?'

Motley answered very quickly. 'No, no.'

Sessions kept on. 'Let me remind you, Mr. Motley. You don't have to answer any questions. You don't have to even talk to us. And you can have a lawyer any time you want.'

Motley was not only white, he was sweating. 'No, no. Listen, I have nothing to hide.'

Remick, one foot on a chair, leaned forward, elbow on knee. 'Why does a nice-looking young fellow like you want to come in here and tell lies to the police for? Wasn't Monica Glazzard your friend? Don't you want to help her?'

Motley nodded. 'Yes, I do.'

'Well, then, just tell the truth. That's all you have to do. Tell us what you know about Monica. Is that what you called her? "Monica"?'

'Yes.'

'And you were her boyfriend, right?'

Motley looked frightened again. 'No. No.'

Remick was solicitous. 'What's the matter, Motley? You afraid of shocking us? You don't have to worry about something like that. Now Mrs. Glazzard paid the rent on your apartment, didn't she?'

'No,' Motley said, licking his lips. 'Of course not.'

'We're going to look at your lease first thing in the morning. Do you want to sign a sworn statement tonight that *your* name and not hers is on that lease?'

Motley brushed a distracted hand over his brow. 'No.'

'She pays the rent, right?'

'Yes. She pays the rent.'

Remick smiled at him. 'O.K. Now you told the truth. And you see? Lightning doesn't strike you dead. The earth doesn't stop turning. In fact it's pleasant. I smile. Even Frank here smiles . . . Well, he feels like smiling even if he isn't. Everybody feels good.' The sergeant spread his hands. 'You see how easy it is? Now just keep it up and everything'll be fine. Before you know it you'll be back home in bed.'

Sessions said, 'She buys your clothes for you too, right?'

Motley nodded.

'And gives you spending money? A hundred and fifty on April seventeenth, a hundred and ten on the twenty-sixth?'

'Those are loans.'

'What were you going to pay them back with? She wasn't expecting to be paid back, was she?'

'No,' he said sullenly.

'How much spending money would she give you?'

'No set amount. It depended on what we spent it on.' He grew a little more communicative. 'You see, actually, I was sort of a companion to Mrs. Glazzard. She was a single woman and needed an escort. I served in that capacity. So, of course, she had to equip me for the role. I mean, that's why she paid for the apartment and for the clothes and gave me the money. She'd give me the money so that I could pay the bills when we were out together.'

Sessions' reply to that was, 'Was she sexually demanding?'

It made Motley blink. 'I think you've got the wrong idea,' he said.

'Yeah, we've got the wrong idea. You got a key to her apartment?'

'No, of course not.'

He held out his hand. 'You want to let me see your keys?'

Motley started to reach, then started to object, and then said, 'Oh, all right. I've got a key. I wasn't just her escort, I also ran errands and did odd jobs for her. I was a second secretary. Of course I have a key.'

'And you were her lover.'

Motley let out a yelp. 'No!'

'Come on. A woman doesn't give a young man a key to her apartment so he can do odd jobs. You were her lover and we know it. Why don't you want to admit it?'

'Because it wasn't like that.'

Sessions looked at Remick. 'Jesus, Sarge. I've known some liars in my day.' He reached in his pocket and pulled out the packet of letters Ecklin had found. He held them up. 'You know what these are, Bobby?'

Motley sank back in the chair and for a moment looked as if he would faint. Sessions stuffed them back in his pocket and glowered. 'Now I'm going to tell you something, Motley. You've been lying your head off when you've had no reason to that we could see. You're told this woman is dead and without even knowing how she died, you start lying like a fool. I don't know what it is you're afraid of, mister, but I'm going to find out. Now I'm going to tell you again. You don't have to answer any questions we ask you and if you're guilty of having something to do with Mrs. Glazzard's death, you'd better not answer any questions at all. You get me? You'd better keep still and get an attorney. Now is that what you want to do?'

With great effort Motley managed to pull himself together. 'No,' he finally whispered hoarsely. 'Honest to God I've got nothing to hide. Honest, I didn't do anything to her. I'll tell you anything you want.'

'All right,' Sessions said coldly, 'start in by telling us why you've been lying if you've got nothing to hide.'

'Yes, sir.' Motley lighted a cigarette and took a quick, deep drag. 'What you've been saying is the truth. It's all the truth. I've been trying to hide it to protect Monica.' Then he hunched forward and stared down at the floor. 'And I'll be completely honest with you. I've been lying to protect myself, too. I didn't want to admit I'm a gigolo. And I didn't want to admit that she hired one.' He looked up then and took a slower drag on the cigarette. 'So there you have it. Only I might as well tell you I'm not even a good gigolo. I said I escorted her places. That was another lie. We didn't go out together in public—or if we did, it was only to places where she wouldn't be known. I wasn't kept for anything except that she was in love with me. And it's a soft life and, let's admit it, she was quite a gal. Maybe I wasn't as much in love with her as she was with me, but I cared. We liked each other.'

He made a display of hands. 'We had to keep it quiet. With her reputation it would be very damaging for her to marry a man sixteen years younger than she was. She was so smart and witty and brilliant, it would be so obvious what such a marriage was all about. It would show her up as a sex-hungry old fool. With all the wealthy, smart, talented people her own age around who adored her and would have leaped at the chance to marry her, I would be a terrible choice. She couldn't defend it.

'Of course, that's not the way she put it, but I'm not so dumb I'd think I could compete in her league. The way she put it, and what was also part of the reason, was that marrying anybody would cut into her freedom of action too much. If she had to drag a husband along everywhere she went, she'd lose out on the variety of escorts she had—different people for different occasions. Also she'd no longer be the femme fatale, if you want to call her that. What I mean is, she liked being swarmed around by males of all kinds. And she liked her independence. She would have hated marriage.

'But, let's face it, she also liked the physical side of life too.' He gestured with his cigarette toward Sessions' pocket where the packet of letters lay. 'I guess you read those. She was earthy. She liked sex and saw no reason why she shouldn't. It was our little secret. I guess it's not going to be much of a secret any longer. So, all right.' He pulled on the cigarette and mashed it beneath his foot. 'What else do you want to know?'

'When'd you see her last?'

'Night before last. Monday night, that is. She went out to a dinner party and a private showing of some of sculptor Jon Majznik's things. I went over to her place about half past twelve and watched television until she came in. I wanted to see how the evening went. Besides, she liked having me sort of be there when she came home at night. She liked having somebody to talk to and tell about the night's doings to. I wouldn't do this every night, but I'd try to anticipate when she'd want me to, if you know what I mean? Sometimes she'd be bringing people home and then I'd stay away, of course. Other times, though, she'd be going out with people she didn't particularly enjoy, or would be coming home early and wouldn't be tired yet. So I'd be likely to be around and she might have a drink with me and she'd dictate her column for a few minutes—that wouldn't take long, and then we'd talk or make love or whatever and then I'd go home.'

Remick said, 'You'd go home? You wouldn't stay over?'

'She has this secretary who comes in in the morning and wakes her up for lunch. She's been doing that for years—since before I came on the scene. So she doesn't want the secretary knowing too much about me. I mean, I'm around and the secretary knows me, but it's not like her finding me in Monica's bed every few days when she brings in the breakfast tray. Monica was discreet about things.'

Sessions said, 'So you saw her Monday night. How come you didn't see her last night?'

'She was expecting to bring some people home with her.'

'What people?'

'I don't know. Friends she went to the theatre with, I think.'

'She didn't tell you?'

'She didn't tell me.'

Sessions said, 'So what *did* you do last night?'

'Oh, me? Nothing. I just stayed home.'

'What do you usually do when you aren't seeing Monica?'

'Stay home.'

'You don't have any friends of your own, people to go see, relatives or anything like that?'

'No, I don't.'

'You don't see or date anybody except Monica?'

'No one.'

Remick said, 'Come on.' He held out his hand and wiggled his fingers. 'A young buck like you and you're going to tell us you never go to bed with another dame?'

'That's right.'

'You want us to believe you don't have some cute little number stashed off out of the way who comes to your apartment sometimes maybe on nights when Monica is going to be entertaining? Or maybe, during the day, when Monica's got her parties and things . . . ?'

Motley flushed. 'No. Absolutely not.'

Remick said gently, 'Hey, come on, Motley. What're you telling us a story like that for? We aren't going to squeal on you. Monica's dead. Hiding it isn't going to do you any good now.'

'Absolutely, there are no other women. None.'

Con Devlin spoke then. 'Do you like *men*, Mr. Motley?'

Motley's flush deepened. He called Devlin a name.

'O.K., no need to take offence.'

'Why not, when you accuse me of things like that?'

'Nobody was accusing you of anything, Mr. Motley.'

Sessions said, 'You don't like homosexuals, Bob?'

'I think they're scum.'

'Mrs. Glazzard knew a lot of them, didn't she—homosexuals?'

'I don't know.'

'You must know who her friends were. A lot of theatre people in there, weren't there? People in the various arts? A lot of them are fags, you know. You *do* know that, don't you, Motley?'

'Only by reputation. I wouldn't associate with such people myself.'

'What did Mrs. Glazzard think of people like that?'

'We didn't discuss such matters.'

Boxton scowled at him. 'She doesn't discuss this with you, she doesn't discuss that with you? What the hell did you discuss?'

'Well, we didn't talk much together.'

Sessions said, 'What about those letters you wrote her? Tell us about those.'

Motley swallowed and forced a tiny smile. 'I wrote those back when we first started going together. Before she—before I became a gigolo. She liked them. She liked that kind of thing. So I tried to please her.'

Sessions moved to background next and the questions came quick and fast. 'Where're you from? What's your hometown?' 'Were you born there?' 'Parents' names?' 'Where do they live?' 'When did you come to New York?' 'Why?' 'How did you meet Mrs. Glazzard?'

Motley tried to slow the questions by thinking carefully about his answers, delaying them, altering their spacing. He could tell the game the detectives were playing—trying to keep him off-balance so he'd either cross himself up or tip them off by his hesitations when he was lying. He wasn't going to let them run him like that. He was going to keep a certain amount of control over proceedings. He was born and raised, he said, in Sacramento and his parents lived there till they died, his father six years ago, his mother two years. The police threw him a curve by asking what county Sacramento was in and he couldn't answer. 'I just never paid any attention,' he said. 'I don't know what county New York is in either.'

He graduated from high school and went to work in a filling station for a while, then got a job selling real estate for a successful but small real estate operator. The man's name? 'Charles Sumner.' The name of the filling station operator? 'That was, uh, Jerry Greenbaum.' More boldly—'Any other names you want to know?'

He continued in the real estate business, he said, and after his father died was his mother's main source of support. His father had been a streetcar conductor and later a bus driver and he wasn't able to save anything. Pensions? 'Well, they didn't have a pension plan until right near the end.'

After his mother died, he had taken what money there was and come east to New York. This was two years ago in August of 1965. He got himself a room down in a loft off Avenue B which cost twenty-five dollars a month. He had enrolled in September in the New School, taking art courses. He had always wanted to paint but had never had the chance before. He also began haunting art galleries.

How did he get to meet Mrs. Glazzard? It was at a party given by Mrs. Carolyn Dines Stevenson. In her apartment on Washington Square. 'Mrs. Stevenson introduced us, in fact.'

Sessions got Mrs. Stevenson's address down and said, 'How did you get to meet Mrs. Stevenson?'

'We were both interested in painting. We ran into each other in art galleries.'

'How old is she?'

'Mid-forties, I suppose. Her husband is quite wealthy.'

'What was your relationship to her? You her protégé?'

'No, sir. No relationship. Just friends. In fact, hardly that, for we hadn't known each other long. It was the first time I was ever in her apartment. And, because Monica and I met, it was the last.'

'All right, you met. What happened?'

'We hit it off. We liked each other. When the party ended, she brought me back to her apartment and we talked a long time. It started with her planning to do a column about me but we got off that subject. And we saw each other some more and it went on from there. It was a year ago February when we met. Then she didn't want me living in a loft way down on Avenue B so she moved me into an apartment closer to hers and signed a two-year lease.'

Remick said, 'You kind of liked each other? You mean you kind of liked her money?'

'No, I mean I liked her.'

'And you still want us to believe you didn't have any girl on the side? That maybe Monica didn't find out about this other girl and maybe you and she quarrelled about it?'

'No. That's absolutely not true.'

'Suppose we ask over at your building, talk to the super and the elevatormen and the doormen. Will they tell us you never had any women up to your apartment?'

'You're damned right they will.'

Remick shrugged and looked at Sessions. He turned around, opened the door and went out, closing it behind him. Sessions said, 'What were Mrs. Glazzard's views on suicide, Mr. Motley?'

'I don't know.'

Sessions made a face. 'Jesus, Motley. You've practically lived with this woman for damned near a year and a half and you're trying to tell me you don't know a thing about her? Come off it, will you?'

Motley was very cool about it all. He wasn't going to be upset by Sessions' flare-up. 'I don't happen to know her views on suicide but that doesn't mean I don't know quite a lot about her. I know, for example, that she loved Mexican food, she loved murder trials, and she loved pretty clothes. So, you see?'

'And she loved sex?'

'Yes, she liked sex.'

'How many other men did she play around with?'

'None that I know about. If she played with anybody else, you don't think she'd tell me, do you?'

'Why not? What would you have done about it?'

Motley bit his lip and managed his not-quite-happy smile. 'Not much, I guess. But even so, why would she tell me such things?'

'How about her sex life before she met you?'

'She never talked about that either.'

Boxton said bitterly, 'Don't you get it, Sessions? She and he never talked. They just plain didn't talk together.' He fixed Motley with a baleful eye but Motley ignored both the sarcasm and the stare. 'I can't help it,' he said. 'Maybe there are other people she confided in more. That wasn't what she wanted me around for.'

Sessions lighted a new cigarette from the butt of the old. 'That's about it,' he said. 'Just a couple more questions. We don't know yet how Mrs. Glazzard died. It could've been suicide. Would you find this hard to believe?'

Motley thought about it for a moment. 'No, I don't suppose so.'

'Why?'

'Well, I don't know. Her temperament, I guess. She was kind of high-strung, nervous. She had ups and downs. You know, the blues. I'm not saying that's the way she was feeling last night because I wasn't around, but it's quite possible.'

'It could've been murder too. Would you find that hard to believe?'

'That someone would kill her? Yes. I can't imagine who'd want to.'

'She never talked about anyone hating her or wanting to see her out of the way?'

'Not to me.'

Boxton said, 'Don't you remember, Sessions? They never talked.'

Sessions took a deep drag on the cigarette. 'Except about Mexican food, murder trials and clothes. O.K., Motley, let's talk about you. You say you were home in your apartment all last night. What were you doing tonight?'

'Staying home, watching television.'

'When did you first find out Monica was dead?'

'When you called me. What—an hour and a half ago? Something like that.'

'You sure you didn't find out earlier?'

Motley looked genuinely puzzled. 'What do you mean?'

'I mean you're sure you didn't go over this evening to meet her? You've got a key. You let yourself in and you look around and you suddenly find out she's dead in bed. And you get worried and you don't know what to do so you hurry up back home and then call the police and report a body in that apartment?'

'No. That's a fantastic story. I never left my apartment. You can check with the elevatormen.'

'O.K., then how come you didn't show up this evening? You usually dropped in, right? You'd come over and wait for her. You didn't do that last night because she was having people back after the theatre. So why not tonight?'

Motley took a breath. 'I was going to come over tonight. But not till late. She was going to a party at some hotel. Some friend of hers. She didn't tell me the details. All she did was say it would be very late. She thought she wouldn't be home before three at the earliest. Probably closer to four.'

'When did she tell you that?'

'Monday night. The last time I ever saw her.'

Sessions took a final drag on the filter cigarette and added its stub to the others in the tray. 'Last question,' he said. 'What do you do daytimes? When she's not around to check up on you?'

'Oh, lots of things. I go to the movies. I go shopping. I kind of like clothes myself. And there are museums and art galleries and in the summer there's Jones Beach and Coney Island.'

'Who do you go to all these places with?'

'Who? I don't go with anybody.'

'You just go to Jones Beach all by yourself? You visit these museums all alone? You never take a friend along?'

'You're trying to trick me into saying I know some other women. I don't. I don't date. I don't take women out.'

'And you'd never say hello to a girl on the beach or strike up a conversation with some pretty young thing?'

'No. Flatly and definitely, no.'

'Why?'

'What for? What's the point?'

'What're you trying to tell me, that you're afraid Mrs. Glazzard would find out and she wouldn't like it?'

'No, it's just that I felt obligated to her and I wanted to be faithful.'

Sessions said, 'Jesus, you know that's really touching.'

'All right, so you don't believe it. I also happen to like to keep my life simple and uncomplicated. I'm not trying to make myself out to be any Puritan, but you start messing around and things are going to get sticky. What's the point?'

'What's the point? Why, you might fall in love, get married, settle down and get a job. Or maybe you weren't making any plans for the future?'

'Not particularly. I've been content with the present.'

'And maybe Mrs. Glazzard was fixing up your future for you? What do you get in her will, by the way?'

'I don't know. I don't have any idea.'

'Something else you never talked about, huh? We're going to be seeing her lawyer tomorrow and he's going to tell us. He's also going to tell us if you knew. You still want to say you don't?'

'I don't.'

'You got much money salted away, Motley? I mean, she's not going to be sending you any more cheques. What are your plans?'

'I don't have any plans yet, for God's sake. I haven't been able to think.'

'You have any money?'

'A little. Not much. I don't know what I'll do.'

They let him go then and Sessions turned on some of his charm for a change. He walked him out to the gate and thanked him warmly for his co-operation. 'I'm sorry we had to get you down here at a time like this. But I guess you can sleep tomorrow.'

'It's O.K. I'd've come down even if I'd had to go to work at 6 a.m.'

Sessions gave him a big smile and a wave as he went out the door and down the stairs. Remick, Ecklin and D'Amato came over, leaving Dr. Patterson behind in the kitchen. 'Get anything?'

'Out of him?' Sessions snorted. 'With him it's not a question of how much of what he told us was true, it's a question whether anything he told us at all was true. Right, Sarge?'

'He's some boy,' Remick agreed.

'You know what he wants us to believe?' Sessions told them. 'That he lives in a monastery. In the middle of New York City he's living in a god-damned monastery. Never looks at another woman. Never thinks about another woman. Doesn't have any friends, relatives, anybody to talk to except Monica Glazzard. She's his whole life. You got that? His whole god-damned life!' He put his hand on Ecklin's shoulder. 'And you know what? If that isn't enough—feeding us a line like that—he doesn't even back it up. The centre of his life and now she's dead and the son of a bitch doesn't have one tear to shed, one word of regret to utter, one thought as to whether he can help out some way.' Sessions laughed. 'Jesus, he must really think we're stupid.'

D'Amato said, 'You figure he's the perpetrator, Frank?'

Sessions shrugged. 'If you could find him with a girlfriend—and Monica knowing about it—or if he stands to profit by the will . . . Hell, he's got the key to her apartment, he's more likely than anyone else to be around when she's in a nightgown. If there's a perpetrator, of course he could be it. Whether he actually is or not is another story.'

Remick muttered, 'Change the subject. Here comes Patterson.'

And Ecklin said out of the side of his mouth, 'Don't let him start asking questions, Frank. He's a sociologist and he's just discovered the New York Police Department.'

'Well, did you get any clues?' Patterson asked, joining the group.

'We just asked a few questions,' Sessions answered. 'Where's some of that coffee?'

'What are you going to do next?' It was ten after three in the morning but Patterson looked ready to go through the day.

'I expect we'll head back to homicide. There's nothing more here.'

'What're you going to do there?'

'Try to get some sleep.'

THURSDAY 6:30–9:30 A.M.

Frank Sessions shut off the alarm and dragged himself out of his cot in the dormitory at half past six that morning. He lighted a cigarette, tried to tell himself that two hours of sleep was enough to do a day's work on, crossed down the hall to the lavatory and let the cigarette burn itself out on the glass shelf over the washbasins while he took a shower and shaved. He padded, with a towel around his waist, back to the dormitory, got a key to Boro Headquarters, crossed the hall to open that up, poured a bag of coffee into the urn, got water for it and plugged in the cord. He went back to the dormitory, lighted another cigarette, shook Remick, Ecklin and Connager into wakefulness and started to get back into his clothes.

Ecklin groaned and said, 'Ten of seven. God, what time did we finish with those DD5s?'

'You quit at half past four.'

'I hope there's some coffee.'

Sessions laughed. 'Try to hang together till you can fall back into bed at home.'

Remick asked Connager how he made out. Mike said Johnson identified the photo of Trench but they couldn't find him. The owner of the Green Glove came in to the two-eight about half past one and said that the stories he'd picked up were that White and Johnson had robbed a pusher and it was the pusher who did the shooting, but the owner didn't know who he was.

'You ask Johnson?'

'Yeah. I went over to the hospital on the way back and woke him up. He denied the robbery, he denied knowing the pusher.' Connager muttered a four-letter word and got up.

'What time did you get in?'

'Two o'clock. Just as Laird was closing down Boro Headquarters. He said you were over in the one-nine.'

Lt. Joseph Xaviar Sullivan, commanding officer of the homicide squad, came in at half past seven. He was a tall, square-built man in his early forties who weighed a rock-ribbed two-twenty and looked as if he could still make the Fordham football team. His hair was greying, his clothes were as well cared for as Frank Sessions' own, and he had a wife and two young daughters in a home on Long Island.

This was a man who moved carefully among the public as if aware that the image of the homicide squad and the police department were in his care.

He sat down at his desk and listened to a rundown by Remick on the two deaths of the preceding night, what had been done and how things stood. He thumbed through the 'unusuals' and the follow-up DD5 reports which formed the written record of the cases and was satisfied so far. To Connager he said, 'Are you going to need any help, Mike?'

'No, sir. Not yet. It's just a question of ringing doorbells and asking questions trying to find out where Trench is and who knows about the pusher White and Johnson robbed.'

As for Sessions' case, the M.E. would decide whether it involved the homicide squad or not and until that time there was nothing special to be done. 'You'll be there for the autopsy, Frank?'

'Yes, sir.'

'Call me as soon as it's over.'

Sessions poured himself a cup of coffee when the briefing was through and by now Boro Headquarters, Manhattan North, had come alive again. Charlie Gallagher was on the desk, the burglary and youth division men were in their offices, homicide detectives Andy O'Dell, Roger Donnelly and Bill Cantrell were on hand for the eight to five shift, and the phones were starting to ring.

Assistant Chief Inspector Harry Nyborg, head of the Detective Boro for Manhattan North, came in a little before eight and Sessions went into his office as soon as he was settled. Nyborg, a tall, grey-haired man with a gentle face, tilted back his chair and clasped his hands behind his head while he listened to Frank's story. On the corner of his desk was the latest edition of the *News* and Monica's death got the front page black headlines.

When Sessions was finished, Nyborg said, 'You print the whole apartment?'

'Yes, sir. Every room.'

'Send them all down to Washington. Every last one. Sometimes you'll turn up a big surprise.'

'Yes, sir.'

Nyborg sat up, straightened the sleeves of his coat and looked up at the detective. 'This will get a lot of publicity if it's a homicide, Frank. My phone's not going to stop ringing. I'm going to be getting calls from everybody, from the mayor on down about this. Therefore I'm going to want to know everything that's going on. I want to be kept up to date and I don't mean just putting DD5s on my desk. I'm going to want to be on top of this thing all the way. So that's one of your little extra assignments, Frank. Keep me posted.'

Sessions said he would. He went out and had another cup of coffee and phoned Con Devlin at the nineteenth. Devlin said safe and loft had been notified and a radio car was waiting at the deceased's apartment to pick up Nettie Sandhurst when she arrived for work. He and two other detectives were going after all the other elevatormen and building employees. 'You get much sleep, Frank?'

'Two hours.'

'Geez. I thought I was bad. I got three and a half.'

'Yeah. Keep phoning in, Con. I'll give your boss the M.E.'s verdict as soon as I get it.'

'You're going to watch them cut her up? I don't know how you can stand it.'

'Hell, she's fresh. It's the ripe ones that are tough to take.' He hung up and got off the desk in the homicide section between the banks of lockers. Connager came out of the office. 'I'm going to get some breakfast and start pushing doorbells. You going to eat?'

'I don't have time. I gotta be at the M.E.'s in forty minutes and I don't know how I'm going to get there yet.'

'The boss is having Andy drive you.'

The headquarters of the Chief Medical Examiner of the City of New York was a recent glass and glazed blue brick structure adjacent to Bellevue Hospital. Sessions, chauffeured by Andy O'Dell, got out of car 299 in front of the building at a little after nine, went up the steps, through the glass doors, around a corner and up some steps into the lobby. The attendant passed him through and he went into a hallway, pulled open a heavy blue door, went down a flight of steps and pulled open another door. The tiled corridor down there was lined on one side with huge metal drawers and a Negro attendant was loading a corpse from an open one onto a metal cart. It was the body of Alfred White.

Sessions went around the corner to the door at the end where the corridor doubled back. 'Main Autopsy Room' was painted below the glass in faded letters and in the vast room beyond, bodies lay on four of the eight autopsy tables. A woman pathologist from Thailand was investigating causes of death on two bodies at the end, a white male, elderly, and a Negro female, young. A Negro male was being loaded onto another table from one of the carts and Monica Glazzard's body, white and gaunt, was already stretched out on the table nearest the door while a Negro assistant prepared her head.

Dr. Ballou was at the phone on the window ledge and Peter Quent, the homicide detective on permanent assignment to the M.E.'s office, was leaning against one of the empty tables smoking a small cigar. 'Hey, Frank,' he said. 'You going to attend this thing? Good, then I won't.'

The sound of the assistant's electric saw cutting bone made a low whine and Quent raised his voice a little. 'I'm supposed to tell the doc what's what and I don't even know. He's telling me.'

Ballou came away from the phone, popped a plastic bag and withdrew a pair of rubber gloves. 'Well you came, eh?'

Sessions said, 'Yeah. I'm here. Any DOA's I'm involved with, I'm going to be at the autopsy. I don't want to just hear how they died, I want to see.'

Quent said, 'Brother, you can have it. He's as bad as Ray Eklin, Doc. Ray brings his lunch in here.'

The phone rang and another attendant answered. He called, 'Is there a Detective Sessions here?'

'Yeah.' Frank went over, putting a cigarette in his mouth. He picked up the phone. 'Sessions.'

'This is Con, Frank. We talked to the maid but there's nothing there. She doesn't know anything. A real stupid type.'

'Maids usually know a lot more than anybody else. You're sure she's not conning you?'

'Oh, no. She's dumb. She cleans the place, picks up after parties and all, but she doesn't know any of the deceased's friends. She doesn't see them. She didn't work her parties. If the deceased was having a big party, she hired others to cater and clean up . . .'

'You get a make on the caterers?'

'She doesn't know them. Millie probably would. Anyway, this woman only came in two days a week, only went around cleaning up the place, and only saw the deceased, her secretary, and sometimes that guy Motley.'

'Yeah.' Sessions leaned against the wall and kept his eyes on the table and the attendant at the opposite end working with the saw. The whine grew louder and Devlin said, 'What's the noise?'

'Nothing,' Sessions said. 'They're cutting her skull.' He studied the white, thin body clinically. No visible marks or scars. It was too thin a body. She must have worked hard to keep her weight like that. There'd be massages, workouts, carrot juice cocktails, starvation diets, and a daily study of the needle on the expensive bathroom scales she had.

Devlin said, 'Listen, call me as soon as you get something, O.K.?'

'Sure.' Sessions hung up and thumbed through the directory beside the phone, copied the lawyer's number into his notebook and rejoined the others. The attendant took a hammer and chisel to loosen the section of skull he had cut. Sessions turned over one of the dead woman's hands, took a final drag on his cigarette and exhaled smoke. 'She's been printed already?'

Quent said, 'Printed and identified. We're way ahead of you.'

'Identified? By the daughter?'

'And by the patrolman who found her. She was in an hour ago. He came in when he went off duty.'

Sessions said to Ballou, 'What about her fingernails?'

'I got some scrapings but it doesn't look like anything. She didn't scratch anybody. What else? The nails are false and, judging from the tobacco stains on the index and middle fingers, she was a heavy smoker.'

'The chief wants all the prints sent to Washington. I suppose that means hers too.'

Ballou went around the other side of the table and adjusted the block under the body's head. 'What would Washington want with her prints?'

'Nothing. The chief just has a thing on fingerprints.'

'It could be worse,' Quent said. 'Remember Captain Delehanty and the licence plates?'

Sessions said, 'I heard of him,' and moved to watch Ballou remove the section of skull. Ballou said, 'What about the plates?'

Quent moved away a little. He laughed. 'It seems that when Delehanty was a rookie patrolman he cracked a homicide by writing down the licence numbers of every car parked within a block of the scene and checking them out. That gave him his start and ever after, no matter what the case was, his first order was, "Copy down the licence numbers of every car in the area and check them all out." Christ, the hours we used to spend!'

Dr. Degnan, short, grey-haired and balding, came in with another doctor in tow. 'This is the main autopsy room,' he was saying and gestured at the general activity. 'Here,' he said, approaching Ballou's table, 'is a case—apparent overdose of barbiturates but we suspect manual or ligature asphyxiation. As a matter of fact, this woman was a prominent newspaper writer. She interviewed me once and wrote me up in her column, back at the time of the Malcolm X shooting.'

The visiting doctor, who was an oriental, said, in hard to understand English, 'But if it is asphyxiation you suspect, what is it with removing the brain?'

'It will have to be tested for barbiturates anyway.'

'But wouldn't you go first to the throat?'

Degnan laughed. 'Well, I'll tell you, Doc, we're not just involved with the medical, but with the legal. Not just causes of death, but courtrooms. Suppose you have a man shot twelve times and you don't do his head, you just probe for bullets. It's the bullets that killed him, right? So then you get up on the stand and the defence lawyer says, "Do you know what a subdural hematoma is, Doctor?" And you say, "Yes." "Would you describe it, Doctor?" So you describe it. "Can it be fatal, Doctor?" "Yes, it can." "Did the victim experience a subdural hematoma, Doctor?" "I don't know." "Why don't you know, Doctor?" "Because I didn't examine his head. I took it for granted the bullets killed him." "Oh, you took it for granted?" ' Degnan laughed. 'That's the way to spend a very unhappy afternoon in a witness chair. It's easier to do the job thoroughly and do it right.'

Dr. Ballou had meanwhile switched his attention and his scalpel to the body itself, opening it and removing the sternum. Now he examined the underside of the flesh of the throat. 'Look here,' he said and Sessions, Degnan, and the visiting doctor came close. The flesh had been damaged and there were contusions. When Ballou removed the windpipe, a little fluid spilled which he made no attempt to save. Then he pointed to the rest of the evidence. There were two dark spots on the sides of the larynx. 'And take a look here.' He pointed with his scalpel. 'The cricoid cartilage is fractured.' Sessions looked, Degnan said, 'Umhmm. Well, well.' The visiting doctor bent close with great interest. Sessions said to

Ballou, 'Come on, Doc, say something. Make it official. Homicide, right?'

Ballou nodded. 'It's a homicide. Manual or ligature asphyxiation. Probably manual.'

Sessions went to the nearest phone and dialled the homicide number. 'Boss? Frank. It's a homicide. The M.E. just called it. Strangulation. Just as we figured.' He listened and said, 'The nineteenth? O.K., as soon as I finish up here. I want to see what else there is to learn. Specifically, I want to see if there's any semen.'

THURSDAY 10:15–10:45 A.M.

Sessions came through the doors of the nineteenth at quarter past ten and took the stairs rapidly, but one at a time. He felt momentarily light-headed and slightly dizzy and gave his head two quick, hard shakes in an attempt to clear it.

Upstairs in the squad room everybody was there. Sergeant Trager, Con Devlin and three other detectives in the nineteenth, Lieutenant Sullivan, O'Dell, Donnelly and Cantrell from homicide. The lieutenant and the homicide men had their jackets on, the nineteenth squad men were in shirt sleeves. All were standing or sitting around at the desks there, talking, and the conversation was Monica Glazzard's murder.

'Was there intercourse?' the lieutenant asked when Sessions came through the gate.

The detective shook his head. 'No intercourse. The time of death is still any time after she came home the night before last till as late as noon yesterday. We'll get a report on her stomach contents in a few days and if we can find out when she ate what's there, we're in business.'

The lieutenant said, 'You're off the block, of course, and we'll give you all the co-operation you need, all the men you want.'

Trager said, 'I can put five men on it today, counting myself and Devlin. And we can get men assigned from other squads . . .'

'I don't think we're going to need that many,' Sessions said. 'It doesn't look like one of those sex or burglary slayings where anybody could be the perpetrator and we need mass coverage of an area. This looks like the close friend or relative type, which should be a lot easier to crack. The perpetrator is probably someone close at hand, maybe one of the subjects we've already talked to.'

Sullivan said, 'Don't count on it being too easy. It doesn't look like a spur-of-the-moment killing. This was planned, which means a lot of care's been taken to remove clues or leave false clues.'

Sessions nodded. 'Yeah. And the big one was strangling her with gloves so it wouldn't leave a mark and pouring barbiturates down her throat. We can be pretty sure the fluid in her stomach is going to be barbiturates. So the whole aim appears to be to fake a suicide and right away that tells us a few things.'

Trager said, 'What things are you thinking about?'

'The perpetrator isn't familiar with the way the M.E.'s office handles questionable deaths in New York. He or she is very likely not a native New Yorker.'

Donnelly said, 'I don't think that follows, Frank. New Yorkers don't know how the M.E.'s office operates either.'

'I admit I'm reaching, but I'll still stand on it. Because there are a lot of places in this country where you could work a phony suicide like that and get away with it. You know, where the coroner is a political appointee, maybe not even a doctor, or where autopsies are pretty perfunctory. It sounds like the kind of M.O. a perpetrator would use if he'd worked it before somewhere or heard about somebody working it. But it wouldn't be here. Not in New York.'

'You might be right on that,' Sullivan agreed. 'Now there are a couple of things I want to say and then we'll get back to what your views are on this thing. There's going to be a lot of noise about this one. Now I'm not going to tell you to look good because you always look good. Just see that you stay that way. Let's keep the goofs down to a minimum. One reminder. I want all DD5s right up to the minute. The moment you report in, get those DD5s done. It's the only way we have of knowing what's going on, who's doing what and when. It's the only way of keeping from going over the same ground twice. All right, that's my say. Frank, you and Devlin are the only ones who have the complete picture up to here. Tell us what you know and what you think. Then we'll kick it around.'

Devlin deferred to Sessions and Frank flipped open his notebook. 'You know the general set-up so I'll skip that. The M.E. says there's no skin under the deceased's fingernails. So we aren't looking for a perpetrator who's got scratches on his face. The way it looks to me is he must have seized her from behind. I further make it that she was in her nightgown at the time. That would presumably make the perpetrator either a close relative or intimate friend.'

Donnelly questioned that. 'If the idea was to establish suicide by an overdose, the perpetrator would want her in a nightgown, so he'd put her in one. Therefore she might have still been in her clothes when she was killed.'

That question was kicked around for a bit, the general view being that while it was possible Monica Glazzard had been killed while dressed—and perhaps in a different part of the house—in all likelihood she had been murdered in her bedroom in her nightgown. Sessions went on.

'If safe and loft tells us the locks were picked, that'll change things. Right now, though, it looks like the perpetrator got in with a key or was let in by the deceased. If she was attacked from behind in her boudoir, either it was by an intimate friend she didn't suspect wished her any harm, or it was by someone unexpected, an attacker she would have feared but didn't know was there. While the latter is a possibility and someone unknown to us has a key, this isn't very likely. The evidence is that the attack on the deceased was perpetrated on her as a person rather than as, say, a sex-object or a source of money and so forth. We can assume, therefore, that the homicide was committed by someone too close to her to escape police attention. Workers in the building are possible suspects, naturally, since, despite what the super says, it's quite possible for them to get hold of a key. They don't look like good suspects at this point, again because there is no rape and no theft.'

Donnelly said, 'The reason there was no rape or theft might well be because the perpetrator didn't intend to kill and fled when he saw what he'd done. Just because there wasn't any doesn't mean there wasn't supposed to be.'

'But the perpetrator didn't flee. He dissolved sleeping pills and poured them down the deceased's throat and tucked her into bed.'

'We can't be sure of that.'

Sessions laughed and lighted a cigarette. 'You're right, Rog. But I still don't figure your idea's likely. It's hard to see an amorous building employee working out a plot like that, knowing where to look for the barbiturates and all that.'

Sullivan said, 'So who do you suspect?'

Sessions hitched his shoulders in his nervous way. 'Right now, boss, I'd say there're four logical suspects. The daughter, the secretary, the lover and the friend, this Archibald Patterson. Presumably all have keys except Patterson.'

O'Dell said, 'What about the maid? Doesn't she have a key?'

Devlin answered that one. 'Yes, the maid had a key but she couldn't strangle a fruit fly.'

'Yes,' said Donnelly, 'but that doesn't mean she couldn't

have brought a strong friend with her, or lent the friend the key.'

It was an angle, the others agreed, but, at present, not a likely one. Sullivan said to Sessions, 'Anything seem to you to point at anyone in particular?'

Sessions shrugged. 'It's hard to say. Take the daughter. We presume she inherits. Is that motive? Even if it is, we don't have anything putting her near the scene. The secretary? We've got no known motive. Presumably there's opportunity. Patterson? We've got him on the scene but again there's no motive. The lover? Again no motive, also, presumably, no alibi. In fact he loses out by her death—unless, of course, he's mentioned in the will.'

'It doesn't sound as though you like any of them.'

Sessions laughed. 'I like all of them. It's my guess one of them's it. We just haven't found out enough about them yet to know which.'

'Any guesses?'

'For what it's worth, I like the boyfriend, of course. He's got the most involvement with the deceased and that's the stuff motives are made of.'

The lieutenant turned. 'What about you, Devlin?'

'Well I agree with Frank. And besides his reasons, there's the fact that the boyfriend is the only man in the case. I would think, in a strangulation, it would be a man rather than a woman.'

'Isn't Patterson a man?'

'He's an old man. Physically I'm lumping him in with the women.'

'And you don't think the women are capable?'

'Of strangling the deceased? The maid's not. The secretary I suppose is strong enough. She's rather burly. And the daughter is young and looks able. The question is whether they'd think of it. Seems to me Patterson and the women would come up with a different method of killing.'

'Except,' the lieutenant said, 'there's the second part of the plot—the attempt to make it appear like suicide. There's more to it than a person merely thinking how best to kill. It's, "how best to kill and make it look like suicide".'

'Yeah. Yeah, that's right, Lieutenant.'

They talked then about the paths of the investigation. All suspects would be checked through BCI, of course, to see if they had a record. This would include employees in the building, some of whom had already been checked, as well as the special friends of Monica Glazzard. Sessions wanted Sacramento police contacted in case Robert Motley had a record there. More than that, he wanted to find out if Motley ever came from Sacramento, a claim he doubted. Monica's lawyer was on the list. Sessions would see him about the will. Devlin would be responsible for the other elevatormen—what they could tell about Monica, what they could tell about each other. O'Dell would go to Lindy's and see what he could learn about Monica's appearance there after the play—what she did and what she ate. Cantrell would see Frederick and Florence Lyle, Donnelly would get a guest list from Gregory Buckingham. Then there was Linda Glazzard, of course, and Millie, and the question of who had transcribed Monica's last column. That meant going to the syndicate offices and finding out who the messenger boys were and what the people there had to say. And, of course, what kind of a guy was this Archibald Patterson? Who thought what about him?

Behind that, of course, was Monica's address file and the hundreds of names there which could be contacted if nothing else developed. Or a check of Monica's toll calls over the past few months. Lots of eye-openers came out of that area of investigation.

The Monica Glazzard case might not require the efforts of hundreds of detectives working around the clock but there were enough leads in the beginning to keep the present crews busy.

THURSDAY 11:10–11:20 A.M.

The offices of Stockton, Bates and Pierce were on the fourteenth floor of 507 Park Avenue overlooking 59th Street. The receptionist's room was modern—metal, plastic, and pastel shades. The office of Lawrence Stockton, senior member of the firm, was Edwardian: panels, leather and oil portraits. Stockton, who rose and came around his desk to shake hands when Sessions was shown in at quarter past eleven, stood better than six feet, carried two hundred and twenty-five pounds nicely girdled, and looked as if his grey suits were cleaned as often as his shirts.

'A very sad occasion,' Stockton said, holding a heavy green leather chair for the visitor. He got back behind the desk and pushed a humidor of expensive cigars across to Frank. 'I saw in the paper this morning that she had died mysteriously. But then you call me and say she was murdered. That is shocking.'

'Yes, sir, it is. It puts a different light on things, wouldn't you say? Now we want to know who hated her. And we want to know who profits by her death. That, as I explained on the phone, is why I'm here.'

'You want to know who is named in her will?'

'That's exactly what we want to know.'

Stockton picked up a pad of foolscap and fumbled for a pair of glasses. 'Do you have any suspicions yet, Mr.—ah—Sessions?'

Frank, ignoring the cigars, lighted a cigarette and crossed his legs. 'We're being open-minded about it, Mr. Stockton.'

'I might as well tell you, the daughter is the main beneficiary. Will that mean trouble for her?'

'Probably not. The daughter would be expected to be the principal beneficiary. How large an estate is involved, Mr. Stockton?'

'I couldn't tell you. She has some property, of course. She owns the apartment she lived in outright. The mortgage on that was paid off last year. And she owns a farm in Connecticut. That is mortgaged but the mortgage is insured so that is automatically paid off on her death.' He referred to his pad and went on: 'She has an interest in an inn in New Hope, Pennsylvania. A one-third interest, that is. She has some stocks and bonds and investments but I'm not her investment counsellor and I can't tell you about those.'

'Do you know who is her counsellor?'

Stockton pressed a button on the intercom and asked his secretary to look it up. 'And I don't know about bank balances or what her income was. I have a copy of her contract with the News Features Syndicate. She gets so much for each paper that subscribes to her column. And it's carried by quite a large number of papers. Then there are other sources of income, her lectures, her television appearances, her endorsements. I would say that her income was very substantial.'

'And who else gets it besides the daughter?'

Stockton smiled a little. 'I daresay you're going to be disappointed in what I tell you. I'm afraid you're not going to get any clues here.'

Sessions said, 'Don't worry about it, Mr. Stockton. Whether we get any clues out of it or not isn't the point. The thing is, we have to find out.'

'Well, all right, for what it's worth.' Stockton adjusted the glasses a little better. Behind his back the Venetian blind was raised but all that was visible was the face of the building on the other side of the street. 'I noted it down before you got here so we could dispense with a lot of "whereases" and "therefores". First, there's a thousand dollar outright gift to Nettie Sandhurst. That's her cleaning woman.'

Sessions put his cigarette in the large desk ashtray and wrote that down.

'Then there's one month's salary to Mildred Butelle, her secretary. There is a gift of one hundred dollars to the New

York Journalists Club Contingency Fund . . .'

'Excuse me—do you know what Miss Butelle's salary is?'

'It's one hundred and seventy-five dollars a week—at least it was when the will was made out in nineteen sixty-four, for it states seven hundred dollars as the month's salary.'

'Nineteen sixty-four,' Sessions said and wrote.

'There's another bequest,' Stockton went on, 'of three hundred dollars to the Anti-Vivisectionists' League. Five hundred has been left to the Actors' Fund. Her papers, letters, manuscripts and writings go to Boston University and everything else goes to her daughter, Linda.'

Sessions got that into his notebook and asked about any possible enemies. Stockton didn't know of any. In fact, he hadn't seen his client since the making of the will.

'And she's never, since that time, called you or spoken to you about possibly drawing a new one?'

'No. Never.'

A buzzer sounded and Stockton picked up the phone. He handed it across the desk. 'It's for you, Mr. Sessions.'

It was Devlin. 'Are you going to see Linda Glazzard today?'

'Sometime today. Why?'

'Because I've got a couple of bombshells which may change your plans a little. You want to know who transcribed Monica Glazzard's last column for her? Millie Butelle. The woman who claimed she had the day off. That's who.'

'Where'd you get that?'

'Carl Mancini. One of the elevatormen. He's on ten in the morning till seven at night. So I ask him who comes in and goes out and the first thing he tells me is that just about twelve noon, down the stairs—she doesn't use the elevator, she uses the stairs—comes Millie Butelle. And out she walks.'

'And that was yesterday at twelve?'

'That's right. Yesterday.'

'When'd she come in?'

'That's what I haven't been able to find out yet. Because

Lester Fritz, who's the guy who'd know, is off till Friday and I can't reach him at his home.'

'What about the other guy—who came on last night? The one who made Patterson?'

'Caligliaro. He's on from one till ten in the morning, but when Fritz comes on at eight, Caligliaro goes out for an hour for breakfast. He wasn't around between eight and nine.'

'What about transcribing the column and leaving it in the lobby for the pick-up? Caligliaro or Mancini see her do that?'

'No. We only have her walking out of the building at noon. But that's not the whole of it. Guess what. Not five minutes after she walks out, guess who walks in! The daughter! The one who says she hasn't seen her mother in months!'

'Yeah,' Sessions said. 'Good going, pal. How long was she around the area?'

'That's why I got to get hold of Fritz. Mancini doesn't know. He didn't see her leave.'

'O.K., I'll see what she's got to say for herself. Got a report from safe and loft yet?'

'Yep, and there's nothing. No scratches on the inside of the locks. They weren't picked, they were opened with keys. It's somebody who had a key. You got anything on the will? Does Motley get a bundle?'

'Linda gets the works. Motley doesn't get a mention. He wasn't in the scene even when it was drawn.'

'Linda, huh? And time of death, Frank! Monica could still have been alive when Linda got there.'

Frank laughed. 'Yeah, pal. But I wouldn't put money on it.'

THURSDAY 11:30–11:45 A.M.

Linda Glazzard checked the last name off the list. All the potential contestants were present, sitting in the little anteroom outside the window to her office. She opened the door beside the window and went out to them. 'You're all very prompt,' she said, smiling at the eight men and women sitting and standing in the cramped confines of the little room. 'You're all here early, in fact, so we might as well get started.' She opened another door to a hallway and led them into the first room on the left which contained a long table set with a dozen chairs. The people sat at the table and Linda handed out pencils and two mimeographed tests. 'If you'll put your names at the top,' she said. 'The first test is, you will notice, a sort of general information test. It's not hard. but it will give us an idea of the sort of areas your general knowledge covers. You are to fill in the blanks with the name that answers the question. You will have ten minutes for the twenty questions. The second test features sample clues of the type you get on the "Guess the Guest" programme. Is there anyone here, by the way, who doesn't know how that game is played?' There was no show of hands so she said, 'Good. As you will see, there are ten sets of clues. You will have ten minutes for that.' She looked around cheerfully. 'Are there any questions?'

One woman said, 'Well now this first test. Where it says, "What's the tallest mountain in the world?" That's a sensible question. But the second one, "Who plays first baseman for the New York Yankees?" Now I don't think that's a fair question to put on a test like this. I mean maybe there are some men who might know but how can you expect women to know the answer to a question like that?'

'I said this is just a test of general knowledge. If you don't know the answer, just leave it blank.'

'But that means you got it wrong. I don't think that's a

fair question. I mean who's going to know the answer to that outside of men who live in New York and who like the Yankees instead of the Mets? If you asked who the Mets' first baseman is it'd be fairer because more people like the Mets.'

'It's all right to leave a blank space, I assure you. It's quite likely no one will know the answer to all twenty questions. That's the way the test is made up.'

'I don't mind not knowing. I mean I don't think the question is fair. Now farther down you've got, "Who is the ruler of Egypt?" Now that's my idea of a fair question. I might not know who it is, but that's a fair question.'

Linda smiled. 'I'm sorry if you don't like the test but it was devised by psychiatrists especially to screen applicants for this show.' She glanced at her watch. 'If there are no further questions, you may all start—now.'

The eight would-be contestants on the 'Guess the Guest' show pitched in. Linda leaned back against the doorframe. Her smile faded and she bit her lip. She felt almost physically sick. It was that detective again. Detective Sessions. There was something about him that terrified her. She had recognised his voice the moment her extension had rung and she had picked up the phone. How could you describe his voice? Could you call a voice 'gaunt'? That's what it was. Gaunt like the man. And you picked up the phone and said, 'Hello,' with sweetness and charm in your manner and suddenly there was that voice saying, 'Miss Glazzard?' and suddenly it was all back with you again. It was last night and hearing questions and knowing you were suspected of things they wouldn't mention. You felt trapped and you felt guilty and you sensed they knew you were guilty. Especially that Detective Sessions. 'I tried to reach you at your apartment,' he had said to her. Nothing about his tone condemned her. Nothing betrayed surprise or suspicion. It was a dead tone and maybe that was the way to describe his voice. It was a dead voice. Like the man himself. He looked too thin. He looked, to use the old high school cliché, 'like death warmed over'.

But he had tried to call her first at her apartment and only when there was no answer did he call her at work. And how do you explain that, my pretty girl? Your mother had just died. The funeral arrangements haven't even been made yet. Nothing has been done. No tears have even been shed. Yet here you are at work, giving out tests to argumentative women who don't know that their complaining ways have killed them deader than not knowing where Mickey Mantle is spending his time these days; you're smiling at them, being gracious to them, meeting nice people, smart people, appreciative people to be sure, but every so often the lemon in the crowd who should never have passed screening far enough to take these tests. And there you are, as if nothing had happened at all last night. And maybe that's what you're trying to pretend is the situation, but you don't say that to a detective. He's going to wonder about the lack of tears, about the Spartan return to work when she could have the rest of the week off. And he's going to decide this girl, Linda Glazzard, must really have hated her mother to be so callous about her death. Hated her, perhaps, enough to kill her.

For that was what it was now. Murder. The detective had said so. He'd made a point of saying so. Linda could tell that. He wanted to talk to her again. He wanted to ask some more questions. Because now they knew that Monica Glazzard hadn't suffered a natural death. She had been helped to it and all hell would break loose.

That was part of Linda's nausea. It's one thing when someone close to you dies of natural or even accidental causes. It's a worse thing when that someone commits suicide. But when that someone is killed, is ripped untimely from earth's bosom or whatever the hell Shakespeare had said or would have said, that's a stunning blow. That leaves you weak and ill. And when you begin to feel that eyes are watching you, that the police have it in their minds that you yourself might be the guilty party, you feel really sick. Strangled, the detective had said. Monica had been strangled. But that meant a man, didn't it? Surely Linda herself couldn't have strangled her mother. Monica was slim, trim, durable, quite strong. Could Linda have done it? Did she have the strength? That wasn't the point. Could she prove to the detective that she hadn't? Oh yes, they were supposed to do the proving, but everyone knew that wasn't the way justice really worked. Everyone knew that in real life you stood condemned unless or until you could prove your innocence. And even then, even when you had proven you hadn't done anything wrong, there were still those who wondered. You went through life from then on tainted.

Now the detective was on his way over. She had had to tell him she'd be through at twelve o'clock. A little before twelve this noon because the group had got a two or three minute headstart in taking the tests.

Lunch. He'd said something about lunch. He was going to take her to lunch, or eat lunch with her, and now she had no appetite. Alone, or with some of the usual gang, she could have managed a little meal—they'd all said their condolences and had understood that Linda and Monica weren't close, that Linda wasn't truly broken up, that there was much work to do at Cowan and Blakeslee. She was part of the team and what she did was important to the operation. Tie up her end or bring in a substitute and everything else would be slowed down. Besides, as she had told everybody, the best cure for the ache of grief is work. Don't sit around feeling sorry for yourself, get out and do something. Make yourself forget. The gang understood but she didn't think the detective would. Rationalisation, he'd call it and wonder what she was trying to hide. Lunch? She didn't know how she'd manage it. Yet she was going to have to eat. She couldn't let him wonder what was the matter. The more nervousness she permitted him to see, the more sure he'd be she knew things she hadn't told.

Linda went out into the hall to the drinking fountain. She didn't want the would-be contestants seeing her without the smile, the full attention to their concerns and interests. David came by. He had avoided her all morning and she hadn't seen him since he had dropped her at Monica's the night before. He said, 'Gee, Linda, if I'd known you were working today—I wanted to let you know—you know, about last night—I mean, how are you?'

He was lying, of course. He knew she was in. Linda said, 'I'm all right.' She wasn't angry at him any more. She didn't have any feeling for him. So he was lying, so he was a coward at heart. It didn't matter. She didn't have that much interest in him. The unbidden thought crossed her mind, 'I've slept with this man. We've taken showers together, each washing the other.' It didn't seem real. It wasn't with this man. It was with someone else. Someone she knew. This man was a stranger. They'd laughed and joked together only last night—twelve hours ago—and that didn't seem real either.

'You know,' he said, 'about your boyfriend . . . I mean, I'll do anything you want. I'm really sorry.'

He really was too. She could tell that. But it didn't matter. The mention of her boyfriend, however, reminded her that some things still did matter. She felt a pang, a sharp stab that went clean through her. Was Randy part of the past too now, like David? A few lying words yelled into a phone and the whole of one's life changed direction. Doors clanged shut closing off the gardens of the future and steep descents into dark caverns took their place. Where there had been trust and understanding and forgiveness, now there was suspicion and the ugliness of evil thoughts. Could these ever be wiped away again or had Randy, in that one brief flare-up, revealed that he could never, after all, separate her from her past? And where did that leave her future? Would someone else ever come along with all those forgiving qualities that Randy had shown and mean them as Randy apparently had not? Or would it be a long succession of empty years with companionship a fleeting thing, the abnormal situation of her life? Maybe if she had remained a virgin . . . ? Oh, for Christ's sake, let's be reasonable! But, of course, she didn't have to be as promiscuous as she had been. It had been rather much, after all. A boy can forgive up to a point but . . .

But what? What the hell. Those boys didn't mean anything to her. She couldn't even remember them. Not one. She couldn't even remember what it was like, what her feeling was back then. She'd worked it out with the psychiatrist. She'd found out enough of what was goading her at least to enable her to straighten herself out and become a pretty damned respectable and functional, yes and even important, human being. Was she to be damned forever?

She watched David go off down the hall. His generally ebullient manner was only slightly subdued this morning—in deference to Linda's grief. In front of others he was probably the usual David. In fact, he was almost that now and there was in his walk that sense of relief—of having faced up to an unpleasant chore and pulled it off successfully. He wasn't hurt. He didn't lose his mother and the person he planned to marry both in one evening.

She went back to the room and smiled around at the group. Most had finished and were checking over the tough ones. The woman who didn't know the ruler of Egypt any more than the first baseman of the New York Yankees looked very unhappy. She was sensing she wasn't going to get past the first hurdle. Not that it mattered. She could be the smartest woman in the state, she wasn't the kind you picked for participation on game shows in front of a television camera.

Linda said, 'Is everybody finished or do you want the full ten minutes?' The woman wanted the full ten minutes and Linda told her she had a minute and a half left.

'I think it's more than that,' the woman said. 'I made sure I looked at my watch before we started.'

Linda had had this before, though fortunately not often. 'If you'd like extra time,' she said sweetly, 'you may have as much as you'd like. Meanwhile, so we won't hold up the rest of the group . . .'

'I don't need any extra time,' the woman said, pushing her paper over. 'I've done all I can. But I do want to say I don't think these questions are fair. "Who wrote the words to the 'Star-Spangled Banner'?" Now really. I know as much as the next person but I certainly don't clutter up my mind with a lot of unimportant information.'

With the papers in hand, Linda let the members of the group run through the answers to satisfy themselves that the Nile was the longest river in the world, that Dean Rusk was the Secretary of State, that maple syrup came from sugar maples but 'trees' was acceptable. She asked if there were any other questions before they started the second test and a thin, youngish woman said, 'Your name is Miss Glazzard, isn't it?'

'That's right.'

'Are you any relation to Monica Glazzard, the columnist who died?'

Linda said, 'We're distantly related. Shall we go on?'

THURSDAY 11:57 A.M.–12:45 P.M.

At three minutes of twelve Linda collected the mimeographed tests and thanked everybody warmly. 'If you don't hear from us within a week to ten days, you probably won't, so I wouldn't count on it after that.' She showed them back into the tiny anteroom that exited into the hallway and Frank Sessions was there. She knew he would be but her heart flipped and sank a little anyway and she could feel her knees tremble. She had planned to be coldly efficient with him: the 'I can only give you a couple of minutes' sort of thing, but the look of him made her know she couldn't pull it off. Not that he didn't seem friendly enough, smoking a cigarette and smiling pleasantly at her and her mother-hen role as she shepherded out the chicks. But the smile was business and so was his presence. He hadn't come in to meet a girlfriend, he hadn't come in to try out for the television show. He didn't even care whether the show went on the air or not. All he cared about was who had killed her mother. That's why he was there, smiling at her and reading her at the same time, reading the kind of work she did, reading the people she was saying goodbye to, interpreting what he read in the context of however many years he'd had in the detective business and what he had experienced and learned in those years. She wouldn't be able to dismiss him with a firm tone. In fact, in his presence, it was all she could do to keep a quaver out of her voice when she thanked the departing group one last time and told them goodbye.

His smile faded now as he put out his cigarette in one of the ashstands between the collection of odd chairs that lined the walls of the little room. He seemed somehow grim as he took her arm and said, 'I expect you like French food?'

They went by cab to a small restaurant on 58th Street where he had a table reserved. It was at the rear of a long, narrow room where he sat with his back to the wall, she with her back to the other customers. She found that she liked his making the decision on lunch, where it would be and what, instead of asking what she wanted. She also approved of his decision. The restaurant was too far away from the Seagram Building to attract her crowd and if she had to undergo a grilling, it wouldn't be in front of her friends. Her appetite was coming back too, which was good, for this would be better than her usual fare. And it might work to her advantage in other ways. It was possible that over food the detective would lose some of his commitment. It was possible that the detective would start to notice that she was a comely woman. Linda had no illusions about her looks. She wasn't a beauty queen, but there was no point in excessive modesty either. She was very attractive and enough men had chased her (even after she had quit being everybody's bedmate) for her to know it and walk in the confidence of her powers of appeal. That was one area where she didn't feel subservient to Monica.

Now, in the dim inner fastness of the restaurant, with a drink in front of them and a menu in their hands, she began to assess her fearful opponent more carefully. At Monica's apartment last night, he was just a face, figure and voice of no particular shape and sound, asking and probing in ways that frightened her, but she was too numb really to understand. Now she could see that Detective Sessions had brown eyes that were really quite good-looking if you could somehow forget the policeman's gaze that came out of them. His hair was dark brown and flawlessly combed, his clothes were really much more expensive than she would have expected a policeman to be wearing. It led her to wonder how much money a man in his position made and what his financial responsibilities were. He might be married with a wife and family. Cops did marry, after all, she realised, though she found it hard to imagine what it was like to be the wife of a policeman. He was taller than she had at first thought. He was all of six feet though he seemed shorter. And he wasn't as thin as he looked. Part of what passed as gauntness was fatigue. He needed ten pounds, but he needed sleep even more.

They ordered over drinks and she noted that he didn't seem ill at ease in a pretty fair French restaurant. Why was it she thought a policeman was out of his depth the moment he entered any eatery more posh than a Nedick's counter? He knew what food he wanted and he knew how he wanted his martini. He even ordered wine without asking the waiter's advice. He was quite the man of the world in a French restaurant, but there was a little-boy quality to him too. Linda could see it in the weariness he ignored. He needed somebody to take care of him, to tell him that it's not just clothes that make the man, it's the man himself and he should mind his body as well as his suits. And the way he smoked cigarettes—God, it was a wonder he had any lungs left. Sitting opposite her, he looked like a poor little motherless child who aroused the maternal instinct in the female breast.

But then she remembered that this same motherless child carried a revolver on his hip, that he knew how to use it and when to use it. And he hadn't got to be where he was in the police department just by studying his lessons and putting in his time. In the police business you had to arrest people—sometimes dangerous people. You had to take risks and go forward where the average man hung back. A policeman wouldn't watch out the window while Kitty Genovese was being stabbed to death in the street. A policeman didn't turn away because he might otherwise get involved or he might get hurt. This detective might be motherless but he was no child. Anything that painted him in such colours was deceptive. 'Watch out, my girl,' Linda reminded herself as she sipped her Manhattan and awaited his questions.

Frank Sessions took a little of his martini. His last cigarette had been snubbed out less than a minute but already he was lighting another. 'Why didn't you tell us about yesterday, Miss Glazzard?' he said by way of breaking the ice. It was the kind of abrupt and unexpected question that revealed a good deal through its effect on the receiver.

In this case, all the question got him was a slight start and puzzled frown. But there was an overtone in there too. Some pang of guilt somewhere seemed to have touched her. 'Tell you what, about yesterday?' she asked.

'That you went to your mother's apartment yesterday noon.'

'Oh?' She smiled a little. She should have known that was something he'd find out quickly. He wouldn't believe it, of course, but she really hadn't thought to tell him. 'I didn't think of it,' she said, telling him the truth and waiting for his disbelief.

He didn't say anything to that. He hitched his shoulders nervously and took another drag on his cigarette. 'What happened?'

'Nothing. I went over there. I rang the doorbell. Nobody answered, so I came away again.'

'Just like that?'

Now his voice was expressing disbelief all right. She could feel its cold cutting quality. 'Just like that,' she said back.

'Why didn't you use your key?'

'I don't have a key.'

'Come again?'

'I said I don't have a key.'

'It's your own mother's apartment . . .'

'What if it was? Just because Monica was my mother didn't entitle me to invade her privacy. She doesn't have a key to my apartment either.'

'Monica? Is that what you called her?'

'Yes. Is that strange?'

'It's not usual.'

'Monica wasn't the mother type. I can't imagine anyone calling her "mother". Neither could she, which was why I was brought up to call her by her name. Also, from the vanity standpoint, I'm sure she wouldn't like having a twenty-nine-year-old woman indicating by the "mother" bit that she was a generation older than that.'

Sessions nodded. 'Getting back to the key . . .'

'Look, I said I don't have a key. Would you like to see my key ring?'

'Sure.'

She didn't think he'd take her up on it and she fumbled a little getting it out of her purse. The ring didn't hold many—her own apartment key, one to Randy's apartment, one to her desk in the office, one to the office door and one to her suitcase. 'There,' she said, laying them on the table. 'And if you know what Monica's keys look like . . .'

He put his finger on one. 'What's this for?'

'My apartment.'

'And this?'

It was Randy's key. She said, 'That's—uh—one for, ah, the outer office door. This other one is for the inner office door.'

The waiter came and started serving the first course. He removed the cork from the wine bottle with proper flourishes and set it in front of Frank. He poured a touch of wine into Frank's glass, got approval and filled both. By the time he went away Linda had her keys back in her bag.

Sessions took a first mouthful of food, killed the rest of his martini, and said, 'Let's finish up with this key business, Miss Glazzard, if you don't mind. You have no key. What did you do with it?'

I didn't do anything with it. I never had a key.'

'Miss Glazzard, you're twenty-nine years old. You told me last night your mother bought the apartment eleven years ago. That would make you eighteen. Presumably, at eighteen, you were still living with your mother. Do you expect me to believe you had no way of getting into that apartment?'

'But that was years ago.'

'Sure it was. What did you do with the key?'

'I don't know.' She looked at him querulously. 'Why, is that important?'

'It's your alibi, isn't it?'

'My alibi?'

'You're telling me you didn't go into the apartment, aren't you?'

She said with sudden fright in her voice, 'Are you suggesting I might have—killed her?' She may as well use the word. All along she'd sensed she was under suspicion about something—even before she knew how Monica had died. But not until this moment had it occurred to her that she might be suspected of murder. She'd played with the thought but it was only play. That sort of thing couldn't really be happening. But the police got ideas and fixations about things and if this detective really thought she were guilty, she'd have an all but impossible time shaking him out of his conviction. That he might be looking at her as a murderess made her breath catch and her lip tremble.

He watched her closely, though he appeared casual. He said, 'You might have—if she was still alive. You might have found her body if she was dead.'

'But I didn't go in. I rang the bell and nobody answered. I don't know what happened to the key. That was so long ago. It's probably on some childhood ring in some trunk somewhere. Or maybe it got thrown out when I left home.'

'What did you go there for?'

'I wanted to tell Monica something.'

Sessions said, 'You certainly make a person ask a lot of questions, don't you? You're not on a witness stand and you're not being interrogated and you're not being accused of anything. What are you acting like a hostile witness for?'

Linda lowered her eyes. His gaze was too penetrating, his manner too intense. He shot off too many sparks. How could she have felt he needed mothering? She'd as lief mother a full-grown lion. 'Because I'm under suspicion,' she said to him softly.

He changed his manner completely. He smiled at her. He sipped some of his wine and pitched into his food. 'I didn't mean to play rough,' he said with that little-boy quality that wasn't little-boyish at all—only by interpretation. 'I have to ask a lot of questions. I have to look a lot of places. I have to talk to a lot of people. Right?' He grinned at her. 'A detective has to find out a lot of things. It's your mother and she's been killed. This is a homicide. You understand that? Somebody killed your mother. We have to find out who that somebody is. And you want to help, right? So would you tell me all about this visit you made yesterday noon to your mother's apartment? What you went there for, who you saw there, what happened? The whole bit?'

Linda sighed. She finished the first course and let the waiter set the entree in front of them. 'All right,' she said, 'if you want to hear a lot of irrelevant details. I'm engaged to be married. This is to a boy my mother hasn't met. Until a week and a half ago she didn't even know about him. Of course, then she wanted to meet him. She decided to have him and me over for dinner. This was going to be tomorrow night. She had tickets to something or other that's opening off-Broadway. We were to have cocktails and dinner with her and go to the theatre and to a party afterward.

'Well, what happened was, his aunt in Pittsburgh took seriously sick and he's her favourite nephew and principal heir and he had to go to Pittsburgh in a hurry. How long he'll be there I don't know, but he wouldn't be coming home this week. So I went to tell Monica that we couldn't keep the dinner engagement, that we'd have to make it another time.'

Sessions said, 'And you went to her apartment and rang the doorbell and then what happened?'

'Nothing. I gave up and returned to the office. Oh, I got a hamburger to take in with me.'

'And you didn't do anything more about cancelling the engagement?'

'Yes. I tried to phone several times during the afternoon. But there wasn't any answer.'

'Where'd you phone from?'

'The office. I have an outside line.'

Sessions took out his notebook and wrote something. 'There'd be a record of those calls anywhere?' he asked.

'No.'

'Why did you go to see her during your lunch hour rather than call?'

Linda hesitated. That was another one of those hard-to-explain things like the key she once had. It seems perfectly logical to oneself but weird and unnatural to anyone else. 'Well,' she said, 'it's really kind of difficult . . . You see, Millie

Butelle, Monica's secretary, is there until Monica has lunch and that's anywhere from twelve-thirty to one-thirty. And if I called and Monica wasn't awake, Millie wouldn't wake her. Millie tends to be spiteful that way. She doesn't like me very much.'

'Why?'

'I don't know. I just don't think she likes *people* much.'

'What kind of an answer is that supposed to be? Why doesn't she like *you*?'

Linda made a face. 'Well, if you must know, back in my teens she did like me. In fact, when Monica wasn't around, she liked to hug and kiss me. But I didn't like it and she stopped and hasn't liked me since. Do you like that answer better?'

'I just wondered if that was it. Go on.'

'Well, if I tried to insist on speaking to Monica, she'd want to know what I wanted to talk to her about and a lot of other nosy things. And also I hadn't seen Monica in a couple of months . . .'

'I thought you told her about being engaged.'

'That was on the phone. Anyway, it was my lunch hour and it was just the kind of thing you'd kind of like to talk to your mother in person about. I'm sure you don't believe it, but that's the truth.'

'Why shouldn't I believe it?' Sessions said and took another mouthful of food. He washed it down with wine, replenished their glasses from the bottle in the basket, and went on. 'Who was the man who answered your phone last night when I called you?'

Linda shivered involuntarily. Oh, God. He was onto that now. Was she going to have to explain about David next? And from there would she have to go into her three years on the psychiatrist's couch and then into the reasons why she went to the psychiatrist in the first place? Damn it, a girl was entitled to *some* privacy even if her mother was murdered. 'I don't think,' she said coldly, 'that that's any of your business.

That has nothing to do with my mother.'

'It might have something to do with your boyfriend, though. That wasn't him, was it?'

'No.'

'What was the man's name?'

'I'm not going to tell you,' she said and realised instantly how guilty that made her sound. 'Why do you want to know about my personal life?'

Sessions said, 'Believe me, it's not your personal life. It's your mother's personal life. I'm trying to figure the angles. You had a guy up in your apartment last night. Maybe he's a friend of your mother's.'

Linda almost laughed. 'Is that what's worrying you? He's not. He's a man who works in the office. Randy—that's my fiancé—and I were going to the theatre last night. Then his aunt got sick. He came to the office to tell me and he gave me the tickets. He told me to take a friend. I did. I went with a friend from the office.'

'And you don't want to tell me his name?'

'His name is David Allison.'

'What's your fiancé's name?'

'Randy's? Randy Benson. Why?'

Sessions wrote that down in his book. 'Address?'

'Now wait a minute. He doesn't know my mother either.'

'So you've got nothing to worry about.'

'But what do you want to know about him for?'

'He's going to marry a girl who's going to inherit a lot of money because her mother's been murdered.'

She put her hands to her face. She was almost in tears. 'Oh now that's too much. Well if that's what's worrying you, you can forget it. In the first place, his aunt is very wealthy, and in the second place, there probably won't'—her voice broke—'won't be any wedding.'

'What's that mean?'

'We broke up and I don't want to talk about it.' She got out a handkerchief and blew her nose. 'So,' she said, 'tomorrow night—instead of Randy and me being with Monica, I'm going to be with Monica alone. Only she's not going to know it.'

'What's that?'

'Her funeral. The viewing is tomorrow night and I have to stand beside the bier.'

'You arranged that?'

'Monica's agent, Dick Morton, arranged it. He called me up this morning and offered to have the agency handle the whole thing. He's been her agent for years. They'd know what to do and how to do it. All I'm to do is what they tell me.'

THURSDAY 1:20–4:15 P.M.

Sessions, after dropping Linda, rode the cab to Fifth Avenue and the Richard Morton Agency which was on the tenth floor of the corner building on 45th Street. He spent twenty minutes there, learning what a blow Monica's death was to everyone, what was being done about the funeral, that they'd handled Monica's business interests for over twenty-five years. He learned nothing that shed light on the cause of her death.

At one forty-five he walked down to Madison and got an uptown bus, reflecting as he showed his shield that this was a more customary means of getting around town. He could imagine the snorts of laughter that would greet the costs of the cabs he'd taken should he put them on an expense sheet.

At 66th Street he got off, turned up his coat collar against a starting rain, and walked back to the nineteenth station house and the detective squad room. There he read what DD5s he hadn't seen and, at Sergeant Trager's request, talked to two reporters who were hanging around, letting them look over his shoulder as he made out his own DD5s. When the reporters left, he called Chief Nyborg with a briefing and by then Con Devlin was back.

They sat around for a cup of coffee while Devlin said he'd got hold of Lester Fritz and had it confirmed. Millie Butelle had come in a little after eight on Wednesday. She gave him the copy for the messenger service about half past ten. The messenger boy picked it up as usual around eleven.

Devlin typed up his own 5s and at three-fifteen they left together in a raging downpour and drove to 419 East 52nd Street to see what Monica's erstwhile secretary had to say for herself.

Millie Butelle's apartment was on the fourth floor. The living room was to the right off an entrance hall. It was small, but adequate, neat and nondescript. It had a parquet floor and a view of the apartment across the street. As for the woman herself, she was wearing tan slacks and a loose blouse. One of those new, 100-millimetre cigarettes was dangling from her lips and the ash was ready to fall. She didn't give quite the same impression she had the night before, that 'tight ship' all-efficiency way she had around Monica. In her own place she let down a little. In her own place it didn't matter if slacks were unflattering to a stocky figure, or the girdle stayed in the drawer.

The detectives had their shields out. 'Just a few questions, Millie.' They wiped their feet carefully and took off their coats before entering and Devlin shook the rain from his hat. They had parked their squad car in front of a hydrant two doors down but it was pouring hard and even the few seconds it took to run a hundred feet was enough to dampen their clothes.

She gave them a stony stare but let them pass and the two men walked through the hall and into the living room with that certain striding way that becomes a policeman's trademark, the result of thousands of enterings into thousands of differing situations, always as the man-in-charge, or the man from whom something is expected, always as the man prepared to deliver whatever that something is.

In the living room they looked around without seeming to, except that Sessions parted the curtains over the large window in the far wall to see what the view was like, whether there was a balcony or fire-escape, how the window opened. It was a habit as natural as instinct now to validate all the means of entrance and exit from a room before settling down. It was the same way he and all the other detectives sat in restaurants with their backs to the walls, their faces to the doors and if that opportunity were denied them, they were conscious of the fact.

'You live alone?' Sessions, asked, turning away from the window and flipping open his notebook.

She stood just inside the room, tense and straight. 'Yes.'

'Where's your home?'

She answered the routine questions about home and family. She came from Poughkeepsie but her parents were dead and an aunt and three cousins were the only connections she still had with that city. Her nearest living relative was a brother in a sanatorium for the mentally retarded. He had been there most of his life.

Sessions' questions were routine and his voice offhand, but there was no smile on his face, no cajolement in his manner. Whether Millie sensed it or not, this was no fooling. 'Last night you told us,' he said, getting to the real business, 'that you didn't go near Mrs. Glazzard's apartment all day yesterday, is that right?'

Millie sat down slowly on the couch as though she knew what was going to come next. 'I may have,' she said cautiously and concentrated on brushing cigarette ash off her blouse.

'And that was a lie, wasn't it?'

Millie didn't quite know the proper reply to that one so she tried a question of her own. 'Was it?'

'Tell her, Con.'

Devlin said, 'Lester Fritz, doorman at the apartment, says

you entered the building shortly after eight yesterday morning and went up to Mrs. Glazzard's apartment, that you came down about half past ten with an envelope for the News Features Syndicate messenger boy. You returned to the apartment and remained until about twelve noon when you were seen to leave by both Lester and Carl Mancini, who was also on duty at the time.'

Sessions, standing with his feet planted, said, 'You're carrying the ball now, Millie. What do you want to do? You want to tell us about it? You want to go down to the station with us? You want to call a lawyer? You want to plead the Fifth Amendment?'

She looked at him levelly. 'Suppose I refuse to say anything at all. Then what will you do?'

Sessions' look matched hers. 'I'll tell you what we'll do. Inasmuch as this is a homicide case and we're looking for the person who murdered your former boss, the first thing we'll do is decide you have guilty knowledge. We'll figure that either you're the murderer or you know who the murderer is and are trying to shield him. So we'll start collecting evidence against you to present to a Grand Jury . . .'

'Wait a minute,' she said with a touch of alarm in her voice. 'I didn't murder her. I didn't know she was murdered. Honest, I didn't know she was murdered.'

'What do you know?'

She came to her feet and paced in a circle, touching, patting and rubbing her face with one hand. Finally she took a puff on the cigarette and turned around. 'All right. I'll tell you everything. I'll tell you everything that happened.'

'That's the smartest thing you can do, Millie. Get it all off your chest.'

She sat down again, stared for a long moment at the coffee table as if collecting herself, then put the cigarette in the ashtray there and examined her fingernails. 'That wasn't true about the day off,' she said with a sigh. 'I made that up. I went there just like any other day. Same time as usual.'

'What time was it yesterday?'

'A little after eight. I went in and Lester was there. He took me up. He'd just come on. I went in.'

'What did you say to Lester?'

'Nothing.'

'Nothing? You didn't even say hello?'

'Well I guess I said hello.'

'And that's all?'

'I don't generally make it a habit to carry on conversations with elevator operators.'

'Go on.'

'I went in. I remember there were some glasses and dirty ashtrays in the living room. I cleaned them up.'

'How many glasses?' Devlin asked.

'I don't remember. Four, I think.'

'Lipstick on any of them?'

She looked up at him. 'I didn't notice, but I had the impression that there had been two couples, that Mrs. Glazzard wasn't the only woman.'

'Lipstick on the cigarettes?'

'Yes. I remember that now. Some had lipstick.' She reflected for a moment and went on. 'I cleaned up and put those things away. Then I went into the office off the dining room. The belt with her column was on the dictaphone. I played it and transcribed it as I always do. Then I put it in a pick-up envelope and took it downstairs and gave it to Lester.'

'What time was this?'

'Around ten-thirty. A little before.'

'Go on.'

'Then I went back to the office and did some other odds and ends. There really wasn't much. I rearranged some files, and then, about half past eleven, I took some coffee and fruit juice up to Mrs. Glazzard. She had a luncheon engagement with Sarah Little, the poet, at one o'clock. Well, I knocked and entered and put the breakfast table on the bed, but she didn't stir. I called her twice more, and then I put my hand on her shoulder, and she was cold. I knew immediately she was dead. So I took the breakfast things back down to the kitchen again, cleaned up and went home.'

Sessions said, 'Just like that, huh?'

'Well I didn't want to stay around the house with a dead body.'

Devlin put his hands on his hips inside his coat. 'Why didn't you call the police?'

'I don't know.'

'What do you mean you don't know?'

'I mean I suppose I should have but I didn't want to get involved. I don't know. Maybe I was afraid I'd get blamed for her being dead since I was the only person around.'

'Why did you think you'd get blamed?'

'I just told you. Because there's nobody else but me around.'

'You knew, then, that she didn't die of natural causes. You knew somebody had killed her.'

'No. I thought she committed suicide. The bottle was right there on the table, totally empty, and it'd been filled only a week ago. I thought she'd taken an overdose.'

'If you thought she'd committed suicide, why did you think you'd get blamed?'

'I don't know. Maybe that's not what I meant to say. I didn't want to get involved. People might think I could've stopped her or something. I don't know. I just know I didn't want to report it that she was dead. I don't know what I was afraid of. I guess I just panicked.'

'You panicked?' Sessions said.

'Yes, that's right. I panicked.'

'When was the last time you panicked?'

'I don't know.' She looked at him narrowly all of a sudden. 'Why?'

'Tell the story straight, Millie. You lied before. Don't lie this time.'

'I'm not lying,' she said testily. 'I can't tell you exactly why

I didn't call the police. I just didn't want to get involved. I was shocked. I just didn't know what to do except get as far away as possible, let somebody else discover the body.'

Sessions said, 'All right, go on.'

'I just came back here and I stayed here. I guess what I was hoping was that Robert would find Monica and report it to the police. And I waited to hear that she had been found. Well, nothing happened. It got to be evening and late in the evening and still there was no word. I was sure I'd be notified as soon as she was discovered. But there was no word. So I went out and walked by the place, across 72nd Street so Harry, the doorman, wouldn't notice me. And everything was quiet. You have to realise that at this point I thought she had deliberately taken an overdose of sleeping tablets.

'So I came back here and I didn't know what to do. I was afraid she wasn't going to be discovered that night at all. I thought when she didn't show up to her appointments people would try to phone her and then they'd have somebody break in to find her but nothing like that happened. Nobody seemed to notice and I suddenly realised that—well, she might not be found all that night, and then what? What was I going to do the next morning—this morning? I couldn't very well not show up to work, but I couldn't go through another day pretending I didn't know she was dead. So finally I called the police anonymously and told them there was a body in the apartment. And then the police found her.'

She looked up at the two detectives belligerently.

Devlin was the first to speak up. 'You said you panicked. I think that was the term. This is not what Lester and Carl told us. They said you looked in perfect control of yourself. You want to call them liars or do you want to change your story?'

'Of course I "looked" in control of myself. You don't think I'm going to let them see me upset, do you?'

Sessions said, 'You wear gloves to work?'

'Sometimes.'

'You wear gloves yesterday morning?'

'No.'

'Why not?'

'No reason. I don't always wear them. Like I told you.'

'Do you remember the times you wear them?'

'I can remember I didn't wear any gloves yesterday and I'll swear to that in court. I know what you're trying to do, Mr. Detective. You're trying to frame me.'

'Frame you?'

'You're trying to get me to admit I had gloves and then you're going to try to claim that I wore the gloves and strangled Mrs. Glazzard for some reason I can't even guess at. Because that's how she was killed, isn't it? She was strangled, wasn't she?'

Devlin said, 'That's a good guess, Millie. How'd you come to make it?'

'Are you trying to make something out of that? She's dead and you tell me she was murdered. There's not a mark on her, no blood, no wounds. What else am I going to think except that she got strangled?'

'How did you and Mrs. Glazzard get along?'

'We had a mutual regard for each other.'

'Is she being good to you in her will?'

Miss Butelle snorted. 'If she is, I'd be very surprised. I'm not expecting anything out of her will. I can't imagine why she'd have me in it.'

Sessions said, 'You went into the apartment at eight o'clock. When did you discover Mrs. Glazzard's body?'

'I told you. Half past eleven.'

You didn't go to her room before that for any reason? There was no phone call for Mrs. Glazzard, there was nothing you needed to disturb her for?'

'My instructions have always been very explicit. Under no circumstances was I to disturb Mrs. Glazzard before noon. And that means for phone calls too. If the King of Siam called up, I'd tell him he'd have to call back. Yesterday I went up early with the tray because she had given me instructions to waken her at eleven-thirty because of her luncheon date. She usually didn't make luncheon dates, but Sarah Little was a special occurrence. Mrs. Glazzard was willing to get up early to have lunch with Miss Little.'

They asked about Miss Little, who was staying in town at the Plaza. Then they asked about Motley. Millie said the first time she saw him was when he arrived at the apartment at half past two on a cold February afternoon to go shopping with Mrs. Glazzard. The shopping, Millie later found out, was for him. Then Monica got him an apartment and there was talk at one time about his having a car, but nothing came of that. 'But,' she said, 'that's about the only time he lost out.'

'You don't like Motley. Why?'

'Because he's a fourflushing, no-good gold-digger. That's what he is. She's been keeping him and any man who lets a woman do that is no man. He didn't care two hoots in hades about her either. It was the money. She paid him well to hang around and that's why he did it.'

'And that bothers you?'

'Why shouldn't it bother me? I worked for the money she paid me. He got his for smiling at her, for buttering her up. I'll bet Mr. Prettyface has never done a day's work in his life.'

'He and she ever quarrel?'

'Not around me.'

'Where's he from?'

Millie didn't know that. She had nothing on his background at all. She didn't see him all that often and when she did, they'd passed few words. Nor had Mrs. Glazzard ever talked to her about him.

'Know any reason he might strangle her?'

She shook her head. 'But if he did, I'll bet it's for money.'

'What about Mrs. Glazzard's daughter, Linda?'

'You mean would she strangle her mother? She could all right. There wasn't any love lost between them, I can tell you.'

'You don't care much for the daughter either, do you?'

The woman snorted. 'Her and her nice, prissy, respectable ways. She'd like you to think she's quite the lady, wouldn't she? Well I can tell you things about her that would fry your liver.'

'Like what?'

'Never mind. I'm no squealer. But you just ask the men in town. Any man. Any town. She needn't try those airs with me. I knew her when.'

'And what about this Dr. Patterson? Where does he fit into things?'

Her contempt was less but it was there. 'He's the old friend, the comfortable companion. Old reliable Archie. He wasn't in her league mentally, but he was handy and he was her best audience and I expect she liked that. And, if she needed an escort or an extra man, she could always get him.'

'And what did he get?'

'Glamour, I expect. She saw and did exciting things. He liked getting in on it.'

'Was he in love with her?'

'I think he was a worshipper. He admired her wit and her brains. He appreciated her. And, of course, Mrs. Glazzard felt flattered. But she knew him for what he was. He couldn't fool her. Only that Robert Motley could fool her and I don't know that she was so much fooled as willing.'

THURSDAY 4:15–11:00 P.M.

Con and Frank left the secretary at four-fifteen and went to the Plaza to talk to Sarah Little. She was a tiny, birdlike creature of nearly ninety who hopped and chirped, who was horrified at her friend's murder and fascinated at being questioned by the police. She had met Monica perhaps four times in her life, but there had been correspondence and they kept in touch. When the columnist failed to keep her luncheon engagement, Miss Little had called her apartment two or three times and when that got no answer, she assumed there had been some mistake and went on about her other affairs.

It was an interview that supported and explained but contributed nothing new to the investigation. The two detectives returned then to the nineteenth squad, typed up reports, made some phone calls, and went off again on more interviews. This time they pinned their shields on their coats and rang the doorbells of all the people who lived on Motley's floor. Then they drove all the way across town to Morningside Heights and repeated the process in Dr. Patterson's neighbourhood.

It was quarter of nine and still raining when they got back in the car after the last call. Con started up and said, 'You married, Frank?'

Sessions laughed harshly. 'Once. A long time ago. Jesus, don't remind me.'

'I was wondering. I called my wife back at the squad room to hold dinner, but I didn't think we'd be going this long. I gotta call it a day. I'm beat. I only got three hours' sleep last night.'

'Yeah. We'd better go back to the one-nine. Your wife'll think you're out with another woman.'

'You going home? I got a car over there. I can drop you.'

'Cantrell couldn't get a meet with those actors today. I thought I'd go down to the theatre and hit them in an intermission.'

'You want me along? I live in Stuyvesant Town. It's down in that general area.'

'Hell no, but I'll take a ride as far as you go.'

The first intermission break was nine-thirty to nine forty-five and Sessions had his interview but he didn't learn anything new. The rain was only a drizzle when he came out of the backstage door and he walked through it to the nearest Seventh Avenue subway kiosk and an uptown train. When he came out at 96th Street, it was pouring again, but he flagged a passing radio car and rode the few blocks to the twenty-fourth precinct and Boro Headquarters.

When he walked in it was ten-thirty and all was quiet. Homicide Sergeant Lou Monast was sitting on the front desk talking with duty officers Sergeant Bill McVey and Ed Higgins of the three-two squad.

Monast said, 'Well look who's here,' and asked Sessions how he was making out.

'We don't have anything yet. What's doing here? Where're the boys?'

'In the dormitory. It's all nice and quiet. Nothing like a drenching downpour to keep people honest.'

'Not honest, Sarge. Indoors.'

'It's the same thing.'

Sessions laughed. He went back to the homicide section, got out the DD5 sheets, the carbon paper, his notebook, and started typing. He pecked away laboriously for twenty minutes, put the results on Lt. Sullivan's desk and went back to the others. 'The hell with the rest of them. I can't see the keys any more.'

Joe Riley came in from the dormitory room, clapped a hand to his forehead and said, 'Oh, Christ, it's Sessions. Say, Frank, don't you ever go home?'

'I'm going. I've had it. My goddam eyes are burning holes in my head.'

McVey said, 'I didn't know he had a home. I thought he just slept standing up.'

'He's got a million beds in this town,' Riley said. 'With a different broad in each one.'

Monast grinned. 'Where is my wandering boy tonight?'

'Jesus,' Sessions said. 'What a bunch of comics.' He sat on McVey's desk and opened his notebook. 'By the way, did

Connager get a make on the perpetrator in that Harlem shooting last night?'

Monast said, 'Not yet. He thinks now that the aided—what's his name, Johnson—really doesn't make the perpetrator.'

'Yeah? No kidding.'

Higgins held up a copy of the next morning's *News* so Frank could see the headlines. 'MONICA MURDERED' they read and Higgins said, 'You really rate, Frank. Connager's case didn't even make the obituaries.'

'I'll take his. Two reporters had to have interviews. I got to brief the chief every time I go to the john, I got to tell the whole story to Captain Conklin tomorrow morning—I was supposed to see him this afternoon but we didn't get back. Jesus, it's bad enough trying to do a job.'

'But you got your name in the paper. It says, "according to Homicide Detective second grade Frank Sessions, there are no signs of breaking and entering and police believe robbery was not the motive for the slaying".'

Sessions laughed. 'How do you like that for a nice non-committal quote?' He dialled a number and rested his cigarette in an ashtray. 'Fred?' he said into the mouthpiece. 'Frank Sessions. Say, where the hell have you been all day? Every time I tried your office your secretary said you were expected back any minute . . .' He listened and laughed and said, 'I would too,' then he picked up his cigarette for a drag. 'What I wanted is some help from the phone company. And I figured you could cut through some of the red tape. Can you get me a record of Monica Glazzard's toll calls over the last four months? . . . That's right, Monica Glazzard. . . . Yeah, I'm on the case.' He listened for a bit and said, 'O.K., tomorrow noon. I'd better call you. I don't know where I'll be.'

When he hung up, Higgins said, 'You think her toll calls have something to do with it?'

'I wouldn't know but it never hurts to look.'

Alfredo Rodriguez and Bart Mannion came in from the dormitory. 'Who's for some coffee? Hello, Frank.'

Lou Monast said he was getting hungry. He got off the desk. 'You eaten, Frank?'

'Jesus, you know? I was going to pick up a hamburger when I finished down at the theatre and I clean forgot.' He dialled another number.

'You'd better come along with us. Build up your strength.'

Sessions put a hand over the mouthpiece. 'I'll let you know.' He listened and got an answer. He chuckled and said, 'Did I wake you up, Sweets?' He laughed again. He put out his cigarette. 'I'm at the office. . . . Listen, I'm not kidding.' He covered the receiver again. 'She thinks you guys sound like a bar.' Into the phone he said, 'Sergeant Monast is here, Bart and Joe Riley, Alfredo and a couple of guys from the three-two. Listen, you got any coffee in the house? . . . Because if you've got some coffee I'll come around in about half an hour and have a cup. First I got to go to my place and change my shirt . . . I want to stop off there anyway, see if there's any mail. Give me three-quarters of an hour.' He listened. 'No I haven't eaten—well, I ate lunch. . . . All right, three-quarters of an hour.'

When he hung up, Monast was taking orders from McVey and Higgins. 'We'll be down on Broadway,' he said. 'What's the name of the place? Probably Stanley's. Right, Joe?'

Riley said, 'Stanley's. Sounds like Sessions has a better place to go.'

Monast said, 'She must make a hot cup of coffee.'

Alfredo said, 'I think he likes her company better than ours.'

Riley said, 'Especially the plumbing facilities.'

Sessions said, 'Face facts, fellas. I like you but I don't love you.'

They moved out to the elevator and Riley said, 'Is it true, Frank, that she's really eighty-three years old, but she types up your DD5s?'

'Jesus,' Sessions said. 'Don't remind me.'

Outside, instead of walking down to Broadway, the men insisted on getting into the car and driving Sessions home. His home was a walk-up apartment on Third Avenue between 92nd and 93rd, across and beyond the old Ruppert Brewery. When he got out, they told him they'd be glad to wait while he changed and drive him to that cup of coffee. 'She might have a few extra cups.'

'It's no use. She hates cops. Her first husband was a cop.'

Sessions waved and crossed the sidewalk. The front door was between two shop windows and had a small glass pane in the top. It opened into a short entrance hall leading to a couple of steps and another door. Sessions let himself through the inner door with a key, walked around to the foot of the steep staircase and went up slowly. His apartment was on the fourth floor and consisted of a small living room, bedroom, kitchenette and bath. The living room and kitchenette had windows looking out onto the back court, the bedroom and bath looked into a narrow air shaft.

Sessions went through the apartment throwing on lights. The place was comfortably furnished and reasonably neat. The bed was unmade, but that was traditional. Sessions only made the bed when he changed the sheets. There were a couple of dirty dishes in the sink, a glass and a few pieces of silver.

Sessions opened the icebox and drank the rest of the bit of milk that was there. He opened a cabinet under the counter beside the sink, took out a quart bottle of Canadian Club that was half empty, poured an inch of it into a fresh glass, added some water and took that into the bedroom to sip while he changed his clothes. In the bathroom he ran a quick shower, finished it cold, then examined his face in the mirror. It was pale and drawn, the eyes dark and unhappy. To him it looked like a hideous face—even worse because his hair wasn't combed and the start of a stubble was forming on his chin. He rubbed the sandpapery skin with his hand. His fingers were long and slender—artistic. The nails were manicured and well kept. The calluses were few, the palms and skin soft.

He blinked his eyes. The shower made him feel better but the eyes still burned with fatigue. He got out his razor and some aerosol foam, whisked his chin smooth, and got into all fresh clothes, including a different suit and different shoes. He checked his money, his gun, his supply of cigarettes, drained the rest of his drink and went through the apartment turning off all the lights as he left. He'd been in there just under twenty minutes.

Downstairs in the hall, he unlocked his mailbox. There was a bill from his tailor and a letter from his brother's wife in California. He left them there, went out onto the street and hunted for a cab.

FRIDAY 7:30–7:50 A.M.

When the alarm went off, Nora Hensen propped herself on an elbow and tried to blink her eyes open. Her tousled hair was dark, her cheeks pink, her eyes a lighter brown than Frank's. Her lips were full, her teeth white and strong, her face round, and scattered with freckles. When she got her eyes open enough to see, she reached out to shut off the noise. Then she pushed away the covers and sat up. She was the kind of girl who could be called 'pleasingly plump'. Her breasts were large, which was good, but pendulous, which was bad. Her arms and legs were well fleshed out, particularly the upper arms and thighs, so that she couldn't call them slender, but they weren't fat either, not by a damned sight, and she did have very nice ankles even if she did say so herself. She wasn't happy about her stomach though. If she lay on her back it stayed down pretty flat, but sitting, as she was just then, it ballooned out in a most ugly fashion. And when a girl slept raw, as she did, there was no hiding the fact from any pair of eyes that happened to be around. At the moment, though, hers were the only eyes in the room. Frank wasn't in the bed and she gained an impression that he hadn't been in the bed for quite some time.

Then he appeared in the doorway, fully dressed except for tie and jacket. Instinctively she straightened a little and tried to suck in her stomach. 'How long have you been up?'

'Since five. I woke up and couldn't go back to sleep. Say, don't you have anything in this place to read? I've had nothing to do but look at the late late late late show and drink coffee.'

Trying to hold herself straight was a strain and it didn't look natural. She slumped again. The hell with her stomach. That was about the least interesting part of her anatomy to Frank anyway. Besides, he'd seen her six ways to Sunday. There wasn't a position she could take or a way she could move that would be new to him. And how long had they known each other? Three months? It seemed like three years. It seemed almost like forever.

'There're a couple of paperbacks on the television.'

'I read those. They only took twenty minutes apiece.'

'Well you should have waked me up. I could've entertained you.'

Sessions laughed. 'There isn't any question about that.'

'In fact I still could.' She lay back on the bed and tucked her hands under her head. She looked good that way and she knew it. Her stomach was flatter and she showed more. 'I don't have to be at work until nine.'

'Yeah, but I have to be at work at eight.'

'I thought you had the next two days off.'

'That was before the Monica Glazzard homicide. Now I'm

going to be working all day every day.' He gestured at her. But I'll take a raincheck.'

'Any time.' She got up and went for a robe. After all, if a man can't do anything about it, it's mean to tempt him. She followed him into the kitchen where he'd been drinking instant coffee and was heating the water again. 'How about tonight, Honey?'

Sessions set down a cup for her and measured coffee for both. 'I don't know. I don't know where I'll be or how I'll feel or when I'll be through.'

Nora let him pour the hot water into the cup and pass it to her. She stirred in some sugar and picked up the milk. 'How're you going to get by on three hours' sleep?' she wanted to know.

'Don't worry about it, Sweets. I'm fine.'

'You know, Frankie, I had an uncle who used to say that. Those very same words. And you know what happened to him? He dropped dead one afternoon. Right out in the street.'

'No kidding?' Sessions said. 'That's too bad.' He looked at his watch and lighted a cigarette.

'That's all right, he wasn't a close uncle. But what I mean is, you need somebody to take care of you, Frankie. Get you on some kind of schedule.'

Sessions laughed. 'Are you proposing to me, kid? Forget it. I make a lousy husband.'

'We'd be good for each other, Frankie. You know we would. We're good right now, in fact. You've got to admit that.'

'That's right. So why change it?' He reached over to put his hand on hers. 'So let's not rock the boat, huh?'

'What I mean is, Frankie, sure we're good for each other and this is a fine arrangement. I'm not knocking it. Believe me, I'm not. But what I mean is, I'm twenty-six. You know that's not exactly young any more. . . . No kidding. Don't smile, I mean it. I know you're older but you're a man.

Twenty-six is very old for a girl. It makes her start wondering. You know what it makes her start wondering about, Frankie? About settling down. Is she going to get married? You know a girl doesn't want not to get married, Frank.'

'You were married. And you told me the first time I took you out that nothing was worse than marriage.'

'Marriage to somebody like Andy, yes. That wasn't settling down. He was after every skirt he saw. He went to bed with a whore on our honeymoon. I mean it literally. That's what he did. All right, maybe I wasn't as good then as I am now, but God damn it, that really hurts.'

Sessions said gently, 'I chase skirts too, Nora, and you better know it. In fact, I've been doing it for thirteen damn long years now.'

'You think I don't know? I'm one of them, aren't I? But that's what I mean. If we got married, you wouldn't have to any more. I'd keep you happy. Believe me, you wouldn't have strength for another woman.'

Sessions leaned forward. 'Sweetie, I like the present arrangement. I thought you did too.'

'Oh, I do, Frank.'

'We're free individuals this way. Why do you want to tie us together with knots? What's that going to do?'

She said earnestly, 'There's one good reason for doing it legal, Frank. That's children. A woman wants to get married so she can have children. You know, when I was born, my mother still hadn't reached her twentieth birthday? And here I am, twenty-six and there's nothing even on the horizon. If I don't get married pretty soon, nobody's going to want me. And then there won't be any children.'

Sessions smiled at her tenderly. 'And that's what the problem is? You want to find a husband? Look, if my coming around is queering things for you . . . If I'm keeping other men away . . .'

'No, no,' she said hastily. 'You don't come around that often anyway. Forget about the kids. Honest, Frankie, I only mentioned it out of selfishness. I figure if we were married, I'd see you oftener. This is the first time in a week and I get lonesome. I don't mean I don't have other dates—especially on weekends—but that's not like being with you, Frankie. I get wondering, when the days go by and you don't phone, who you're with, what you're doing, if she's prettier than me—you see, Frank? I know I'm not the only girl in your life. But I'd like to be. So I made a pitch. You know.' She shrugged. 'So I struck out.' She thought of something. 'Hey, listen, I was going to cook you some breakfast. And here I am gabbing my head off—and me the one who says she hates gabby women.'

But Sessions was on his feet. 'I can't, Sweets. It's quarter of eight. Make it next time, huh?' He kissed her on the mouth.

'A raincheck?' She smiled at him. 'Like in the other room? Like that?'

'Just like that.' He kissed her again in the doorway and she kissed him back and clung. He had to make a move to free himself. Her robe was mostly open, she noted, when he went to the elevator and if some man were to come out of one of the other apartments just then, he'd get quite a show. Even so, she took her time gathering the robe about her again. It would be good for Frank to leave her with the picture of semi-nudity in his mind. It might help counterbalance that clinging bit where she held onto him too long. That, on top of the talk about marriage and children, could be enough to chase someone like Frank Sessions away for good. You can't hold a man to you with your hands or with chains or laws or appeals to his sense of obligation. It wasn't that easy. You had to hold him to you with your personality and temperament, plus your interest, plus, if possible, better sex than he could get anywhere else. But that was very very hard. If you weren't born with the knack, it was devilishly hard to acquire.

She waved and blew him a kiss when he got on the elevator and she let him see a big smile. Then she closed the door, let the robe fall open at random and went back to her coffee.

She wasn't smiling now. Her face was melancholy as she analysed events. He might just have kissed her off at the door. No question but she shouldn't have talked marriage to him at quarter of eight in the morning. But when the hell was she supposed to get to such subjects? When else did they do anything but make love? Three hours of sleep he'd had. And two the night before. And he'd been working steadily all that day. The autopsy in the morning, the lunch with the daughter, the interviews . . .

Nora, thinking about that, realised they did do other things than make love. Frank talked. He told her things. And, of course, that was good because he wasn't the type who'd just tell anything to anybody. But she didn't get to tell him things. Except over this breakfast when she figured he ought to be in a pretty weakened condition. All the work, all the lack of sleep, all the sex last night—better than two hours of it. If any time was going to be the time to feel him out about marriage, this morning should have been it. And if she'd chased him away instead of roping him in, well she played it wrong and she shouldn't have done it. But what the hell? Was she supposed never to gamble for the stakes she wanted? Was she supposed, instead, to keep herself available for a lost and footloose detective who didn't really seem to know what to do with himself when he wasn't working?

He wasn't any bargain, she told herself, hedging against the possibility that he'd never come back. Marriage to a guy like Frank Sessions? God, she probably wouldn't see any more of him than she did now. But, of course, with marriage she could have children. That would make it easier if not all right. But what a man to fall in love with! What did he have? He was nice-looking but you wouldn't call him handsome; he made a very good salary as a detective second grade. It kept him in luxury, but with a wife and family it wouldn't go so far. His job was the kind that your friendly neighbourhood life insurance dealer wouldn't be quite so friendly about. Three detectives shot in Brooklyn only a few weeks ago. A detective shotgunned to death by a narcotics peddler in Harlem back in March. A woman could lie awake nights worrying if her husband was a detective.

Of course he could make love like nobody she ever dreamed of. But this ability might be commonplace. She wasn't all that experienced, since, before Frank, there had only been two boys back in high school and her erstwhile husband.

But, whether she could rationalise him as a catch or not, she wanted him and now she'd made her first move. She'd planted the seed. It might grow—the ground should be fertile. From what Frank had told her, just about every one of the twenty-four other men he worked with was married and had children. In fact, in some cases, their children had children.

And maybe he was getting tired of chasing. Maybe he was ripe for catching. If only she didn't have so many freckles. Maybe if she weighed a little less, if her stomach wouldn't stick out so much when she sat down without a girdle.

She decided she'd go without breakfast.

FRIDAY 11:30–11:45 A.M.

By half past eleven Friday morning, when Sessions presented himself at the Washington Square apartment of Mrs. Carolyn Dines Stevenson, he'd already put half a day's work under his belt. He had personally briefed Chief Nyborg on the status of the case, gone over results and worked out the day's schedule with Lt. Sullivan, Devlin, homicide and nineteenth squad detectives, told the results of the meeting to Captain Conklin personally, given an interview to the press, told Nyborg what was going on, made an appointment with Mrs. Stevenson, brought his DD5s up to date and spent a half hour in travel time between West 100th Street and Washington Square.

As for the results of the first day's investigation, it was established that Monica and Dr. Patterson had arrived together at Greg Buckingham's party in the Biltmore Hotel about six. Thirty-four other people also attended. There was a buffet dinner which the guests of honour, Frederick and Florence Lyle, couldn't stay for since they had to be at the theatre well in advance of curtain time and since they also never ate before a performance. After the performance Buckingham, the Lyles, Patterson, Monica, the director, producer, author and the main angel were seen together at Lindy's where they ate and waited for the early editions and the reviews. The reviews had been disappointing to those connected with the production and the party broke up almost as soon as they'd been read.

Actually, the nine people did not make a merry little group. Monica, asked her opinion of the play, had been frankly critical. The author, in defence, had questioned her taste and there was a distinct coolness between the two parties. When the reviews confirmed Monica's position, she didn't mention it but the author, who had been quite rude, and his friends stalked off. The Lyles, however, who had fared well at Monica's hands, stayed and when the party broke up, were persuaded to return with Monica and Patterson for more talk which would be the basis of a column. They stayed late but Patterson stayed later. They did not know what his and Monica's relationship was except they seemed at the very least, good friends, at most, even lovers. Certainly the Lyles could see no murder in their relationship. They couldn't even see ill-will. The author, director, producer and angel were among the people the police would attempt to interview this day.

As for the other areas of investigation, neither the three people closest to the dead woman, her daughter, secretary and lover, nor any of the building employees had committed felonies in New York City, at least under their present names. Nothing Millie Butelle or Robert Motley had said about themselves was refuted by any of their neighbours. Motley, however, didn't fare so well with the Sacramento police. They not only had no arrest record for such a man, they could find no record of his ever having lived there. Which was the main reason why Frank Sessions was calling on Carolyn Dines Stevenson, the woman who brought Motley and Monica Glazzard together.

Mrs. Stevenson was plump, grey-haired and bouncy and her apartment looked like the back alley of a supermarket. She was a heavy investor in pop art and stacks of empty toilet tissue cartons, specially piled and glued for her by some pop artist, decorated each side of the fireplace. There was a ten-foot-square collage of labels from the cans and boxes found on grocery shelves, a three-by-ten-foot canvas painted a solid, hideous pink, two yard-square examples of op art that, on prolonged viewing, could induce seasickness, and an array of less imposing and intrusive works covering most of the available wall space.

'My husband won't set foot in this apartment,' Mrs. Stevenson said. 'He calls it my museum and complains bitterly every time I buy another work of art. But he'll find this a worthwhile investment. Great art improves in value as the years go by. This isn't money wasted as he seems to think it is by any means.'

'It's an interesting room, Mrs. Stevenson.'

'May I see your badge again? Is that what you call it?'

'Shield, ma'am.' He opened the leather case and exposed it.

'Now that's just beautiful. That shield is a work of art. Did you know that, Lieutenant? That's what art is all about these days. Appreciating the beauty of design and feeling that's been put into the most commonplace articles. How much do you want for the shield?'

'What?'

'I'd like to frame and display it. I think over the fireplace would be good. Perhaps with a baby spot to make it dazzle. Is it real gold, Lieutenant?'

'It's not real gold and it's not for sale. I'm sorry . . .'

'How about a thousand dollars? Even if it were real gold that would be a pretty good price, don't you think? One thousand dollars. Cold cash. Right now. Twenty brand new fifty-dollar bills in your palm in one minute?'

Sessions laughed and put the shield away. 'I can't sell it without the commissioner's approval. You ask him.'

'Well that's a lot of bother. Whereas, one thousand dollars . . . ? You could always say you lost it.'

'The commissioner. Now shall we talk about the man I asked you to think about, Robert Motley?'

She got interested in Robert Motley then and gave a lengthy recital on the subject. She had first come across Robert Motley in one of the art galleries she habituated. This was two Octobers ago. She began running into him in other galleries and conversation started. She learned he was studying art at the New School, lived in a converted loft over on Avenue B, had little money but was obsessed with the desire to paint. He showed her some of his work and she was impressed. She gave him a little money to help him over the bad spots—tuition for the second term at school, for example, for he had no family or relatives he could turn to.

Early the following year, she invited him to one of her parties. She lived alone most of the time because her husband had received a government appointment and worked in Washington and she wouldn't leave New York. As a result, she gave frequent parties for one purpose or another, to honour this person or that one. This particular party was for a writer she knew and wished to give a push to—that was, after all, the function of a patron of the arts—help the gifted get started. She had invited Robert Motley, another talented unknown, because at this party there would be people, like Monica Glazzard, whom it would help him to know. And since Motley was personable as well as gifted, she made a special point of introducing him to Monica.

The meeting, however, went strangely, Mrs. Stevenson said. She left the pair together and was busy greeting and talking to others when she ran into Monica again at the punch bowl. She asked how Monica liked the young man and Monica had laughed and said he was an utter phony and where had she found him?

'Well,' Mrs. Stevenson said, 'I didn't know what to make of that remark. "He's not phony at all," I told her. "He's a painter and a good one." And Monica said to me, "He's the biggest phony I've seen this decade. If he's a painter, I'm a channel swimmer." '

Monica, she went on to say, apparently changed her tune, for later on that evening Mrs. Stevenson saw her and Motley in deep and prolonged and serious conversation. Later they were laughing together, and ultimately they left the party together. And she never saw Motley again. He dropped out of the New School—at least they didn't know anything about him there when she made inquiries—and he didn't appear at the art galleries or anywhere else she went any more. In fact, when she tried to get in touch with him a couple of months after that, he'd moved and left no forwarding address.

'And you made inquiries at the New School?'

'Yes, after I couldn't find him at the loft. But all they could tell me was that he wasn't attending any classes there.'

FRIDAY 8:00–10:00 P.M.

The funeral home in which Monica Glazzard's mortal remains were to be displayed was on Lexington Avenue between 84th and 85th Streets and the viewing was reported in the paper as Friday night from 8 p.m. and Saturday from nine in the morning until 2 p.m., when a service would be held. What was not announced in the paper was that Monica's earthly fate was cremation according to her own wishes as expressed in her will.

The viewing on Friday night was held in the suite of rooms on the fourth floor and four of the rooms were required, two connecting rooms to handle the line, two others where mourners could congregate. It was a staggering turnout, and the flowers that came in were almost as numerous as the people. The huge mahogany coffin with its white satin lining was almost hidden by flowers and the rest were already being put around the chapel on the second floor where the next day's viewing and final services would be held.

Linda Glazzard stood in the room with the coffin but over near the exit door so she wouldn't have to hover around the body. Monica, lying in repose in a high-necked purple velvet gown with a rhinestone pin on her breast, both purchased by the Morton Agency (with some advice from the funeral home), looked serene and quite lovely if not completely real. In fact, Linda, bearing it alone in the beginning, standing and shaking hands and receiving sympathetic kisses and remarks from people she had for the most part never seen before, couldn't help thinking drily, 'I'll bet they think she looks better than I.'

Admittedly, Linda was feeling sorry for herself, but she was depressed. She had no sense of loss about her mother. Her mother belonged to the public, not to her, and it was the public that was grieving. Some who gazed at the corpse shed real tears and while most were close friends who had genuine feeling for the columnist, it was obvious to Linda that many had never laid eyes on Monica and only loved her through her columns.

But it wasn't the number of her mother's friends that depressed Linda. It was that she herself had no one at all. If only Randy had been there to lean on. If only she could have felt the warmth of his presence even if he did nothing. But there was no Randy and it looked as if there never would be again. He had not even sent a telegram of condolence.

But Dr. Patterson, bless him, came to the rescue. He arrived at quarter of nine when the line was still in the embryo stage and he stood with her thereafter to greet the mourners.

Another who came, Linda noted, was Detective Frank Sessions. He wore an expensive dark suit and a subdued, grey and white tie. But the disguise, she felt, didn't fool anybody. He didn't go through the line, he didn't mingle or talk with anybody. He was only there to watch, to see who was there and what was going on. It made Linda wonder about his ability as a detective. To her he had 'cop' written all over him.

What Linda did not know was that the sedate young man in the black suit who handed the guest book to each new arrival to sign was also a detective. The names of everyone who attended the viewings and the service were going to be carefully scrutinised by the police department—and in some cases the handwriting—before Linda Glazzard would have it given to her by the funeral home.

As for Frank Sessions, who was responsible for the guest-book ploy, he didn't care whether anybody knew he was a detective or not. He only put in an appearance because he had to. Captain Conklin, the fourth district commander, was very edgy about the Monica Glazzard case. If it weren't solved in a reasonable time, a great deal of public dissatisfaction might be roused. The police department might come under some heavy fire. And the way one usually handled dissatisfaction in any organisation was to order a shake-up. Captain Conklin didn't wish for any shake-ups in his district because the head-rolling might start at the top.

When he learned of the viewing, therefore, he promptly inquired of Sessions and Devlin which one of them planned to cover it, and he was not quite pleased when they said neither. Did they not think any information could be derived from the viewing, from the people who came or who didn't come? They told him about the guest-book arrangement but he was still dissatisfied. There was nothing like on-the-spot measures, particularly by those who formed the central nervous system of a case. Both detectives really ought to attend the viewings—both Friday and Saturday—and keep their eyes open. However, since other leads needed checking out, it would be enough for one man to go to each and stay as long as necessary to make sure no possible clues were overlooked. For Frank Sessions, twenty minutes was as long as it took.

He rode a bus back down to the nineteenth and climbed the stairs at quarter of ten. Boxton was out in the main room in his shirt sleeves gabbing with two other detectives. No one was in the cage and the room was otherwise empty. Sessions said, 'Where's my partner?'

'Con?' Boxton answered. 'He went home a couple of hours ago.'

A detective named Nichols said, 'How was the wake?'

'Oh, Jesus. Ordeal by grief. Who the hell thought up the idea of showing off dead bodies? They're nothing but rotting pieces of meat for Christ's sake.'

Boxton said, 'Careful, Frank. You want to make us all puke?'

Nichols said, 'He sounds like a communist.'

'You ought to hear him on religion sometime.'

Sessions laughed. 'Try me on marriage. I'm very good on marriage.' He lighted a cigarette. 'You got anything for me? Any new fives?'

Boxton showed him what they had and he sat down and scanned them at a glance. Most were interviews with guests at the Buckingham party. One said he'd taken pictures which he'd show the police as soon as he got them back from being developed. No one else had even that much to offer.

Boxton sat down facing Sessions and tilted back a chair. 'I hear you're concentrating on Motley. You think he's the perpetrator?'

Sessions shrugged and put a foot on the desk. 'He's a fake, a fraud and a phony. That doesn't make him the perpetrator but it does make you think about him that way.'

'What've you found out?'

Sessions laughed. 'Oh brother, plenty. First I talked to this dame who first introduced him to the deceased. Carolyn Dines Stevenson. Jesus, is she from Freaksville! I get it from her where he lived in this loft. That checks with what he told us. I get it about the New School—the courses he's supposed to have taken. So I go over and they never heard of the guy. He's never taken any courses in anything.'

Sessions sat up to mash out his cigarette. 'Then let me see. I picked up a list of the deceased's toll calls for the first four months of this year. Jesus, she makes almost as many toll calls as a bookie. There must be two hundred . . .'

Boxton said, 'Yeah, I know. I saw the slips. That'll keep a few people busy.'

'And then I go over to the loft Motley used to live in. One guy who knew him was around. Three others weren't. This one who knew him is a painter and he says one thing significant. Motley offered part of his room for this painter to store his canvases in. That's where Mrs. Stevenson got the idea the subject could paint. He palmed another guy's stuff off as his. So he's a con-artist. He's trying to fashion himself a soft berth and it looks like Mrs. Stevenson was supposed to provide it but something better came along.'

Nichols said, 'I don't know why the Glazzard dame didn't see through him.'

'The evidence is that she did and took him on anyway. So, anyway, what else? I'm trying to find out where this Motley comes from. He lied about Sacramento, which means he doesn't want us to know where he's from, which makes it important to me that we find out. So I try the post office for change of address cards. Nothing. I check to see if he ever tried to collect unemployment insurance or get on welfare. Nothing there. I try the employment agencies, but he hasn't left any tracks. All of a sudden he appears in New York without any previous life—like Venus on the half-shell or an amnesia victim regaining his memory. And it's damned hard back-tracking on the son of a bitch.'

'Maybe if you go talk to him . . .'

'I tried that after I had some supper but he wasn't in. I thought he might be at the viewing but he wasn't there either. So I'm thinking that's kind of interesting. I got it from one doorman that when Motley went out, he was carrying an attaché case—like an executive going to work. In the middle of the afternoon, that is.'

'What would he have in an attaché case? Pyjamas and a clean shirt?'

'That's the obvious answer. So what is he doing, running? Or is he giving up the monastery and going calling? And if so, who's his friend?'

FRIDAY 10:15 P.M.–SATURDAY 12:15 A.M.

Sessions left the nineteenth detective squad at quarter past ten that Friday night but he didn't get to his own building, almost exactly one mile north, until quarter of twelve. He took a bus up and got off a block from home to go into Paddy's Bar between Ninety-first and Ninety-second. There he drank two mugs of beer, smoked five cigarettes, watched the end of the Yankee ball game on the television, gabbed with a couple of men around, suspected the fat, fifty-year-old woman on the make in there of syphilis, saw no one else, and finally faced up to going home.

In the front hall he stopped again to open his mailbox and found that the tailor's bill and letter from his sister-in-law had been added to by a plug for a new laundromat opening around the corner. Frank stuffed the junk mail and bill in his pocket and ripped open the letter from his brother's wife. He read it quickly under the dim hall light. It was two pages scribbled longhand on both sides but Sessions was through with it in less than thirty seconds. It was a sad letter. The real estate venture they had gone into with such high hopes wasn't working out well. They wouldn't be able to pay back the money yet. In fact, if they couldn't borrow some additional money from somebody pretty quick, she didn't know what was going to happen to them. Ken was too proud to write to his big brother and ask for more money when he already owed so much, but if Ken was too proud, she, Kathleen, was not. There were two children involved—little Frankie Sessions, named for his big detective uncle, and Barbara, named for her paternal grandmother, Frank's own mother—and Kathleen had no intentions of letting pride stand in the way of their welfare, regardless of Ken. Could Frank let them have five hundred dollars for six months? He could afford it, after all, being a single man earning better than twelve thousand a year. And she'd be glad to let him have her diamond engagement ring as security. Granted it wasn't worth five hundred dollars (Frank happened to know Ken paid a hundred and fifty for it, for he'd lent him the money) but in sentimental value it was worth twice that.

One corner of Sessions' mouth tightened and he stuffed the letter into his pocket. He wouldn't have minded if Kathleen had really begged for the money but he knew her better than that. He knew them both better. It was Ken's doing. That namesake bit clinched it. He'd made Kathleen write. Ken knew Frank had always liked Kathleen, had always thought Kathleen got the raw end of the deal. Ken was trying to be clever but he was only being awkward. It was the story of his life—always the would-be entrepreneur, the man who would have made a million only a) the war started; b) the war stopped; c) the big shot died; d) the big shot was lied to and turned against him, e), f), g) and the alphabet. Ken would try almost anything to make a buck except work.

Sessions fitted his key in the lock of the inside door and as he did, the outer door opened and, to his surprise, Linda Glazzard came into the little, poorly lighted hall. She looked distraught and nervous, showing not quite the icy, steadfast calm she had exhibited at the viewing. But otherwise she was the same—same clothes, same hair, same makeup. She was, in fact, one hell of an attractive girl and for a quick moment, Sessions was aware of it. Then he remembered that she was the daughter of a murder victim, a suspect in the case and quite possibly a murderess. At the very least she was a hapless civilian, dependent upon the police for help and the police in such cases weren't people, they were automatons created and maintained for purposes of assistance and nothing else. 'Well hello,' he said in the little-boy way he sometimes had when he wasn't acting in an official capacity. He gave her a smile and held the door. 'You waiting to see me?'

She nodded. 'I thought you were never coming. I went to the precinct after the viewing and they said you left about quarter past ten and were going home. I've been calling you and everything.'

A woman with a poodle came through the door Frank held and went between them. Frank said to Linda, 'You want to come up? It's more private. Or would you rather talk here?'

'I'd rather come up. I'd like to sit down. I've been standing since eight o'clock.'

He let her precede him up the long flights of stairs, opened his apartment door and switched on the light for her. He followed her in and turned on other lights. She paused and looked around. 'It's a man's apartment,' she said.

'You're a detective yourself. You want a drink?' He went by her to the kitchenette.

'Some rye. On the rocks, please. I don't see any flowers or fragile vases or anything like that. You do have curtains. You know, I had a bet with myself that you wouldn't. But they're plain and heavy. They look utilitarian rather than decorative.'

'Which,' Sessions said, 'is the difference between men and women. How'd you find out where I live? They tell you at the one-nine?'

'No, I found you in the phone book. I didn't want to ask the detectives there. They'd want to know what I wanted you for and I've had some experience with the way you detectives ask questions. You go through a person's defences like a trip-hammer. If I told them it was something to do with my mother, they'd want me to tell them what it was. If I said it wasn't, that would be worse.'

Sessions got out the whisky from the cabinet in the kitchenette and poured some into two glasses. She came to the doorway beside him. 'Canadian Club,' she said, impressed.

'The glasses aren't the best, but the whisky is.' He got out ice. 'So what did you want to see me about, and why me?'

She opened the cupboard door to observe the rest of his liquor supply. 'You know, you're funny,' she said. 'You wear very nice clothes. I was noticing that at lunch yesterday. They're expensive clothes. And you buy only the best brands of liquor, yet you live in a fourth-floor walkup way up in Germantown. Could I ask what you pay for rent?'

'Sixty-two sixteen a month. There's been an increase.' He put ice in the glasses and filled his glass the rest of the way from the faucet.

'A little water for me too, please. What I mean is, that doesn't make sense. How long have you lived here?'

'Since about three months after my divorce. Thirteen years. And it makes perfect sense. All I need is a place to store my clothes and sleep once in a while.' He gave her the small glass, held his up and said, 'Cheers. Let's go back in the living room and sit down and you tell me what this has to do with your mother.'

They went into the small living room, Linda taking an

easy chair facing Sessions who slumped on the daybed, tossed his cigarettes out beside him and fished for one of the few that were left. Linda held up her glass and said, 'To you.'

He laughed. 'Yeah, let's drink to me. Now why is it you wait up for me to come home just so you can tell me something to do with your mother that you don't want to tell the other detectives working on it?'

'I've asked myself that,' she said, staring into her glass before taking another swallow. 'The answer is that when a girl is suspected of killing her own mother, she—she becomes afraid of strangers. Of course I know you suspect me—probably more than any of the others do—but I feel as if I know you better. I feel that if I tell you something that might throw suspicion away from me, you'll be more apt to accept it than the others.'

Sessions lighted the cigarette and drew on it heavily. 'You're feeling sorry for yourself. So you lost your mother. So it happens to everybody. Nobody's singled you out for special blighting.'

'I know that. And if I am feeling sorry for myself, that's not the reason. I'm not weeping over Monica. She's crammed more into her forty-eight years than most people cram into eighty-four and since I seldom saw her anyway, I can't claim that her death is going to alter my way of life measurably. She was murdered and that's something of a shock, but any sorrow I felt would be for her, not for myself. So if you really want to know why I feel sorry for myself—I'd rather say I'm melancholy, it sounds better—it's because I've just had a good dose of being chambermaid to Monica's queen again. That hasn't happened much in recent years—since I got out of her orbit and started fending for myself—and I'd almost forgotten what it was like.'

'Give me an idea,' Sessions said, watching her and pulling on his drink.

'You saw it. You were there. The people coming to see Monica—by the hundreds. Now I don't begrudge her that, believe me. I must sound awfully selfish and self-centred, but I'm not. In fact, that's the one thing I've never been able to be. What is it I heard a minister say once, "Anybody who doesn't believe in Original Sin has never seen a baby. Look at a baby, born totally selfish and self-centred. He fully believes himself to be the centre of and most important thing in the universe." And he went on to say that the path to goodness is struggling to get away from this self-centred attitude. Well he happens to be wrong because if that's goodness, then I'm an angel. Because I, Mr. Frank Sessions, never believed that I was the centre of the universe. So far back that it's before I can remember, I learned that Monica was the centre of the universe and I was a useless piece of baggage that happened to be dumped in the vicinity. In fact, the psychoanalyst I went to had to try to get me to put myself in the centre of my universe so I could then go about learning that I wasn't the centre in a more normal fashion.'

'How'd he make out?'

'He had some success. I'm a reasonably normal human being now. Except that I'll never have the kind of confidence that comes from being good and knowing you're good. For instance, I'm sure there are things I'm good at, but I don't dare think I'm good for fear I'll be wrong and am nothing but a fool.'

Sessions got up to get an ashtray. 'So Monica has her hour in the limelight—for the last time. And everybody pays homage to her and not to you. So what? You're alive and she isn't. And I don't know of anybody who'd swap your place for hers, including her.'

Linda frowned. 'You make everything I say sound awful. I don't begrudge her anything. I wish I could bring her back to life in fact. But it's the loneliness of being ignored. It's standing there and being greeted by people who don't know you, who perhaps didn't even know Monica *had* a daughter till that moment, or maybe didn't even know what I was doing there in the first place. When Dr. Patterson came and helped, that made it better. But, well it's lonely.'

'Yeah,' Sessions said, resuming his position on the daybed. 'You didn't have a boyfriend around to help you over the hard parts. Is that what's really back of it?'

'Maybe. I don't really know. All I know is that my only relative goes at the same time my fiancé goes and I suddenly realise that's all there is in the world. Maybe I'm feeling sorry for myself because it's a little tough to take.'

'That's as good a reason as any. Now let's get back to this thing about your mother which you think I'll believe but other detectives won't.'

'I didn't mean it like that.'

'How did you mean it?'

'What I meant was—well, this is a very important case. It's one you've got to solve. In order to solve it, you need a guilty party, don't you? And who looks guiltier than the daughter? So if the police suspect me, they're not going to be very happy discovering evidence that I'm innocent. They're going to suspect that kind of evidence because it might ruin the case they're building up against me.'

Sessions laughed. 'But I won't. Is that it?'

'Well, you know me a little. I mean I'm a human being to you—at least I think I am. I'm not just a name to go in the record book. Therefore you might like to think I'm innocent. Therefore you'd look at the evidence more kindly.' She looked at him hopefully. 'Do you understand?'

'Yeah, I understand. It's a miracle, but I managed it.' He sat up and put his feet on the floor. 'You're a nice kid,' he said, 'except you've got mixed-up brains and you really are wallowing in self-pity. Now I'm going to try to straighten you out a little. In the first place, what the hell do you think a detective is, some monster from Mars? Do you think all we're looking for is a fall-guy to hang the rap on? Do you think we've got no feeling for people at all?'

Linda chewed a lip. 'Well you don't show a great deal. A person dies and you come around asking questions of the bereaved relatives as if you couldn't care less about their sorrow. You don't show one shred of sympathy.'

'When we come around, Miss Linda Glazzard, it's because somebody has been murdered and our job is to find the murderer. And since, more times than not, murders are committed by near relatives, we're not going to be impressed by who's doing the crying. And when we ask questions, it's not to get the answers the subject wants to give us, it's to get the truth. Therefore we're not going to soothe him, we're going to cross him up, keep him off-balance. We're going to be rough because if we aren't, some fast talker will con us. And this is homicide, remember. And we can't let that happen.'

'All right, but a woman's dead. Never mind that it's my mother, that's not the issue. She's dead. And the lot of you go around treating the whole thing in the most cavalier fashion. It's only a dead person. Who cares? So why not hang the daughter for it? Who cares?'

Sessions laughed. 'Oh, Jesus. Drink your drink, will you? Do you know how many bodies a year we go out and look at? Old people, babies, fresh bodies, decomposed bodies, tidy bodies, battered bodies. There was a girl—hit and run victim up in Harlem a short time ago. The car cut her in two. He must have been going a hundred miles an hour. One half of her was at one intersection and the other half was a block away at the next intersection. And you see worse things than that. You simply can't get personally involved with every dead body you see. Even if you wanted to, it's a physical impossibility. You see too many of them.

'So we don't tiptoe around and whisper. So we do laugh and joke. How else do you think we could handle this kind of a job? But we don't joke about the dead person and we don't joke about death. Because in our business, that is not a joke.'

She was silent for a moment. Then she said, 'What you're telling me is that policemen are people too.'

'What I'm trying to tell you is that we care who killed your mother. And we care about catching that person. If it happens to be you, we'll get you for it. Homicide is the one crime you're stuck with. It's the crime all the money in the world, all the influence, all the tears in the world won't get you out of. On the other hand, if you're innocent, you've got nothing to fear. We don't want you.'

'Which do you think I am?'

'As of right now, innocent. That's on the evidence so far, but the picture could change.'

'Are policemen really people? Right now you sound cold and utterly inhuman.'

Sessions laughed and reclined again on the daybed. 'I was just explaining the facts of life to you. You could make up to the detective all you want, you could give him your pure white body, but he'll still lock you up if you're guilty. But if you're innocent . . .'

'I didn't come up here to offer you my pure white body,' she said.

He laughed again and mashed out his cigarette. 'That's right. You came here to tell me something about your mother. What is it?'

She set her glass down and leaned forward, putting her elbows on her bare knees below the hem of her skirt. 'Wednesday night, when I was there, they had collected her valuables. Remember? I was told that I could pick them up at the nineteenth precinct station house within the next couple of days, otherwise they'd be sent to the property clerk downtown somewhere and I'd have to go there. So this afternoon I went to the station house after work and got the property and, before I went to the viewing, I had a chance to look it over. And I found there's a thirty-five-hundred-dollar diamond pin missing.'

Frank Sessions raised an eyebrow, took a strong sip of his drink and crossed one shiny black loafer over the other. 'A thirty-five-hundred-dollar pin, huh? Well now that's interesting.'

'Could one of the policemen have stolen it?'

Sessions slowly straightened to a sitting position. 'Everything's itemised. Even the serial numbers on every bill. Did you check the itemised list?'

Linda nodded. 'It wasn't on it.'

'Then it wasn't found in the apartment.' His eyes had changed again. They'd been warm and personal, seeing her as a human being, a female. Now they were a cop's eyes, shrewd and searching, weighing and assessing. 'How do you know she had such a pin?'

'Because I was with her when she got it. It was at a testimonial dinner in 1957 honouring twenty years in the newspaper business. She had it appraised and insured it for thirty-five hundred dollars and I know that because she lent it to me to wear at my senior prom and I was properly nervous about it.'

'When did you see it last?'

'When I brought it back after the prom. That was in June of 1959.'

'That's eight years ago. Jesus, girl. You can't . . .'

'But if she lost it or something, I'm sure she'd make some mention of it sometime.'

'I'm sure. Look, her insurance policy described all the pieces the company is covering and all the pieces described in the policy were found in the apartment. If she still had that thirty-five-hundred-dollar pin, I'm sure The Travelers Indemnity Company would be insuring it along with the others.'

'Travelers? I thought Bertram Fox was her insurance company.'

Sessions' eyebrow went up again. 'Oh?'

'Al Lanard of Bertram Fox. He used to handle her insurance. Some of it, anyway.'

Sessions took out his notebook. 'Some of it? She insured with more than one company?'

'Well I don't really know. But it wouldn't surprise me. You know, spread the business around among friends. That would be Monica. In which case the pin might just be . . .'

'We'll find out,' Sessions said, writing and putting the notebook away.

'It might be more than the pin, too. A lot might be stolen.'

'Let's wait and see.'

She said, 'If some pieces *are* missing, would that change the whole motive for the murder?'

'It might.'

'And you'd be looking for a robber rather than an enemy?'

'Maybe. It depends on what was taken and why—whether it was incidental to the real purpose of the crime or whether the crime was incidental to it.'

Silence fell between them for a moment. A waiting silence. Linda looked at her watch and said, 'It's quarter past twelve. I didn't realise it was so late.'

'That's not late.'

'I should be getting home. You must be tired.' She laughed a little and rose slowly to her feet. 'I think I've intruded long enough.'

'You don't want to finish your drink?'

'I've finished most of it.'

Sessions got up and picked up her glass. He put it in her hands and smiled at her. 'Be a good girl.'

She smiled and lowered her eyes, cupping the glass with both hands. She finished it off quickly, shivered and said, 'Oof.' She handed him back the glass. 'Was I good?'

'You get to take a giant step.' He put it down on the edge

of the table against the front of the TV.

For a moment neither moved. Then she said, 'Oh, I meant to ask you. Did you find out? Did my mother have a boy-friend?'

'Yes.'

'I see. Did anybody know about it?'

'*I* didn't know about it. I don't know who did.'

They were standing very close together, she looking uncertainly at his tie, he looking down on the golden sheen of her hair and the full round way she filled out a dress. She said, 'It's late. I think I'd better go.' He set his glass down and as she started to turn, he took her arms and twisted her back. He pulled her in close and kissed her upturned, startled mouth hard. She didn't try to resist but if she had she couldn't have managed it. His fingers held her arms like steel and she was surprised and overcome by his strength. Those lean, long, artistic fingers that seemed more appropriate on a concert pianist than a detective in the homicide squad.

'What was that for?' she whispered when his lips moved across her cheek to the lobe of her ear.

'For us.'

'It's late.'

His left hand slid up her arm and grasped her chin. He planted his mouth on hers again and she could feel his tongue probing between her teeth. She probed back with hers and his right arm went around her, the left slid away from her chin, down over her throat, around the neckline of her dress, then down over the fabric that covered her breast.

All at once things were getting out of hand. She twisted her mouth away from his and tried to break apart but he was too strong. The arm about her waist held her locked against him, the hand squeezing her breast was demanding. 'No,' she said as he nibbled the lobe of her ear. 'We mustn't.'

Then his muscles relaxed slowly and she was able to pull away. She broke contact feeling a little disappointed. If he had refused, if he had overpowered her, if he had taken her right there on the daybed without so much as a by-your-leave, would she really have minded? Then it wouldn't have been her fault and she could have had her cake and eaten it too.

But he wasn't going to rape her on the spot. He was going to let her go instead. He released her—reluctantly but unmistakably. 'You really are a mixed-up kid, aren't you?' he said sullenly and snatched up one of his cigarettes from the pack on the daybed.

She backed off and sat down on the other corner of the daybed, breathing heavily. 'Mixed up, how?'

His lighter flared and he exhaled a great lungful of smoke. 'You don't know what you want. You move two different ways on two different levels.'

'What's that mean?' She reached for his next-to-last cigarette and put it between her lips.

He lighted it for her and sat on the arm of the chair she had used. 'Let's talk about this boyfriend of yours. Do you mean to stay true to him or don't you? If you do, what are you leading me on for? If you don't, what are you pushing me away for?'

She said defensively, 'Well, really. Just because a girl walks into a man's apartment to give him some help in his work . . . ? I mean you aren't entitled to regard that as leading him on.'

'You didn't just come up to my apartment to help me with my work. You hunted me up. You refused to give the information to anyone else and you waited outside the apartment for an hour until I showed up. It's information that doesn't have to be given to me personally. It's information that doesn't have to be given to me tonight. Now if you want to play the outraged innocent, all but trapped in the monster's clutches, go to hell.'

Linda half smiled and half frowned. 'You know,' she said, 'that's very interesting. I never thought of that. But you may be right.'

He shook his head. 'Jesus, what the hell kind of talk is that?'

She laughed, kicked off her shoes, and tucked her feet up under her on the daybed. 'What I mean is, I wondered myself, while I was cooling my heels, pacing around across the street, corner to corner, what I was doing there, why I hadn't given the story to the other detectives, and why I felt I had to give it to you tonight. And I guess all that business about being under suspicion, I guess that was trying to rationalise my behaviour.'

'Irrationalise it. That didn't make any sense at all.'

She waved her cigarette. 'All right, irrationalise it then. But I really didn't want you to make a pass at me. I honestly didn't. At least not on the conscious level. God only knows what I'm thinking about on the subconscious level. God and my psychiatrist.'

He laughed. 'Oh, Jesus. There you go rationalising again. You liked being kissed. It was only when you stopped to think what you were doing that you decided you ought to quit.'

'No, I don't think so, not really. I don't mean I didn't like being kissed, it's quite obvious that I did. I mean it's not that simple. The motive for coming up here wasn't to get kissed. It was to avoid going home. If you really want to analyse it, that's what it was.'

He shook his head. 'You talk a hell of a lot. And you know something? I don't believe you.'

'It's the truth, Frank. Really. All right, let's not pretend I'm an innocent little flower. I was twenty-nine last February and that many years represents a fair amount of living. But I'm not promiscuous. There was a time—I'll be perfectly honest with you, and I don't know why I should be except it's the only way I can face myself and that's something I have to do to get along. There was a time, quite a few years ago, in my late teens and very early twenties, when I thought sex was some kind of cure-all for what ails you and a lot of things were ailing me.' She shrugged and took a drag on the cigarette. There was a faint flush on her cheeks and she didn't look at Frank. 'After a while I discovered it wasn't a cure for anything and a psychiatrist straightened me out. Since then I've been a more average-type girl. On those occasions when I have stepped off the straight and narrow, it was as the result of mature reflection—to the extent that I am mature—and with some concern as to why, when, and what I expected to get out of it. I am not, in other words, anybody's pushover. I want you to understand that, Frank.'

'Sure,' he said. 'I understand. But what are you telling it to me for?'

'I'm trying to explain that I really didn't come up here to have you make a pass. I feel it's important that you know that.'

'All right, so you play love by the numbers. The first date you tell each other the story of your life. The second date you hold hands. The third date you kiss, the fourth, neck.'

'It's not by the numbers. It's not like that.'

'I thought you were trying to explain to me that you can't decide anything without mature reflection and that means we've got to know each other and see each other a number of times before you work around to the mature reflection bit.'

'No, you aren't listening. I'm trying to tell you that I'm not interested in that sort of thing. I have a boyfriend—well I guess I don't have a boyfriend really. Not any more. You remember the night you called me and a man answered the phone? Well, it's not what you're thinking it was. He was a friend who'd gone to the play with me and we came back for some coffee and he tried to get fresh and then my fiancé called up and he—this friend—got on the phone. And that killed it. My fiancé isn't my fiancé any more. I can't make him believe it was all innocent.'

Sessions picked up his drink and swallowed half of what was left. 'You know something, Miss Glazzard, the more you talk the less sense you make.'

'Oh, it's Miss Glazzard now? How formal for someone who's kissed the girl and explored rather intimate parts of her anatomy.'

'And been rebuked for it. You still don't make sense.'

'I'm trying to. Try to understand. I'm alone. I'm at a viewing. It's my mother's body there. It's a reminder that she's gone. She'll never be with me again. My father died years ago, I've got no siblings. My grandparents are all gone. There's nobody. And this is the one night when I'm most aware of it. All the people coming to see my mother's body. That accentuates it. And my fiancé. He's gone too.

'So the viewing ends and what is there left to do? Go home to an apartment whose emptiness is bad enough every other night, but will be absolutely unbearable tonight? What can I do—go to a bar and drink? Get Dr. Patterson to take me out someplace? He's very kind right now. He's the only person who's been aware of me, who seems to care about me, but he's old enough to be my grandfather. He won't do. And there's the stolen jewellery I've got to report. It seemed as if reporting it would be a way of keeping from going home. Now do you understand?'

'Sure I understand. You're not sure whether you've got a boyfriend any more or not so you're not sure how free you are to do what you want to do.'

'And what is it I want to do?'

'Get over the loneliness.'

'And sex isn't the answer, Mr. Frank Sessions. I found that out a long time ago.'

'Then why did you kick off your shoes?'

She looked at them on the floor. 'Because I wanted to be comfortable. I didn't want to put shoes on your coverlet.'

'Because you wanted to stay for a while. Because, whatever the answer is, you think you're going to find it here.'

'You know something, Mr. Sessions? You're quite an egotist.'

'So it's Mr. Sessions, is it? You're being pretty formal for a girl who's been kissed and explored.'

She got up off the daybed and he rose with her. In her stocking feet, the top of her head only came to his chin. She said, 'I should hope I would be formal with a man who suggests that I'm making a pass at him. Besides, it's now after half past twelve. I've got to be back at the funeral parlour at nine.' She turned away and felt for her shoes with her feet.

He put his hands on her shoulders and gently pulled her back against him. He kissed her cheek. She trembled. 'You're supposed to let me go.'

She pushed one foot into a shoe and he kissed her again, closer to her mouth. She said, 'I have to get up for the funeral parlour . . .'

'There's plenty of time. You don't want to go back to that empty apartment yet.'

'Oh, God, I don't. Do you know what it's like to be alone?'

'Everybody's alone.' He turned her around and when he kissed her this time, her arms went around his neck.

They strained against each other, their mouths working, and he found the zipper to her dress. When he got it open, he slipped his hand inside her slip and over her bra. She pulled away a little to give him room.

'Your dress is in the way.'

'Isn't that why girls wear dresses?'

'That's why they take them off too.'

'Oh? And I thought it was to keep them from getting wrinkled.'

'It's to keep them from getting torn off.'

'If I have a choice, I'd rather take it off, please. It's very brand new.'

'I'll let you. Come here.' He took her by the hand into the bedroom where the bed was unmade. While she pulled the dress over her head and laid it across a chair, he took off his gun and holster, put them and his shield in the top righthand drawer of his bureau, which had been fitted with a lock, and turned the key.

'Do you know what time it is?'

'I haven't been paying much attention, no.'

'Sce, on your wristwatch? It's quarter past two.'

'And now that we have found out that vital piece of information . . .'

'I ought to get home. I can't stay here all night, after all. It would scandalise the elevatormen back at 302 East 57th.'

'I'll see you home when the time comes.'

'Look, let's have some coffee. Would you like some coffee?'

'All I've got is instant.'

'That's all right. I'll make some.'

'On one condition.'

'What?'

'I don't want you to put any clothes on.'

'Why?'

'I like to look at you.'

'Yes, I know you do. And the way you do it! You know something? You make a girl so totally aware of being a girl. You make her feel so completely female. And so glad of it.'

'I can't find anything to object to about that.'

'Neither can I. You know, Frank, I'm not really in love with you. I think I could fall in love with you if I wanted to.'

'Don't. I'm bad news.'

'You're the best news I've had all week.'

'I'm poison. I'm warning you. Don't get involved. I'm not the marrying kind. I'm lousy husband material. I bring nothing but grief.'

'I didn't say I was going to fall in love with you. I said I could. I meant it as a compliment. I think you're quite a guy.'

'In bed or out?'

'Both. You're a good detective, aren't you? I mean really good!'

'What's that mean? Like the other guys, I work at it. Some

cases we solve, some we don't. We investigate everything we can find to investigate. We figure everything there is to figure. If it's enough to make an arrest on, we make an arrest. If it isn't, we don't.'

'Who killed my mother, Frank?'

'I don't know. And I wouldn't tell you if I did.'

'Do you suspect anybody?'

'I don't discuss cases with unauthorised personnel.'

'Do you regard a girl you just slept with unauthorised personnel?'

'I told you I was bad news, kid. I don't mix business and pleasure. If you're smart, Linda, you'll go back to your boyfriend.'

'That's funny, isn't it? This is just what he accused me of doing, and now I've done it.'

'But you wouldn't have if he hadn't accused you, so it serves him right.'

'He shouldn't have accused me. He had no right. He should have trusted me. How can a person not trust someone they're going to marry?'

'I don't know, but I thought you were going to make some coffee.'

'Yes, except you want me to do it in the nude and it's cold.'

'It'll be warm by the stove.'

'All right, but you've got to come with me and you can't put on any clothes either.'

'I'm with you, let's go.'

'You know, when I get home I'm going to have some job trying to get myself straightened out after tonight.'

'I thought tonight was starting to unmix you a little.'

'In some ways, but life's got a lot more complicated in others.'

'Don't think about it.'

'But I have to. That's the thing about me ever since I underwent analysis. I'm always asking myself why I do things. Why did I really come up here tonight? Was it for this? Did I know it would happen? Did I seduce you or did you seduce me? How do you turn on this stove?'

'Here. And what the hell difference does it make who seduced who?'

'A lot of difference if you want to understand yourself. Don't you want to understand yourself, Frank?'

'I sure as hell don't. I told you I'm bad news. I don't like reading bad news.'

'Listen, there's no shade on this kitchen window.'

'It's all right, we can heat the water in the dark.'

'But there's light from the living room.'

'You sure do worry, don't you?'

'Well, how do I know—Frank, you're only supposed to look, not feel.'

'If you're sucker enough to believe that . . .'

'Frank, if you want coffee . . .'

'I didn't say I wanted coffee.'

'Oh God, you make a girl hot!'

'You give a man a lot of ideas too, kid. How'd you like to get laid on the daybed?'

'You have nice ideas. They're so direct. Just let me turn off the stove.'

D.D.5 (REV. 9-66)

SUPPLEMENTARY COMPLAINT REPORT

19.PCT.	22.U.F.61 NO.	YEAR	DET.SQD SER.	STATUS OF CASE	DATE THIS REPORT
19	#6434	1967	19	Open	May 13, 1967

DETAILS AS REPORTED BY FOLLOW UP INVESTIGATING OFFICER

With Mr. Allen B. Lanard, Bertram Fox Insurance Co., compared list of valuables found in subject's apartment with list of 5 items insured with Bertram Fox Insurance Co.

Determined the 5 insured items, as described below, were not found in subject's apartment.

Investigation continuing.

DESCRIPTION OF LOST OR STOLEN PROPERTY – SEE APPENDIX G OF R&P

ARTICLE (NAME ONLY)	QUANTITY	VALUE	DESCRIPTION
Pin	1	$3500	16 white stones from 0.5 to 1.1 carats in cluster around one 3 carat stone in center.
Ring	1	$250	1 carat blue white stone, yellow metal setting. Inscription: "Monica-Bill 3/10/37 and forever."
Pin	1	$1100	1 carat green stone in yellow metal filagree setting.
Necklace	1	$7500	31 white stones varying in size from 1 to 3 carats.
Watch	1	$600	Yellow metal Movado watch. Inscribed inside cover: "To Arthur Gray Lining Professor of Literature DePaul University 1918-1943." Case No. 621311 Movement No. /J787415

Investigating Officer's Signature

Frank G. Stoving

Commanding Officer's Signature

J. X. Sullivan

D.D. 5 (REV. 9-66)

SUPPLEMENTARY COMPLAINT REPORT

19. PCT.	22.U.F.61 NO.	YEAR	DET. SQD SER.	STATUS OF CASE	DATE THIS REPORT
19	#6434	1967	19	Open	May 13, 1967

DETAILS AS REPORTED BY FOLLOW UP INVESTIGATING OFFICER

Interviewed Mildred Butelle re: disappearance of 5 items of jewelry belonging to Monica Glazzard.

a. Subject denies any knowledge of disappearance.

b. Subject claims ignorance of what valuables deceased owned. She denies ever having seen the missing pieces.

c. Subject denies having seen Bertram Fox insurance policy in deceased's files, but concedes it could have been there.

d. Subject does not think it remarkable that the stolen property includes the policy as well as those valuables, and only those valuables, the policy covered.

e. Subject was extremely nervous during interview.

f. Investigation continuing.

Investigating Officer's Signature

Frank G. Ssssings

Commanding Officer's Signature

J. K. Sullivan

Romolo Romero, an official in the Detective's Endowment Association as well as a senior member of the homicide squad, was explaining the DEA's present plans to Jim Murtry, Ed Kelsey, Ray Ecklin and Sergeant Lou Monast in the homicide office when Frank Sessions walked in at four o'clock that Sunday afternoon. Romero, with twenty-eight years in the department under his belt though still shy of fifty, finished up and said, 'Hey, it's Frankie-Boy. God's gift to lovelorn women.'

Sessions said, 'Jesus, are you yakking about the DEA again?'

'Family men like Kelsey and Ecklin and the rest of us like to hear about such things. Who're you going to leave all your benefits to, Frankie, when you pass on?'

'Haven't you heard? I'm taking them with me. I've got a special arrangement with the Almighty.'

'I thought you didn't believe in the Almighty, Frankie.'

'That's what the arrangement's all about. I believe in Him and He lets me take in anything I want.' He laughed, picked up the phone and dialled a number.

Ecklin said, 'If anybody can take it with him, I'd bet on Frank.'

Monast grinned. 'If he could, heaven would be lopsided with broads.'

Sessions, with the phone at his ear, growled at them, 'Jesus, this place is getting to be like Television City. Nothing but comics.'

'It keeps our mind off our work.'

'Yeah. How's Mike doing on the White case?'

Monast said, 'All right. He's got a make on the perpetrator.'

'No kidding? Johnson break down?'

'Not Johnson. It was another source. Johnson apparently was clean. The perpetrator mistook Johnson for the man who had robbed him with White.'

'So now it's a question of locating the alleged perpetrator?'

He turned and said into the phone, 'Chief Nyborg, please. . . . Oh, Frank Sessions, Chief. We may have a lead on where Motley came from. A girl he knew in the loft where he lived remembers him writing out a cheque on an Allentown, Pennsylvania, bank. . . . Yeah, it's a funny thing to remember but maybe it's all right. Her story is he and she were sharing the rent and he gave her the cheque as his share for the first three months. She says she noticed it because he never said anything about his past and she was wondering where he was from.' He lighted a cigarette and said, 'I figure we'll try to check out banks in Allentown tomorrow. Mostly, though, we got to hit pawnshops or any place where that jewellery might have been sold. . . . No, Property Recovery doesn't have anything on it, but we think it's been sold anyway. We don't think the perpetrator took it to wear. So we'll poke around a little and after that we'll see what we get in Allentown. . . . No, I don't think we're going overboard on Motley. We're looking at the other suspects too. In fact, Devlin's up in Poughkeepsie today and I'm going over now to talk to the head of the sociology department at Columbia. . . . No, Motley hasn't shown yet. . . . No, he wasn't at the viewings or the funeral service. . . . Yes, we're watching for him, but that's all we can do. We can't tell him he can't come and go as he pleases.' He listened a bit, said a couple of 'Yes, sirs,' and hung up. 'I can't figure it,' he said. 'One minute Nyborg sounds like he thinks I'm spending too much time looking into Motley—blinding myself to the other possibilities, and the next he sounds like he thinks Motley's the perpetrator.'

Romolo said, 'What do you think?'

Sessions lighted a new cigarette and mashed out the old. 'I like him too, but I'm not going overboard on him while that secretary's acting up.'

'What's she doing?'

'She lies all the time. First she lied in saying the deceased gave her the day off. Then she lied about the jewellery, about not knowing some of it was insured with Bertram Fox. She was the dame's secretary, for Christ's sake. Who the hell does she think she's kidding? But you can't shake her. You catch her in one lie and she's got a new one to give you to explain the old one. Either that or she keeps clinging to the old one even when it's an obvious lie. She's hiding something but whether it's to do with the homicide or the theft we can't say. Did she kill the deceased for the jewels? If so, why didn't she take them all? Or at least take all the ones insured with Travelers instead of the five that weren't? Did she kill the deceased for another reason and take the valuables as an afterthought? Did someone else strangle the deceased and Millie find the body and take the jewels? Or did someone else perpetrate the homicide and the theft and she knows who and is covering for him? Or did she work with someone else, giving him the key, expecting him only to commit a theft, but he does a homicide as well? We don't know.'

Romero, frowning, said, 'Anything in her love-life? Any man she's mixed up with?'

'On the surface, no. The elevatormen in her apartment claim they've never seen her with a man. She goes out a lot but never seems to have anybody come in. That's as far as we've followed that line but we'll be digging into her background now. That's what Devlin's doing up in Poughkeepsie and we may get a new slant on her when he gets back.'

'What about the boyfriend? Why do you like him?'

'Because he's a liar, like the Butelle dame, but he does it in ways she doesn't. For instance, that first night we talked to him he told us he came from Sacramento, California. That's a lie and what's interesting is, he tells us that lie before there was any talk of homicide, when, for all we knew, it was an overdose of sleeping pills and deliberate suicide. He's telling us a lie before he's supposed to feel he might have some reason for wanting to lie to us. So why? Is it because he sneaked into the apartment behind the doorman's back and strangled the deceased when she got ready for bed—all for reasons we don't know? Or could it be he's a guy with a record who's latched onto a good thing and when it turns sour, he's afraid he's going to get the blame because of his past trouble? He doesn't show up at the funeral parlour at all, and Friday he ducks out with an attaché case and he hasn't come back since. Why?'

Murtry said, 'Maybe he was carrying the stolen property in that attaché case.'

'Maybe, but I don't see it. If robbery is the motive, why kill? If you do kill, why take the time to fake a suicide? And why do you only take five pieces of property and leave cash behind? I have to guess the robbery is incidental and the real aim is homicide made to look like suicide. In that case, you don't dare commit an obvious theft. You only take a few things you don't think will be missed—happening to know in advance, of course, which ones are covered by the Fox policy.'

Ecklin said, 'And figuring, of course, that a thirty-five-hundred-dollar pin isn't something anybody will remember she had.'

Sessions laughed. 'Yeah, and a seventy-five-hundred-dollar diamond necklace. Jesus, it's that damned robbery that louses everything up. Anyway, so Connager and Trafolo got a make, huh?'

'They've got a name and address for the alleged perpetraor, but they don't have the alleged perpetrator.'

'And he's a pusher and White robbed him and he's getting even? That's the thing. Up in Harlem the motives are obvious. It all has to do with junk and fags, or junk and whores, or junk and money, or just junk. You go over on the East Side and, unless it's a fag killing, the motives start getting cute. You might as well be in a different country.'

'Not the motives,' Ecklin said. 'Only the technique. Can you imagine somebody in Harlem strangling a woman and then trying to make it look like an overdose of barbiturates?'

Sessions said, 'I can't imagine them strangling anybody to start with. Cut them. Shoot them. Why mess around?'

Kelsey said, 'What about Motley and the girls, Frank?'

'He's never had any up to his apartment unless the doormen are lying for him. And while doormen may give us a lot of grief, I don't think they'd lie for a tenant in a homicide.'

'What about outside the apartment? He had time on his hands, didn't he?'

'He had lots of time on his hands and one of the things we want him to tell us is how he spent it. One way we know he didn't spend it was sitting at home twiddling his thumbs waiting for Mrs. Glazzard to call. The doormen say he was almost never home.'

Murtry said, 'I'll bet there's another woman.'

'Sure there is. Another woman or a bunch of other women. There's got to be. Monica might have been hot stuff in the bedroom but she's not going to want it as much as he is. She's forty-eight. She's busy with a career. He's thirty-two and he's got nothing to do.

'But even if we find him with a girl on the side—or a whole harem on the side—what does that mean? In and of itself, that's no reason to commit murder. Even if the deceased found out and threatened to throw him out, that's not a reason. We'd have to find more than that to give him a motive and, frankly, I can't think of anything.'

Lou Monast said, 'But you still like him?'

'I like him for the job, but I think that's because I don't like him personally and I can't see an alternative, rather than because I've got any valid reason for suspecting him. But I'll tell you one thing. As soon as he shows up again, I'm going to want him tailed.'

'*If* he shows up again.'

'If he doesn't, then he's running and if he's running, we're in luck. Because if he's running from a homicide charge, he's stupid and if he's stupid the chances are we'll have him telling the whole thing into a tape recorder half an hour after we catch him. If he was smart, he'd just sit still and keep still. We don't have a thing on him—no motive, nobody seeing him in the vicinity of the crime during the hours when it was committed, no evidence, no nothing. He can call in a lawyer and thumb his nose at us. Naw, I don't think he's running. The rent's paid through the end of the month. I think he'll be back.'

SUNDAY 7:15–7:20 P.M.

When the phone rang, Linda's heart did a quick flip. She was in her kitchen eating a supper sandwich, reading the drama section of the Sunday *Times*, and it was the first time the phone had rung all day. On Saturday there had been the services and the nearly five hundred people who had attended. Linda thought it would never end. But then, suddenly, everything was over. The casket was closed, the people were gone and she had found herself deserted. Frank Sessions was nowhere in sight for that final period and Dr. Patterson had not stood by her side. He had been there, but on this occasion he had only had eyes for Monica and he left immediately thereafter. It was all over now and Linda was all alone. No one called her up for the rest of Saturday, no one had thus far called on Sunday. That was the trouble when an engagement broke up. It was hell's own hell getting back into circulation. And the older one got, the longer it took, until sometime there came a day when you never did. Linda wasn't sure but that her own time had come but she wouldn't let herself think about that. Frank Sessions would chide her for feeling sorry for herself. She'd have to be careful about that. Four days ago life had been heaven and she could walk in joy. Then desolation set in. It wasn't Monica's dying that brought it on, it was the earlier event of Randy's sick aunt. If he hadn't left town . . .

Now, however, with the ringing of the phone, her thoughts didn't go to Randy. They went to Frank Sessions. He was the one who was calling. He was the only one in New York this day who knew she was alive or cared. He was the lonely one, like herself, the one who needed and seldom found companionship. She had been carried by Friday night, all day Saturday and most of this day. But the effect was wearing off now and it needed replenishing. Life without Randy wouldn't be so bad if there were Frank.

Frank was, of course, no one to get involved with. Her head told her he was just what he said he was—bad news—even if her heart did have a way of changing its beat at the thought of him. It wasn't love, she told herself, it was the way he made love. It was that little-boy quality that was so fleeting and yet so affecting. But a future with Frank Sessions in it was a grim vista to contemplate. It appeared to be nothing but a long succession of nights climbing the stairs to his apartment early in the evening, coming down with him later and being taken home in a cab.

That was one thing about him. He didn't tell a girl to find her own way out, he didn't even put her in a cab. He dressed up and combed his hair and took her home in a cab himself and made the cabby wait while he saw her to the door and the key in the lock and her safely inside her apartment.

It was a touch she liked. Nothing would have made her feel more like a tramp than to be put in a cab and sent along home. It made it so obvious what had been going on before. This way she felt like a lady. Not that she was one, exactly. What she'd been doing Friday night was hardly ladylike, and she'd queried herself during the lonely weekend hours wondering why she wanted to feel like a lady and whether it was to hide from herself. But, even trying to judge herself severely, she couldn't see much to fault with her behaviour. She was a jilted girl, after all, without future prospects, and a girl did need loving the same as a man did. It was admittedly on short acquaintance but it wasn't a casual affair.

Not on her side it wasn't. No girl could feel only casually about Frank.

She hurried into the bedroom to the phone, arriving after only its second ring. Then she got hold of herself and waited for the third before she picked up the receiver. Let's not appear too eager, my girl. He's a detective and little things like that register. She paused before speaking and managed a very poised, 'Hello.'

The voice that responded wasn't Frank's. It was Randy's. 'Darling,' he said. 'You don't know what I've been going through.'

In that moment Linda's emotions churned like dice in a cup. Now she was totally disoriented. Did she want to hear Randy's voice? She couldn't be sure whether she was glad or sorry, whether she loved him or hated him. 'What?' she said vaguely.

'I said, darling, you don't know what I've been going through these last few days.'

'Where are you?' She was still trying to get her feet back on the ground.

'Still in Pittsburgh, still missing you. Darling, your mother. I've been reading—I'm so sorry. I'm so desperately sorry. A time like that and I have to be away. How are you, darling?'

Linda brushed a hand through her hair and sat down on the bed slowly. 'I'm all right,' she said but she knew this was hardly the way to talk. There might be a marriage after all, a happily-ever-after routine if she played things right. This might be the most critical few minutes of her life, these moments on the phone.

'Darling, will you ever forgive me?'

'You mean for not being here?' she said, still vague in her thinking. 'You couldn't help your aunt being sick.'

'No, no, not that. I mean for losing my temper the other night.'

'Oh.'

'About that friend who was with you. You're so damned

desirable, sweetheart, I guess I just naturally expect every boy you know is chasing you.'

'Well he was.'

'What? I didn't quite catch that, dear.'

She woke up a little. What the hell was she doing, trying to throw everything away? She wasn't doing this for Frank Sessions, was she? God, she wouldn't be trying to swap Randy and what he represented for Frank and what he offered, was she? How insane could one get? It was only that she had succumbed to Frank so recently, when she was so low and lonely that his effect on her was additionally magnified. His impact had obliterated temporarily the effect Randy had always had on her. Think about Randy, for God's sake. Handsome, well-muscled Randy—really an Apollo type, gifted, talented, highly intelligent, kind and gentle, yet earthy when the situation called for it. The only thing Sessions had on Randy Benson was a job. But that was something Randy was in the process of getting and when he did, he'd make Frank's income . . . 'No, no. What I was saying was that, well, he was kind of chasing me. You know, sort of hoping.'

'In vain?'

'Yes, I told you that. I told you when you called.'

'I know.'

'And you wouldn't believe me.'

'I don't know what got into me.'

'You mean you believe me now?'

'Yes, sweetheart. And let me tell you. I never didn't believe you.'

'You damned well sounded as though you did.' There was a note of bitterness but she didn't care. He deserved at least that for the anguish he'd caused her.

'I was distraught,' he said. 'Believe me. Auntie so sick, missing you, and then I call up to gain strength from the sound of your voice, to hear you whisper a few words of love and encouragement, and I get this strained voice saying unnatural things and it made me upset. And then I hear that man, whoever he was. Darling, do you blame me?'

'No,' she said. 'I suppose not.'

'Do you really think I don't know you well enough to know better than that? Do you think I could ever really believe you'd cheat on me the minute my back was turned?'

'No, I suppose not.'

'You could have a man come back to your apartment after the show. You could have ten men come back. Nothing would happen. I know it wouldn't. I not only trust you, I know you. If I caught you walking out of a man's apartment at four o'clock in the morning, I wouldn't turn a hair. I'd know nothing happened.'

Linda shivered. Why did he have to say four o'clock? That was just the time Frank Sessions had taken her home the night before last. And you sure as hell couldn't say that nothing had happened then. There was hardly anything that didn't happen. On the other end of the line, Randy said, 'Hello?'

'Hello,' Linda managed.

'What's the matter? I thought for a second we got cut off or something.'

'No.'

'Did you hear what I said?'

'Yes, I heard it.'

'You don't sound awfully happy about it. You sound very funny, in fact. Don't you like it that I trust you and believe in you?'

Linda pushed her hand through her hair again, roughly and distractedly. Why the hell had she gone to that detective's apartment? Why had she let him lay a hand on her? God, she hardly knew the man and there she was giving herself to him with abandon. What had possessed her? If only she hadn't, then she'd be the trustworthy, virtuous fiancée Randy thought she was. She could sing for joy. The misunderstanding was fixed up. The lovers' quarrel was at an end and things were once more as they were. But now they weren't.

Her fiancé had turned his back and she hadn't remained trustworthy. She'd gone with another man. Of course she thought the engagement was over, that they were washed up, but was that any alibi? Randy hadn't said he was breaking off with her, she'd only assumed it. She hadn't given him a chance to call her back. She hadn't waited. She had leaped.

And now what was she to do? Should she lie and pretend she was the true-blue loyal and restricted girl he thought, or should she tell him the truth and wash the whole thing up? 'I should hope you'd trust me,' she said. 'I've told you enough about myself.'

'I know, darling, and that's why I've been feeling so miserable. I swore to you I'd never hold the past against you and yet that's what I was doing. The girl you were before analysis and the girl you are now are two different people. There's no connection at all. And I was being mean and petty and suspicious in trying to make a connection. I'm sorry. I apologise.'

'It's all right,' Linda said. 'I don't suppose I can blame you. You call up and there's a man in my room. I can't exactly blame you for jumping to the conclusion you did.'

'You're sweet. But I shouldn't have. I know you. You've told me everything. You've bared your soul. I know you'd never keep anything from me or lie to me. That's why our marriage is going to be so great. There'll be no secrets between us . . .'

Linda made an agonised face and put her hand to her forehead. What was she to do, live the biggest lie of all? He'd find her out. He'd sense she was holding something back. But maybe he wouldn't. Girls were clever enough at deception and men were really so gullible. They believed what they wanted to believe and what they wanted to believe and what was the truth didn't necessarily bear any relationship to each other. She could live the lie with him. The question was whether she could live it with herself.

'That's what makes all the difference in a marriage,' Randy

said. 'It's the total trust that breaks down all the walls and really makes two people one. Oh, darling, marriage to you is going to be so wonderful.'

Linda sobbed suddenly. She couldn't help it. She covered the phone and felt the tears come. Randy said querulously, 'Linda?' And then, 'Is something the matter?'

'Everything's the matter,' she sobbed, taking her hand away so he could hear. 'Everything, everything. I can't do it. I can't marry you. Ever.'

His 'Why?' was frantic. 'Linda, don't hang up.'

'There's no use talking about it. It won't do any good. Nothing's any good any more.'

'Linda! Linda! Don't. Talk. Please tell me. What did I do?'

'You didn't do anything.'

'But don't you love me?'

'Yes, I love you. But it's no good.'

'What's happened? Please, darling, tell me what's happened.'

'I can't be trusted,' she cried and the tears flooded down her cheeks.

'You mean,' he said incredulously, 'that that man in the bedroom . . . ?'

'No, not him. Another man. When I thought you'd left me, when I was in despair—but that's no excuse. I'm no good. I wasn't true. I didn't wait to see. I can't lie to you, Randy. Marriage can't be what you want it to be—not marriage to me. I can't do it to you.'

'Linda, maybe we can work something out . . .'

She cried even more bitterly. 'That's the worst thing you could say. I couldn't do it to you. I wouldn't.'

'Linda.'

'No, no, please. Don't say any more. Goodbye, Randy.' She put down the phone and rolled over full length on the bed, sobbing with her face in her arms.

In a moment the phone started ringing again, but she

didn't answer. It kept on ringing and she counted twenty-eight times before it stopped.

MONDAY 1:30–2:10 P.M.

Frank Sessions drained his coffee and put out his cigarette, picked up his chit and took it to the cashier. His luncheon cheque came to eighty-five cents and he took the change back to leave on the table for the waitress. Then he went out into the cloudy, dank afternoon.

Lunch had been a fifteen-minute respite after a hard morning's canvassing of pawnshops up and down Third Avenue and the one or two that were not on the avenue but were also in the general East Side area where the most likely suspects lived. The theft of the jewels was a separate squeal, of course, and did not involve the homicide squad, but Frank was hot to identify the thief and he worked voluntarily with the detectives who caught it. Now, after a fruitless morning, he was set to tackle the diamond district on West 47th Street between Fifth and Sixth.

He started first with the arcade halfway down the block. It was a collection of shop windows and doorways opening into tiny rooms that offered barely enough space for a display counter and the soft-tinted golden wares it revealed, a customer's chair in front and an area behind for the proprietor, his assistant, and the tools of their trade: safe, worktable, trays, drawers, tools, files and the rest.

Sessions walked into the first of these, showed his shield and said, 'Let me see your books.'

The little man behind the counter chewed his lip, turned and pulled a black ledger off a narrow shelf on the bit of wall behind. He put it on the counter facing the detective and spread his hands. 'I got nothing to hide. It's all legitimate.'

Sessions didn't reply. He thumbed through the pages to the ninth of May and scanned the succeeding entries with a lightning glance. He flipped the book closed, said, 'Thanks,' and walked out. The man nodded and watched in silence. He knew it was useless to ask a detective what he was looking for. It was enough that it wasn't found in his shop.

Sessions went into the next doorway and repeated the performance. He went through the whole arcade the same way and it took him a surprisingly short time.

Next he tried one of the jewellery exchanges which were vast ground floor rooms, rimmed and sectioned by counters into a crosshatch of aisles. Two doors gave entrance to the exchange and Sessions paused before going in to scan the displays of gold bracelets, links, chain straps, trinkets, pins and rings in the show windows between the two doors and around the entryway. Signs in each window said, 'The merchandise displayed here sold at the counter directly behind the window only', but none of the merchandise so displayed had been stolen from Monica's apartment.

He went in and looked at more books, starting with the three dealers inside the door who had the choice location that gave them show windows on the street. Next he started on the partitioned counter along the inside wall, tackling the independent dealer in each little section. Eyes were following him now, the same as they had in the arcade. Fifteen or twenty customers were in the exchange, contemplating a sale or purchase, but Frank was there for another reason so a subtle aura spread around him and the dealers, one by one, caught the scent. They turned and watched and worried but they were pinned at their counters like butterflies on a board and they could only wait their turn and uneasily produce their books for inspection.

At the third section, Frank hit pay-dirt. May tenth was the date in the book and it was all there: the diamond pin, the emerald pin, the ring, the necklace, the gold watch, all described even down to the case and movement numbers on the watch. The paid price for the lot was an even three thousand dollars and the name of the seller was listed as 'Monica Glazzard'.

The sign on the counter said 'Herman Levy Inc.' and Mr. Levy was a short, large-nosed man with a thick grey fringe of hair around a bald pate, a pair of glasses like the bottoms of coke bottles, and a smile like a half moon on a mouth the size of a quarter. With him was his daughter, a savvy young girl with auburn hair and a Kelly green dress which she weighed an attractive ten pounds too much for.

Sessions turned the book around and pointed with his finger. 'Stolen property, Herman. What have you done with it?'

'Stolen?' Herman croaked. 'Those pieces were stolen?'

'All of them. Where are they?'

'I didn't know they were stolen. Believe me, sir. My daughter and I—where are they? They must be on display.' Herman went through the business of scanning the banked trays under the glass countertop. 'Maybe they're in the safe. Miriam, look in the safe.'

Miriam frowned over the book, reading the descriptions, then pulled the door of the safe open. They were in a tray with some other pieces and she put it on the countertop. Sessions studied the insurance company description and picked out the stolen items. The girl put the tray away and latched the door of the safe. Herman said, 'But Mrs. Glazzard? Someone like her? I can't believe they're stolen. Are you going to take them with you?'

'Thats' right. Put them in an envelope and I'll make you out a receipt.'

'Will I get them back?'

'They belong to the Glazzard estate.' Sessions started making out the receipt, describing the items as they had been described in the insurance policy.

Herman and Miriam watched and swallowed. Both were pale. 'What about the three thousand dollars?' Herman said.

'I don't know about that. Now what's this business?' Sessions stopped writing to point his pen at the ledger. 'You list the name of the seller as Monica Glazzard but you don't describe her.'

'An oversight, sir. But I remember her quite well. My daughter and I both remember her very well.'

'What did she look like?'

'A short woman. Heavy build. Greying brown hair.'

Frank's lip curled. He wrote on. 'What time was she in on Wednesday?'

'Afternoon. Two o'clock—three o'clock. Around there.' Levy moistened his lips and pasted his half moon smile back on.

'What did she use for identification?'

'She had a charge-a-plate.'

'She had a charge-a-plate,' Sessions mimicked. 'Jesus, you're so smart. You just couldn't resist it, could you? Thirteen thousand bucks' worth of stolen property for three grand.'

Herman Levy lost the smile. Perspiration beaded his forehead. 'Oh no, sir. We didn't know it was stolen. If it's stolen property we were duped. We never dreamed Mrs. Glazzard . . .'

'That wasn't Mrs. Glazzard and you knew it.'

'No, sir. It—she showed us the charge-a-plate. We thought she was legitimate. Didn't we, Miriam? I swear to you.'

Miriam said anxiously, 'We were impressed. She's such a celebrity.'

'Yeah.' Sessions finished and gave the receipt papers to Levy. 'Check them over, will you? Miriam—an envelope?'

She gave him a small manila one and he put the pieces inside and fastened it. He put that in his pocket, got out his notebook and recorded their names, address and phone out in Brooklyn. Levy said, 'Anything we can do to help you catch this woman. I swear we didn't know the property was stolen. Do you think you can catch her?'

'We'll catch her.' Sessions put the notebook away, took out a printed pad from an inside pocket and started to fill in the blanks on the top sheet.

Levy said, 'What is that?'

'That's a summons.'

'A summons?'

'To appear in court.'

'In court?' Levy went whiter. 'What for?'

'Violation of the Administrative Code.'

'I don't understand.'

'Like hell you don't. A list and description of those pieces should have been sent to Property Recovery four days ago. So don't tell me you didn't know they were stolen.'

'Honest, believe me, sir, we didn't know. We did report it, sir. I'm sure we reported it. Miriam, didn't we report it?'

Miriam nodded and licked her lips. 'Yes. I know we reported it. We always report. Maybe it got lost in the mails. That's what must have happened. It got lost in the mails.'

Levy said, 'That's it, of course. Why, if we were the kind of people who'd traffic in stolen goods, don't you think we'd have broken up the pieces? Do you think we'd keep them around?'

Sessions tore off the summons and put it in Levy's hand. Levy said in distress, 'Please, I'm telling you . . .'

'I'm not the guy to tell it to, Herman. Tell it to your lawyer.' Sessions patted the pocket containing the manila envelope reassuringly and walked out.

At a phone in a diner across the street, he called homicide. Riley answered and said the boss was out getting something to eat but was expected back any minute.

'When he comes in, tell him I recovered the stolen Glazzard property.'

'No kidding, Frank? You get the perpetrator too?'

'It's the secretary. She sold them over in the jewellery district on the tenth. Before the DOA was reported, no less.'

'Before, huh? So what're you going to do now?'

'Make a collar. Tell the one-nine, will you? And tell the boss I'll be bringing her there for questioning. We've got her on a felony if we don't have her on a homicide.'

'You think she'll talk?'

'I don't care whether she talks or not. If she clams up I'll stick her in a lineup and bring out my witnesses.'

'You got good witnesses?'

Frank laughed. 'The best. The father and daughter who bought the stuff. They gave the dame three thousand bucks they're going to want back. Listen, Joe, any cars there?'

'Two ninety-nine is. You want to be picked up?'

'I'd like it to meet me at the subject's apartment. It's 419 East 52nd.'

'It'll be there. I'll drive it myself.'

MONDAY 2:45–3:30 P.M.

Sessions and Riley arrived at the precinct house with the prisoner at quarter of three and took her upstairs where Lieutenant Sullivan was waiting with Sergeant Trager and a Detective Harry Lamb of the nineteenth detective squad. Two other detectives in the nineteenth were present, pecking out complaint reports at separate desks while the complainants, one a young woman, the other a middle-aged man, sat beside them murmuring answers to the questions on the sheets.

Mildred Butelle came in with her head bowed, her face white. She was not in handcuffs and Sessions held the gate for her and guided her by the arm like an escort handling a debutante. 'Right over here, Millie. You want to sit here, Millie?' He left her at the bench by the railing and he and Riley joined the others out of her ready hearing. Lamb said, 'Riley I know but I don't think we've met. I'm Harry Lamb.'

'Yeah. Weren't you on detail at the Carlyle when Kennedy was campaigning?'

'That was my older brother Jerry.'

'Jerry. That was it. You look like him.' Sessions shook hands and lowered his voice to Trager. 'Listen, have you heard from Devlin? Is he still up in the wilds of Poughkeepsie?'

The sergeant said in a mutter, 'He's back. He got in an hour ago and went home to change his clothes.'

'He get anything?'

'Nothing that obviously sets her up for anything. Maybe when he gets everything written up we might see some things we don't now. There're indications of lesbianism . . .'

'Hell, I saw that Wednesday night for Christ's sake. But the deceased wasn't one so what's that mean?'

'She wouldn't be jealous of the boyfriend, would she?' Lamb asked.

'I don't know. We can make it anything we want but, without evidence, what's the point?'

Trager said, 'Speaking of thc boyfriend, I hear you found out where he's from.'

'More or less. I called up banks in Allentown and I got one that had a depositor named Robert Motley up till a year and a half ago. I'm going up there as soon as I get a chance—probably tomorrow—unless, of course, what Millie has to say makes it unnecessary.'

'You knew he's back, didn't you?'

'Motley? He's come home?'

'Half past three this morning. That's what Harry here tells me. Attaché case and all. Arrived in a taxi.'

'Drunk or sober?'

Lamb said, 'My sources say he was sober.'

'Anybody talked to him—find out where he went?'

Trager said not yet and Lamb said Motley told one of the doormen he went away for the weekend.

'Got a tail on him?'

Trager said, 'No, Frank. There's no tail.'

Sessions turned to Sullivan. 'What about it, boss? You think we ought to keep him under surveillance?'

Sullivan considered for a moment. Then he said, 'Let's wait and see what we get from this woman.'

'All right.' Sessions went back to the secretary with the others and introduced them all. 'Now shall we go into the other room?'

They trooped down the hall to the room away from the squad room where they could have privacy and Sessions waited until the woman was seated at a table and the door was closed before he spoke. Then he announced, 'Millie here wants to co-operate with us. She's very sorry for what she's done. She admits it was wrong for her to take the jewellery and she wants to tell us about it.' He reached inside his jacket and took out a small packet of 4″ × 6″ file cards, lined on one side and bearing a rubber-stamped legend on the other. He handed her one and said, 'Would you read that while I say it to you aloud? "One. You are hereby advised that you have the right to remain silent and you do not have to say anything unless you choose to do so. Do you understand?" '

She nodded and he continued. ' "Two. Anything you do say may be used against you in a court of law. Do you understand? Three. You have the right to have an attorney present with you during any questioning now or in the future. Four. If you cannot afford any attorney, the court will appoint one to represent you. Five. If you do not have an attorney presently available you have the right to remain silent until you have an opportunity to consult with one. Six. Do you want an attorney?" '

Miss Butelle hesitated a moment and then shook her head.

Sessions said, '"Seven. I have read this statement of my rights and I understand what my rights are." Do you understand all that, Mildred? Good.' He took out a ballpoint pen. 'Would you sign the card there on the top line?'

She hesitated with the pen in hand and looked up at him as he stood over her at the table. 'I don't know if it's wise to do this.'

'Mildred, it's the wisest thing you can do. You've admitted committing a felony to me and to Detective Riley. We have witnesses. This is a serious thing you've done, there's no getting around it, so the easier you make it for us, the easier we can make it for you.'

'I suppose.' She scribbled her name and handed back the pen. When Frank picked up the card and put it in his pocket again, her lip trembled.

'All right, Millie. You want to tell us the whole story? Start at the beginning and tell it all through and we won't interrupt unless we have a question.'

She sat with one arm over the back of the straight chair, the other lying on the table, her fingers playing with a couple of loose shreds of tobacco found there. 'There isn't much to tell,' she said dully, staring at the tobacco shreds. 'I came in to work on Wednesday and when I went to wake Mrs. Glazzard, I found her dead. I thought she'd committed suicide. I was going to leave but then I got thinking she hadn't paid me since the first and she owed me a week and a half's wages and how was I going to get it? A hundred and seventy-five a week I get and it costs me nearly every penny to live. My rent is better than two hundred a month and I spend a lot on clothes. As Mrs. Glazzard's secretary I have to see people. I have to make a proper impression. And I have a mentally retarded brother who's in a sanitarium and I contribute to his support. It could be months before I got the money she owed me—if I ever did—and what was I going to do in the meantime?' She sighed. 'If Mrs. Glazzard fired me, I'd get severance pay. I'd save something to tide me over till I could get another position. This way my back was up against the wall.

'So I looked in her purse. I thought I'd just take out the money that was due me and call the account square, but she only had about sixty-five dollars in cash in there. Then I thought of the jewellery. I decided I could sell some of that and get my money that way. I thought a couple of pieces would never be missed. Nobody would know. But then I thought about the insurance. I don't suppose I would have except the policy with Mr. Lanard had come in for renewal just last week. So I realised that there was a record of everything Mrs. Glazzard had and the only way I could take what was coming to me was to take the record too. And since the policy with Mr. Lanard was a small one—only five pieces—that was the one I took. I thought it would be enough to cover my week and a half's pay and three months' severance.'

'You mean one month,' Sessions said.

'Three months. That's what they give you in the armed forces. I was in the WACs.'

'Thirty days.'

'I thought it was three months. That's the way I was figuring it at any rate. Maybe I was wrong. I might have been wrong, but I thought I was entitled to twenty-five hundred dollars. Maybe it's because I was upset but that's the amount I felt was due me.'

'Twenty-five hundred smackers?' Sergeant Trager said. 'You're pretty expensive to fire.'

'I wasn't trying to steal anything I didn't think belonged to me. That's why I only took five pieces. If I'd wanted to, I could've taken it all.'

Sessions said, 'Tell us the rest, Millie. You took the five pieces and the insurance policy and then what?'

'Well, I didn't know where to sell them so I looked in the yellow pages and saw this ad for somebody named Abraham on West 47th Street and it said that they bought gold and diamonds and everything so I went there and I showed them the watch just to see what would happen and they offered me a hundred dollars for it. I told them it was insured for six hundred and they said they'd go as high as a hundred and twenty-five. I said I thought they should give me five hundred and they laughed. So I walked out and I found there were a lot of jewellery buying places around and I went into this big kind of store and asked at one of the counters and there were two men there and they offered me a hundred and twenty for the watch and when I told them what it was worth, they said it was only worth that if I could find somebody who'd pay that much for it and if I could find anybody who'd pay more than what they were offering, I should sell it to him. Well, I tried a couple more places and that's all they'd offer me. I showed one man the diamond pin, the one worth thirty-five hundred dollars. He said he'd give me seven hundred and fifty.

'So then I showed the pin to Mr. Levy and told him what it was insured for and he wanted to give me seven hundred but when he heard I'd turned down seven-fifty, he said he'd give me eight hundred. He didn't want to but he wanted to maintain a reputation of paying more than other people. So I gave him all the pieces and he paid me three thousand dollars for them. But I want you to understand, all I was trying to do was get what was rightfully mine.'

Trager said, 'You think that three thousand dollars was rightfully yours?'

'I think twenty-five hundred of it was.'

'And what about the extra five hundred?'

'Well, I suppose I wasn't rightfully entitled to that but it's only five hundred dollars and I didn't have any other way to get the money I was rightfully owed.'

Sessions laughed. 'You're a pip, Millie. How much did you really hope to get for selling your boss's jewels?'

She turned to him. 'I don't know what you're saying.'

'You're shocked to find they'll only pay you twenty per cent of the value of the property you're trying to sell. You were expecting a much larger figure. You wanted eighty-three per cent from Abraham on the watch. On nearly thirteen thousand dollars worth of stolen property you must have been hoping to clear almost eleven thousand dollars, right, Millie?'

'Look, I was only trying to get back what was mine.'

'Five pieces of jewellery insured for almost thirteen thousand dollars? Come on, Millie.'

'But I explained that. Those were pieces insured with the Bertram Fox Company. I couldn't take just one, I had to take them all.'

'*And* the insurance policy. *And* one of Mrs. Glazzard's charge plates for identification. That was good thinking, Millie.'

'I know what you're trying to do. You're trying to make it look bad—what I did. But if I'd really wanted to steal, I'd have taken all her jewels. Don't forget that. I could have taken them all. But I didn't. All I wanted was what was coming to me.'

'You wouldn't have taken all her jewellery because then we'd know there was a theft. And you didn't want us to know that, did you, Millie?'

'I'm not a thief. You can't call me a thief. I only got three thousand dollars and that's what I was entitled to. That's why I sold the jewels cheap. I wasn't trying to make a lot of money. I only wanted my twenty-five hundred. And the extra money —you can have it back. I didn't want that. I just didn't know what to do with it.'

'Except there's your brother. You could help your brother with it. That's what you thought, didn't you?'

'Well, yes. I thought Mrs. Glazzard wouldn't mind my using the money for that.'

'And you didn't want to wait till the will was probated to get what was coming to you?'

She shook her head. 'No. I know about wills. Those things drag on and drag on.'

'And you needed money in a hurry. You didn't have much?'

'I had some.'

'You asked Mrs. Glazzard for money, didn't you?'

'No.'

'She wouldn't lend you any, would she?'

'I never asked her for any.'

'What would you do if you needed money in a hurry and Mrs. Glazzard, with all her money and her big apartment and all her jewels, wouldn't lend you any?'

'I don't know.'

'What else did you steal from Mrs. Glazzard?'

'What else?' She looked up. 'Nothing else.'

'Maybe not then. I mean other times.'

'Never anything.'

'This was the first time?'

'Yes.'

'You were desperate this one time.'

'I only wanted what was coming to me.'

'You took a lot more than was coming to you. You wanted a lot of money.'

'I really only wanted twenty-five hundred dollars.'

'When did you kill her? That morning, or the night before?'

Millie turned whiter and shrank. 'No, no. I didn't kill her.'

'You had a big argument with her, didn't you?'

'No, and I didn't kill her. You can't make me say I did.'

'Tell it to us again, Millie. Tell us everything that happened.'

They kept after her until half past three and while they shook her again and again on the jewel theft, they couldn't shake her on the murder claim.

Finally Sessions and Lt. Sullivan went out in the hall for a breather. Sullivan, who had two inches and sixty-five pounds on Sessions, didn't smoke and he watched while Sessions lighted up. 'She sounds like she's telling the truth about the homicide,' he said.

'I know she does,' Sessions agreed. 'She's too mixed up on the stolen property story and too straight on the homicide. There's a sharp line between the two and if she'd perpetrated the homicide to get the property, she'd handle them both the same.'

'I think we'll try to get the D.A. up here to take a statement. This would be a good time.'

Sessions nodded. 'I'll smooth her down a little so she'll co-operate.'

Alfredo Rodriguez came up the stairs and grinned at the pair. In his younger days, Rodriguez had been a lean, dark, handsome Puerto Rican. Now he was thicker around the waist, puffy in the face, and his hair was thinning in back and beginning to fade. He was wearing a raincoat and carrying a photographic envelope which he handed to the lieutenant. 'A Mr. Harper just dropped them off. They're pictues he took at the Buckingham party.'

Sullivan slipped out a dozen $2\frac{1}{2}'' \times 2\frac{1}{2}''$ photographs and negatives and the men started through them. The pictures, on the whole, were disappointing, being small and of crowds of unknown people. 'Is that her from the back in this one?' Then there was one fairly closeup shot of Monica blinking, a cigarette in a holder in one hand, a smile on her face, and Patterson laughing beside her. In one corner was part of the face of Frederick Lyle.

'What's that?' Sessions planted a finger on Monica's dress.

Rodriguez looked. 'A piece of jewellery.'

'Let's get a magnifying glass. That doesn't look like anything on the property list.'

Rodriguez went down to the precinct desk to get the list. Sullivan and Sessions brought the photo in to Millie Butelle. A magnifying glass revealed the piece of jewellery to be a five-pointed star of some kind with a pearl in the centre and Millie said she'd never seen it before. Rodriguez returned with the property list and it wasn't on that.

'And it's not on the insurance list,' Sessions said. 'So

what's that mean? Either it's not valuable enough to insure, or she got it so recently she hasn't had time. What about it, Millie? You lift that too?'

'No, honest. I never saw it before in my life.'

Sessions took up the picture. 'Let me see if I can get hold of Archie Patterson,' he said. 'Maybe he can tell us something.' He went back to the squad room and the nearest phone.

Sessions was lucky on two counts. Dr. Patterson was in and Dr. Patterson remembered about the pin. 'Five-pointed star made of gold filigree,' he said, 'with a large pearl in the centre. Monica had just got it that day from Hong Kong from a family her connections in the Far East had helped get out of Red China. I don't know how valuable it was but she was delighted with it.'

Sessions took the information back to the others. 'And if Millie didn't steal it,' he said, 'the perpetrator must have. I'll take the negative down to photo right now for a blow-up so we can get a flier out on it tomorrow.'

MONDAY 5:30–6:10 P.M.

'Of course there will be the state and federal taxes,' Lawrence Stockton said, 'but when the estate has been probated and everything paid for, I think you'll find yourself quite a well-to-do young lady.'

Linda Glazzard, sitting on the edge of the leather chair in front of Stockton's desk, nodded. It should have meant something to her but it didn't. She made more money on her job than she spent. She didn't need Monica's fortune.

'There's the apartment,' Stockton went on. 'There's nothing

owing on that. That's yours outright. Of course, there's the maintenance fee. That's one thousand a month.'

'Am I supposed to pay that?' Linda said, taking cognisance suddenly.

Stockton smiled. 'No, no. That will come out of the estate. Now there are some other items. Her jewellery. We have a list. There are some pieces stolen, I understand. Of course you won't be taxed for those. But you will be taxed for the insurance payments made on the stolen pieces. You'd understand that, of course?'

'Naturally.'

'There are quite a lot of stocks. My lists aren't up to date. Mrs. Glazzard's broker is supposed to keep me informed but I'm afraid he's rather lax about that and I haven't seen Mrs. Glazzard's own papers yet. I'm hoping to go over them as soon as the police are through.'

Linda thought of the police and it made her think of Frank Sessions. Thinking of Frank made her think of Randy and thinking of him made her unhappy. She'd chuck all this money the lawyer was talking about if she could have Randy instead. She could see herself as a rich old spinster, dry and withered in her marble palace. She'd rather have a husband and live in a tent. And not that marriage was that good, either. For many of her friends, male and female, it had been the horrors. Much could be said for the career girl and her freedom to live as she liked, but Linda still yearned for the lost. For career girls, she told herself, loneliness wasn't the pang it was to her. They'd had parents and siblings to love and be loved by. Affection wasn't dammed up in them crying for an object to expend itself on. They didn't know the hunger of being uncared about. And what was a person to do with all this great sum of money she was getting if there was no one to spend it on or with but oneself? She was getting maudlin, she told herself sharply. It was more of that self-pity bit. It was a fault she just had to get over.

'How much is there? In stocks, I mean?' she asked, feeling

she should show some interest. She could, after all, be far worse off. She could not only be without love, she could also be without means.

'Well, as I said, I don't have an up-to-the-minute report. However, I think I can give you a rough idea. Twelve hundred shares of General Motors. One thousand shares of U.S. Steel. Your mother, I might mention, was very good with money. She invested in solid, reliable companies. This is a benefit you will reap. There's another thousand shares of International Business Machines. Five hundred in AT&T, five hundred in Union Carbide, and a number of lesser investments. In addition, she has a quarter of a million dollars invested in municipal bonds at three point twenty-one per cent. That's a rather small interest rate but it's tax-free and in her income bracket, that's more profitable than five and six per cent.'

Linda was sorry she'd asked. She didn't really want to bother her head with figures. As long as there was enough to pay the rent and buy the things she wanted, she was content. Anything more than that was likely to become a headache and from the way Stockton was talking, it promised to be a large headache. 'Well, I guess it doesn't matter,' she said. 'It'll all get cleared up sooner or later and we'll know what it comes out to and then I can figure out what to do about it.'

Stockton cleared his throat. 'Our firm has handled your mother's legal affairs for nearly a quarter of a century. A condition most satisfactory to both parties. If you do not have a firm to which you are attached, Stockton, Bates and Pierce would be pleased if you would consider us for your legal work.'

'Well I guess you're used to it,' Linda said, smiling slightly at the stuffiness of the Stockton part of the firm. 'And I certainly haven't any other legal connections. I don't lead that complicated a life.'

She stood up and Stockton was quickly on his own feet. 'I think you will find,' he said, 'that life will be a little less simple once you become one of the moneyed class. Stockton, Bates and Pierce, however, would try to keep you from being bothered more than is absolutely necessary.'

'Thank you,' Linda said primly and went out.

The moneyed girl did not hop into a cab when she got out on Park Avenue. She didn't even take the 57th Street bus home. She walked instead. 'That for money,' she said to herself, snapping her fingers, and went the whole distance even though it was starting to rain by the time she reached the canopy of her own building, down a little from the corner of Second Avenue.

Bill was on the revolving door when she came through and he made a comment on the weather, saying the reservoirs ought to be pretty nearly full by now. Linda agreed and started for the elevators and then almost dropped her purse in shock. Getting up from one of the green leather visitors' couches back of the pillars was Randy Benson.

'Oh, no,' she said and her emotions went chasing wildly through her body, shock, excitement, hope, caution, fear, love, every kind of feeling she knew.

He gave her one of those smiles that made a girl ache, and came forward. 'Very cold for May,' he said. 'Since we're talking about the weather. How are you?'

He had her arm and she let him propel her to the elevator. 'I'm fine.' She was, too, except she wasn't sure her legs would hold her. 'Where did you come from?'

'Pittsburgh.'

The elevatorman murmured a greeting and pushed the nine button and the doors closed. Linda smiled at him and said to Randy, 'Are you—is everything—did your aunt . . . ?'

'I have to go back. This is just a quick trip in for reasons that will become evident if I can persuade you to invite me in for a drink.'

She felt warm and gay and a little bit giddy. She smiled. 'Oh do come in for a drink.'

'Why thank you, ma'am, I'd be delighted.'

She gave him the key and he opened the door for her, threw on the hall light and the switch inside the living room which turned on the large table lamps flanking the couch. She went over and drew the blinds against the cold, grey and rainy late afternoon. Then she turned with the room between them and shook her head at him. 'If anybody had told me . . .'

'That I'd be here right now . . . That's what life is all about. Surprises.'

'When did you come in?'

'I flew in this afternoon. And where were you? I arrived down below at five-twenty and expected to find you in. Instead, here it is six o'clock.'

'Monica's lawyer wanted to see me—read me the will and explain all about it.'

'Oh. Is that good or bad—the explaining bit?'

She laughed. 'It's only that it's going to take a lot of time before everything gets settled and I find out how much there is and how much I get.'

'You don't know how much you get?'

'Only that I get everything after her cleaning woman and her secretary and a few bequests are taken care of.'

Randy laughed. 'I hope it's a lot.'

'It promises to be, I guess. The man said I'm to be a woman of substantial means. So pay attention. I'm to be a woman of means.'

'Substantial was the word. Do you think you can manage to stoop to mixing me that drink you invited me in for? The flight wasn't a dry one but the wait downstairs was.'

'Yes, of course.' She went into the bar in the corner for the bucket and took it to the refrigerator for ice. He followed and stood in the doorway. 'I've missed you.'

Her heart stopped and she had to pause before opening the door. The talking was going to start and she didn't want it to yet. For just a few minutes she wanted to have it go on like this—just a little more fond kidding. Just in case the talk was bad talk and there would never be any more anything. 'I, ah—did you?' she said lightly and got out the ice.

'Don't you know I did? I haven't been able to think about anything else but you ever since this started.'

She couldn't think of a light answer now. She couldn't think of anything. She turned her back when she broke out the cubes because her eyes were filling. Randy said, 'It was all my fault.'

She shook her head quickly and dropped ice into glasses. 'No it isn't.'

'I deserted you, darling.'

She turned and went past him, holding the glasses, keeping her head low. She murmured, 'I did worse than that to you.'

He let her put rye in the glasses, then he took her by the arm and led her to the couch. 'Now we're going to sit and talk.' He moved in close beside her, took her free hand in his and said, 'I love you. That's the first thing I want to say. I love you.'

She put her glass down and pressed her fist to closed eyes. 'How can you? After what I've done. After what I am.'

'What you are is the finest, most wonderful, beautiful, desirable girl in the world. Nothing else matters.'

'Other things do matter. Oh, Randy, don't you know? Didn't you understand me over the phone last night?'

'I understood you. You thought I had left you and therefore you did something you would not have done otherwise.'

'But I didn't wait to find out if you'd left me or not.'

'That doesn't matter, darling. It was the way you felt at the time. You were alone and deserted. Your defences were weak. And to cap it off, this occurred at a time and place where seduction was possible and with a man who was interested in seducing you.' He patted her hand. 'Don't fret. Stop thinking you're reverting to the way you were before. That's totally different from what you've told me it was like before treatment.'

'Do you want to know how and where it all happened?'

'No I don't. I don't want to know anything about it.'

He was forgiving her and she knew she should keep quiet but she couldn't. Was it her guilt complexes? Did she have to torture herself and those she loved in order to atone? Or was it honesty; making sure that Randy would know just how bad it had been before he forgave her? Or was she trying to get him not to forgive her—trying to run away from the happiness she thought she wanted? 'I want to tell you,' she said. 'I want you to know. It was—he was a—he's a detective. It was in his apartment.'

Randy was incredulous. 'A detective?'

'The one trying to find out who killed Monica.'

Randy's face grew dark. 'The louse. The scum. Seducing an innocent girl . . . We can report him. He can be broken. I'll get him thrown out of the department!'

She put both hands on his knee. 'No, Randy. Stop. It wasn't his fault. He didn't drag me up to his apartment. I went up there.'

'What for?'

'To tell him about the missing jewellery. Five pieces of my mother's jewellery were stolen.'

'I know.'

'You do?'

'It was in the Pittsburgh papers. But that's the point. You go up there on an innocent errand to help him with the case and when he gets you in his lair, he plays on your loneliness and . . .'

'No he didn't. It was all my doing.'

'Darling, if you're going to defend him by trying to make me believe that you seduced him, well, I'm afraid you're wasting your time. I know what cops are like.'

'But I didn't have to go up there.'

'You did. You had evidence.'

'I didn't have to go to his apartment to give it to him. I wanted to. I waited for an hour for him to come home just sc I could go up to his apartment to tell him about it.' She began to weep. 'I didn't have it in my mind consciously when

I went up there but I think subconsciously I must have wanted to be seduced.'

Randy was sober now and he didn't touch her. 'Are you in love with him?' he asked quietly.

She wiped her eyes and then clutched her hands between her knees. 'No,' she said, staring off at the wall. 'No, I'm not in love with him. I think I just felt an affinity for him. I was so lonely and there he was, the loneliest creature I've ever seen. The loneliest one in the world. I was drawn to him. Maybe I wanted to suffer with him.'

Randy touched her now. He stroked her hair. 'Then it's all right. If you're not in love with him, it's all right.'

'What's right about it? That makes it all the more wrong.'

'No, no, sweetheart. It makes it all right. Because, if you're not in love with him, then I haven't lost you. That's why I flew in today. After you wouldn't answer my calls last night. No matter what happens in Pittsburgh to my aunt, I had to see you today. Wait.' He got up and crossed to the chair where he had lain his coat and came back with a small square box wrapped in white paper with a green ribbon.

He sat with her again, slipping his left arm around her waist and laying the box in her lap. 'I brought you this.'

She said tremulously, 'You brought me . . . ?'

'I don't have a diamond ring to give you yet because I haven't the money yet. This is a substitute. It belonged to Auntie and she's given it to me. She said it's for The Girl when I find The Girl. Darling, if you'll take it, it means I love you and want to marry you and it binds us together forever.'

'Randy.' The tears fell faster as she undid the paper and opened the box. Then she said, 'Oh, Randy, it's beautiful,' and lifted it out.

It was a five-pointed star made of filigreed gold with a large pearl in the centre.

TUESDAY 4:30–4:55 P.M.

Con Devlin walked into the lobby of Robert Motley's apartment building at half past four Tuesday afternoon with a brisk step and one of the newly arrived fliers in his pocket. The flier was what he had been waiting for.

He flashed his shield when the doorman tried to intercept him. 'Robert Motley and don't bother to announce me.'

The elevator was off at some foreign floor and Devlin didn't wait for it but took the service stairs. That was the thing about doormen. Tell one you're a cop and while you're riding the elevator up, he's on the phone to the tenant giving him a chance to sneak down the back stairs. Well, Motley was only on the third floor so he wouldn't have time to go anywhere. And Motley was in his room because Lt. Sullivan had put him under surveillance and he hadn't been seen since the first contact was made—when he had returned to the apartment at half past eleven the night before.

On the third floor he rang Motley's bell and positioned himself before the door so that if Motley opened the peephole, he'd clearly see who it was. Opening the peephole behind the door made very little noise but Devlin was listening for it for he suspected Motley would look before he opened. Motley and women. Most men did not, for they weren't in fear.

He heard the sound and waited for the turn of the lock. It didn't come so he pounded on the metal door. 'Come on, Motley,' he said loudly. 'I know you're in there so open up.'

The lock did turn then and the door opened an inch to where the chain stopped it. Motley's face in the slot had an innocent expression. 'Oh, you're one of those detectives.'

'Detective Devlin. That's right.' He showed his shield. 'Open up.'

Motley opened up without a great deal of pleasure and followed the detective down the hall to the small but nicely furnished living room that looked out on a back court. 'Why'd you lie to us?' the detective said when he turned around.

Motley stopped just inside the room. 'I didn't lie to you.'

'You said you came from Sacramento. That's a lie.'

'No it isn't.'

What's the name of the filling station guy you worked for out there?'

Motley's eyes narrowed and his manner stiffened. His voice got coarser. 'Listen, Devlin, I know what you're after. Monica was murdered and you want to make me the patsy. I've been waiting for that and I'm going to tell you something. I'm not going to answer any questions you ask me without my lawyer being present.'

'You don't want to tell us where you come from, huh? You don't want us to know that, huh?'

'I told you where I come from. If you don't want to believe it, then you tell me where.'

'You sure must have loved Mrs. Glazzard, Motley.'

'What's that remark supposed to mean?'

'You don't show up to her funeral, you don't send so much as a rose, you duck out of town when the final services are being held. You don't want to help the police find who killed her. You don't even care.'

'A lot you know. Just what the hell did you think I was going to do, hang around her bier? She'd love that, wouldn't she? Nobody was supposed to know I existed, for Christ's sake. So I go away for a weekend? What of it? What do I want to stay in town for, with all the agony and grief? As for who killed her, sure I want to find out, but I'll be goddamned if I'm going to help you frame me for the job.'

'Where'd you go this weekend?'

'Sacramento, California. I walked.'

Devlin said, 'My lucky partner. Sessions only had to go to Allentown. I had to come here.'

Motley started just a hair. 'Allentown? You mean Pennsylvania?'

'That's the one.'

'What for?'

'Tracking down clues.' Devlin shook his head and laughed. 'That guy Sessions! When he's on a case, I don't think he ever sleeps. Seven o'clock bus he got this morning and he was typing and studying reports last night till 2 a.m. When he's on the scent, he just goes and goes and goes until he's got his man.'

Motley wasn't reacting this time. He sneered instead. 'What're you trying to do, Devlin, con me?'

'Con you? What would I do that for?'

'All right, Sessions is a big hero. So what else is new?'

'You don't think he's so great, huh?'

'I think you're all great. How many cases *haven't* you solved?'

'We don't get them all, kid, if that's what you mean. Most of them, but not all.'

'And Sessions doesn't solve all of his, does he?'

'Nobody does.'

'O.K., so now what is it you're up here for besides trying to scare me because I won't answer your questions?'

Devlin took the folded flier from his pocket, opened it and crossed the room. 'You knew her pretty well. Where did Mrs. Glazzard get this piece of jewellery?'

The blow-up of the pin was moderately successful. One had to guess at the filigree work and the material but the shape of the piece was obvious and the pearl was unmistakable. Below the picture was the printed description.

Motley licked his lips and held himself in firm control. 'I never saw it before in my life,' he said.

'She was wearing it the night she died.'

Motley handed back the paper. 'Well, you can't prove it by me.'

'What other times did she wear it?'

'I told you I never saw it. And you can get the hell out. I'm not going to answer any more of your questions. If you want to try to arrest me, then I'll get a lawyer and we'll see what happens. But until then . . .'

'You'd better get yourself a lawyer,' Devlin said. 'And quick.' He strode past the man and out.

Motley didn't move until the door had latched behind the departing detective. Then he turned and went down to the door himself, threw the double-lock and put on the chain. Then he went into the small bedroom off the hall and slumped onto the bed, his elbows on his knees, his head in his hands.

He started by swearing heavily and virulently, beating his fists against the sides of his head. That detective had meant to upset him. That mention of Allentown was deliberate. Of course Allentown wasn't the actual town. The real town was Larkspur, but it was adjacent to Allentown and if Sessions had got as far as Allentown, who was to say he wouldn't find his way the whole distance—all the way back to the old woman?

Really, it was all her fault. Old, wealthy Elizabeth Anderson. How she had doted on him. And he had played the gallant. She kept him well too, to the great discomfiture of the nieces and nephews.

It had been a nice life. He'd found girls to play with on the side and Elizabeth was very careless with her money, making it possible for him to steal small sums of cash and even an unnoticed bit of jewellery now and then. Unfortunately, Elizabeth caught on in time and finally the bad day came when she, regretfully, told him he would have to leave.

If only she had paid him off, she'd be alive today. But she hadn't. She was prepared to turn him out penniless—as a punishment for his sins—as punishment for taking advantage of her. She, with several thousand dollars in cash stashed away in various spots around the house. He knew the spots, but he couldn't touch the money without her putting the police on his trail. That was obvious when, finally, even his petty thefts had passed the point of the endurable.

So he had killed her and taken the money and it had worked so well. Strangulation, with gloves, the pouring of barbiturates into her stomach, the absconding with the hidden money. In the little town of Larkspur, it had been called a suicide the moment the sleeping potion was found down her throat. Also there were her fingerprints on the bottle and glass which he'd been careful to preserve. No real investigation was conducted. And, since few people knew of his own existence, nobody was going to make a big deal out of an obvious suicide by dragging him in for any questioning. And, of course, the family was hardly sorry she was dead, especially since they inherited everything. They were only too relieved when he himself didn't try to contest the will and make his relationship public.

It had worked so well that time he was sure it would be equally effective when it became time to get rid of Monica. Monica, who was someone you had to admire, no matter how grudgingly. She had spotted him for a phony at that first party when they met. He couldn't fool her for one moment with that struggling, dedicated artist line and the New School courses. She had a sixth sense about poor men seeking wealthy attachments and she laughed at him.

But she had her Achilles' heel too. If she saw through him, she didn't see through herself. She didn't see, as he did, that the way to win her over was to confess all. The more he admitted to being a fraud, the more he delighted her. It was such a delicious joke, a joke only they shared. That was the start. And in the end, she became the attachment.

Unfortunately, though, being enamoured of him didn't keep her from being wise to him. She didn't leave cash and jewels around uncounted. One false move that way would find him in jail and he knew it. And she owned everything he had, from the apartment she paid the rent on, to the furniture, to the clothes on his back, to the spending money she gave him charily—making it all but impossible for him to play around with anyone else. She had him tied to her all right.

But she tied him too tightly. He was thirty-two now and reaching an anxious age. How long would life go on like this? When would she tire of him? And how much charm would he have left? Would he be too old to find another rich woman to play lapdog for?

The only answer was marriage. To a rich woman, of course —old or young didn't matter. Then he'd have a claim on the estate if he outlived his wife, or he could realise a handsome profit if she wanted to get rid of him. But Monica—how she laughed when he'd mentioned marriage to her. Till the tears rolled down her cheeks, that's how she laughed. Marriage to Monica was out, but the way she kept him under lock and key, it was hard to meet other eligibles.

Until the time he had to hide in another room when Monica's daughter came to call. That was the first he knew of Linda and the first glimpse he had. But from then on it was easy. She didn't have her mother's worldly wisdom and she reacted properly to the struggling artist bit. Only this time he was a struggling writer rather than a painter.

Of course the double game couldn't go on forever. If he could have eloped with Linda it might have been all right. There'd be a wedding licence to contend with when Monica found out. But Linda *had* to tell her mother, *had* to introduce her to the prospective husband. That very effectively removed all the alternatives. Monica had to go.

And so she had, but it wasn't at all like the Larkspur case. He'd pulled the dying-aunt-in-Pittsburgh routine on Linda the next day so that Randy Benson would not have to appear with her in front of people who knew him as Robert Motley. And then he'd sat back to await the suicide verdict in the quiet of his room.

Instead, what he got was a thousand varieties of hell. The stupid Millie didn't discover Monica's remains when she was supposed to and when she did, damned if the police didn't come promptly knocking at his own door. That was the critical moment—when they ordered him to headquarters. If Linda were going to be there . . . But she was back at the apartment, as he phoned to find out.

If he was spared that, other horrors were in store. The police suspected murder right from the first and they really started digging. It wasn't supposed to be like that at all. He had to stay in hiding and finally leave town during all the funeral business to keep out of Linda's sight and away from possible reporters. Fortunately the existence of Robert Motley was kept out of the press and the risk that his picture would get in the papers was eliminated. Nevertheless, he had to keep hopping and bouncing trying to juggle everything right. Like the fight with Linda over the man in her apartment. His outrage was good for it allowed him to cut off communication during the funeral days. But it was bad because by the time he forgave her, she'd committed a genuine indiscretion—with that hideous detective of all people—and she wouldn't forgive herself.

So he had to come in in person and woo her and, to nail her down for good and all, give her a gift. It was a perfectly safe gift. Monica was wearing it the last time he saw her and she told him—before she discovered he was there to kill her—that it had only arrived that day. It was the only thing of hers he had dared to steal and then, since it really wasn't worth a great deal, he had given it to Linda as a down payment on the fortune he'd soon be marrying. Only that damned detective and his picture! They knew about it, knew Monica had been wearing it, knew it had been stolen by her killer. It wasn't safe after all. It was about the least safe thing he could have taken.

And he'd given it to Linda. The police would show her the picture and she'd say, 'Randy Benson,' and in no time the police would discover that Randy Benson was Robert Motley and . . . But he wouldn't think about that.

The question was, had the police got to Linda yet? He looked at his watch. It was ten minutes of five. She was still at Cowan and Blakeslee. The chances were the detective had tried Motley before Linda in the first place and that he wouldn't go to her place of work in the second. He might be waiting for her to come home. In which case . . .

He picked up the phone and dialled, clearing his throat, passing a hand over his hair, acquiring a controlled, calm manner. 'Extension forty-one,' he said smoothly when he got the 'Cowan and Blakeslee. Good afternoon' response.

'Hello, darling,' he said when Linda came on. His voice sounded happy but his face was drawn and sweat was pouring down his cheeks. He had to plan it fast and plan it right.

'Randy,' she breathed into the mouthpiece. 'Oh, Sweet.' Then, 'Where are you?'

'Back in New York again. I may be able to stay now. I'll tell you about it. We'll have dinner.'

'I'd love to. Where will . . .'

'I'll pick you up in a cab outside the Seagram Building in ten minutes.'

She said yes and he hung up. So far so good. Detective Devlin hadn't got to her yet and if he were waiting for her at 302 East 57th Street, it'd be a long, long wait, for she would never go there again.

First there'd be dinner and then he'd take her to the small apartment he'd rented for wooing purposes under Randy Benson's name. But not until after dark. He didn't want people seeing them go in together and him leaving later alone.

He got up and went through drawers for the pair of gloves he'd used before. He'd strangle her as he'd strangled Monica and then what? Leave her in his room? Better yet, there was the roof. Over the edge and into the court. Without identification, of course. They might never find out who she was, let alone how or why she came to be at the end of a six-storey drop.

He'd hate to do it. He really had feelings for her and his love-making with her was not all calculation. And, of course, it was goodbye fortune. Goodbye to the golden dream he had nurtured and worked so hard for. All the effort for nothing.

But it was a question of survival now. Never mind money, never mind his feelings for the girl. That damnable pin he'd stolen. If it didn't cost his life it was costing him everything else.

He put his wallet in his jacket. It contained all the money he had and it wasn't much. And dinner and cab fare would have to come out of it. He'd have to hope Linda had a wad with her.

He hiked down the hall and out to the elevator. Outside, he waved off the doorman to avoid the tip and started hunting for his own cab.

And across the street, a man who had been parked for hours in front of a hydrant made a note on a clipboard, reached forward and switched on his ignition.

TUESDAY 9:00–9:20 P.M.

Frank Sessions walked into Boro Headquarters at nine o'clock that evening. Mike Connager and Ray Ecklin, his regular partners, were on with Sergeant Remick—Connager typing DD5s out in the homicide space, Remick and Ecklin reading in the office.

'You get your perpetrator yet?' Sessions asked Connager as he came in.

'No. Just two false alarms. How're you doing?'

Sessions grinned and took off his coat. 'I got a make, kid.'

That brought Ecklin and Remick to the door. 'On the Glazzard case?'

'Damned right.' Sessions lighted a cigarette. 'All I got to do is find a way to make it stick.'

'Who's the perpetrator?'

'Motley. The lover-boy. Just the way we figured it.'

'What've you got on him?'

'Nothing. That's the damned trouble. At least nothing yet. But he's our boy.'

'How do you know, Frank?'

'Because he did it before. Same M.O. Strangled woman with barbiturates poured down her throat. Out in a place called Larkspur, Pennsylvania.'

'What happened?'

Sessions sat down on the corner of one desk. 'I get out to Allentown around ten and look up this bank that's had an account for Motley. He closed it out a year ago October, but they've got his old record and his old address. It's a few miles outside of Allentown in a place called Larkspur. So I go there, talk to the landlord, the tenants and staff, and I find he left in August of that year. Last week in August. What's more, the lease was signed by an Elizabeth Anderson and had six months to run. Come to find out the estate paid off the lease because Elizabeth Anderson passed away after she paid the August rent and before September's. So who's Elizabeth Anderson? Just the wealthiest woman in Larkspur. Died at fifty-eight from an overdose of sleeping pills.

'So I go talk to her relatives and I get it from them that Motley was milking the old lady and she was keeping him. After the suicide—which they didn't question, incidentally—Motley leaves town and, to them, it's good riddance. As for the suicide—alleged suicide—there's no note but no marks on the body. Like the DOA here. I checked with the old woman's doctor. He's the one who signed the death certificate. He did an autopsy. He found barbiturates in the stomach. Verdict suicide. No further investigation.'

Ecklin took his cigar out of his mouth. 'He didn't study the brain tissues?'

'Hell no. Only the stomach. He didn't do the head at all. Or the throat. You suspect barbiturates, you look for barbiturates, you find barbiturates. Why look for anything else?

You come out with your verdict and all your goddam verdict means is you've been conned. Jesus, I'm used to the way they do it in New York. I forget what it's like outside.'

Ecklin said, 'So Robbie-boy comes to New York and gets himself another sucker?'

'Yeah. And pulls the same thing on her. God only knows what the motive was in Larkspur. Maybe she was throwing him out and he didn't like it. Anyway, God only knows what the motive was here. Maybe he was being thrown out again.'

Remick said, 'You got any evidence, Frank?'

'Against Motley? Not a goddam thing. We can't show a motive, we can't prove opportunity, we can't produce a thing against the son of a bitch. All we can do now is watch him—see how he moves. See if he leads us to anything. That reminds me.' He turned and picked up the phone, dialled and got the nineteenth squad. 'Lieutenant? This is Frank Sessions.' He said a few yeahs and laughed and said, 'And let me tell you. The son of a bitch has done it before. Yeah. He killed another woman in Pennsylvania. Allegedly killed, if you want to be technical. In fact, you can't even say allegedly. Nobody knows he did it. So he's the perpetrator here. No doubt about it. . . . That's right, he's it and we can't touch him. Not unless he helps us. So I think we ought to double up on that watch. We ought to have two men around the clock. Which reminds me. Have you got any reports on him so far?'

Sessions put out his cigarette and produced his notebook and pen. 'All right. Wait a minute. Subject left apartment at four fifty-eight. Taxi to . . .' Sessions stopped. 'Hold on a second, Lieutenant. What's that? He met a girl at the Seagram Building? The Seagram Building? . . . What do you mean why am I getting excited? That's where Linda Glazzard works. Linda Glazzard. That's right. Jesus, did the tail get an ID on the girl? . . . Well what about a description?' Sessions nodded into the phone and put another cigarette in his mouth. 'That's Linda. He was picking Linda up for

Christ's sake. What the hell is going on?'

On the other end of the line, Boxton said, 'Maybe they're in it together, Frank.'

'Jesus, who knows? Anything's possible. All right, then what?' He listened and wrote it down. 'Papa Luigi's Restaurant. Fifty-eighth between First and Second. They walked over from the Seagram Building, huh? Entered restaurant at five fifty-five? They sure took their time. What else? No further report? Then they're still there?' Sessions listened some more, said, 'I see. O.K. I'll call in later.' He hung up the phone, lighted the cigarette and shook his head. 'Jesus. Can you tie that?'

'Tie what?' they asked and he told them. Motley and Linda were a twosome, dining together. The daughter and her mother's lover. 'And she said she didn't know Motley. She didn't even know her mother had a lover.' Sessions laughed bitterly. 'And you know something? I believed her. I must be getting soft in the head.'

Ecklin said, 'You figure they're in it together?'

'It looks that way. The funeral's over now, the heat's off. They don't know they're being watched. They think it's O.K. to start seeing each other again.' Sessions made a face. 'Now the pieces are beginning to fit. And it's not a pretty picture.'

Connager, who knew little about the case since he was tied up with his own, was listening with his hands clasped behind his head, his chair tilted back. 'What would they need to kill the mother for?'

'Her money, of course. Linda inherits. What do you want to bet they get married before the first of the month and he moves in with her?'

Ecklin said, 'You sound bitter, Frank. You act like it's never been done before.'

'It's been done a million times. And it'll be done a million times more. With him, it figures. With her . . . ?' He shrugged. 'I didn't figure it.'

Remick laughed. 'Don't feel bad about it, Frank. After all,

she's a woman and a damned beautiful one too.'

Ecklin removed the cigar from his mouth. 'Stacked is the word, Sergeant.' He put the cigar back in his mouth.

'Stacked is a good word,' Remick agreed. 'So if she takes Frankie-boy for a ride, well, what do you expect?'

Frankie-boy said a four-letter word which made the others laugh uproariously. He looked at his watch and it said nine-fifteen. 'They wouldn't still be at dinner,' he said aloud.

Remick paused in his laughter. 'What's the tail say?'

'The tail's a new guy named Lesgroe who I don't know at all. He's using his own car and it doesn't have a police radio in it. He's got to find a phone every time he wants to report.'

'What are you itching for?'

'I'd like to pick the two of them up. I'd like to run them into the nineteenth, separate them and see what they have to say.'

'Motley won't say anything. Devlin's tried.'

'The girl would talk. I'd make her open up.'

Ecklin laughed. 'I'll tell you, Frank. If you can charm a girl so much that she'll break down and confess a homicide, I'll say you're not just a great lover, you're the greatest lover that ever lived.'

'You're wasting your time,' Remick said. 'I can tell you what both of them will do. They'll sit tight and call for a lawyer. You won't get them to tell you their names.'

Ecklin sighed. 'Ah for the good old days before Miranda. Life was easier then.'

The phone rang out front and the sergeant at the desk came back to say it was for Remick. He went into the office to take it and Sessions mashed his cigarette under his foot viciously. Linda and Motley. He'd never foreseen that at all and it irked him that he'd been taken in. Maybe it wouldn't do any good to bust them up but he wanted to anyway.

When Remick came back, he had his notebook open. 'There's a dead baby over in the three-two. Looks like natural causes but the officer on the scene reports what appear to be a couple of scratches on the baby's face. And with these child homicides they've had over there, McVey wants to be sure. I told him we'd take a look.'

Ecklin and Connager got up and went into the office for their coats. Sessions picked up the phone and dialled again. Remick said, 'You want to come, Frank? Get a bite on the way back—assuming it's not a homicide.'

Frank said, 'Naw, I'm still bugged about this one. Hello, Lieu. Sessions again. Any further report? . . . Nothing? Is Lesgroe supposed to call in? . . . Well they wouldn't still be at the restaurant for Christ's sake. What would they be doing there? They went in at six o'clock. . . . Look, I'll come over there.'

He hung up and intercepted Remick. 'Which car are you using? Two ninety-nine? Then I'll get the keys to two forty-five.'

TUESDAY 9:30–10:10 P.M.

Detective Jerry Lesgroe moved his car down Second Avenue, across 57th Street and pulled into the bus stop in front of the yellow and chrome Liberal Arts High School. Robert Motley and the girl he was with were only slightly ahead of him, walking hand in hand in a leisurely, goalless manner. It was half past nine and dark. They had spent three hours in the restaurant, an incredible length of time which Lesgroe couldn't understand, and now they were walking at a snail's pace down Second Avenue. It was as if they were deliberately killing time.

Lesgroe turned off his lights but let his motor run as he waited behind parked cars until his quarry had crossed 56th Street before he moved out into traffic again. The strolling couple were heading in the opposite direction from Motley's apartment on East 75th Street, out for a walk, but going where?

In a few more minutes, Lesgroe found out. They turned right on 53rd and Lesgroe made the turn, parked the car in front of a hydrant and waited. The couple strolled past the entrance of some new white brick apartments, then turned and went up the steps to the high stoop of a six-storey, old red brick apartment beyond. They went inside and Lesgroe was already out of his car and walking up the other side of the street, watching. He crossed over when he got there, climbed the steps to the high stoop and went into the vestibule. The inside door to the hall and stairs was locked, which meant one of the two had a key and since Motley's name didn't appear next to any of the bells or on the letter boxes, Lesgroe concluded it was the home of the girl, though it seemed a pretty poor dwelling for someone who worked in the Seagram Building.

Lesgroe went back outside, copied the address, came down the steps and crossed the street. What was he to do now? What was this place? Did the girl really live there? Or was it friends? Or was it kept as a love nest? He could guess what Motley and the girl went up there for. A three-hour dinner, a leisurely stroll back to an apartment, and they'd be settling in for some sex. That much you could pretty well guess at. So what should he do? Go up to Third Avenue and find a phone, or sit down and watch the door and wait for however long it took them to come out?

Motley was supposed to be a murder suspect. There were others, but Motley was the one the homicide boys liked best for the job. They had no evidence so they were shadowing him to see what would develop. Well, Lesgroe had been doing the shadowing since he'd relieved Detective D'Amato in front of Papa Luigi's and been shown the man he was to follow. And as far as he was concerned, the homicide boys were all wet. He could testify that Motley didn't look any part of a murder suspect. He looked like a man in love. And obviously he and the girl had gone into the apartment building to do a little loving, after which they'd reappear. He'd presumably take her home and go home himself. Or maybe it really was her apartment and after a while he'd reappear alone and go home.

But Lesgroe's orders were to phone in at every opportunity and maybe Lieutenant Boxton would like to know about this particular address. It meant nothing to Lesgroe but he wasn't even in the nineteenth detective squad. He belonged in the thirty-fourth and hadn't had his gold shield more than a month—which was probably why he'd been called in on extra duty in this case. They were calling in a lot of people for extra duty but the new men would get the heaviest load. Rank, after all, had its privileges.

Well, he'd assume the couple wouldn't be coming out right away and he'd have time to make the phone call. 221 East 53rd. Lt. Boxton could make of that what he wanted.

Linda Glazzard slipped off her coat as the man she expected to marry bolted the door behind them. She said, 'Oh, I feel so stuffed.' She stretched and went to the mirror. It was a small, two-room apartment with a combination bedroom-sitting room opening off the door and a small kitchenette and bath behind.

'That's why I thought we ought to walk,' the man said. He smiled at her primping her hair in the mirror and fondling the filigreed gold pin. He could walk right over to her now, if he wanted, and seize her by the throat from behind. There would be no outcry, only the sound of the scuffle as she'd struggle, but that would end quickly. And, from behind, there'd be no chance of her clawing his face. That's how he'd worked it with Monica and it served him well, for the police were looking at his face less than twenty-four hours later. If there'd been scratches, and then that murder verdict, he could have been in trouble. Elizabeth had scratched him a couple of good ones. Fortunately when he sneaked out of town nobody tried to get him back and murder was never suspected.

But, of course, he couldn't throttle Linda yet. He didn't have his gloves on. They were still in his back pocket. And besides, the apartment was not the place. The damned medical people in New York, in some secret way, knew Monica had been strangled despite the suicide clues he left around. They certainly would know Linda was likewise murdered if he killed and left her here. And maybe he could change names, but his handwriting was on the lease and that couldn't be changed. No, the roof was the place. If he pitched her off, six floors were bound to be fatal. That court out back was pure concrete. Let those damn doctors prove it wasn't suicide this time. Let the damned New York cops find out whom she'd been visiting.

There was only one danger about the roof business. The new apartment next door was fourteen floors high with penthouse. There was the danger of being seen. But the moon was down and how many people looked out? Should he do it now, or wait till later when fewer people would be up? Should he make love to her first, as she was expecting him to do? Or should he suggest they look at the sky? 'How about a drink?' he said.

'No, I've had enough. I'm practically floating now.' She smiled at him and it was a lover's smile. They were alone in a room they'd used for love before. They were engaged. Linda was psychologically ready for love. 'How about some coffee?' he said to stall the matter. However ready she might be, he was not. It wasn't a matter of scruples or even the nervous tension he felt, but the idea of making love to a girl and then throwing her off the roof was totally repellent. Even the thought of touching her was repugnant, knowing what he was going to do. He did not want to kiss her or hold her. He wanted to disassociate himself so that he would be devoid of emotion when the time came, so that he could act without hesitation, without that momentary drawing back that offered her a chance to escape, or might render him totally incapable of going through with it. Yes, there was that possibility. With Elizabeth and Monica there had been no such reaction. But they were older. Though he had successfully feigned love and fascination, they had aroused no feeling in him. But this girl did, and if he stopped to reflect or paused to view her as Linda rather than as a threat to his life, he knew his resolve would waver.

'Coffee,' he said again and moved past her to the kitchenette and the stove.

'Let me do it.'

She came out with him and he stepped aside. 'All right, you can show me how wifely you can be.'

And Linda laughed. She liked that.

Frank Sessions said, 'What's he got?' when Boxton hung up the phone. Boxton sat back in his chair in the office. 'The subject and the girl entered the building at 221 East 53rd Street at nine-forty. You know anything about that address? He says Motley's name isn't on the mailboxes.'

Frank looked at his watch. It was twelve minutes of ten. 'No,' he said. 'I don't know what the hell that's all about. What's the tail's name? Lesgroe?'

'That's right. You going down?'

'It beats going home.'

It was still short of ten when Sessions swung the tan Plymouth into 53rd, headed up the block and pulled in to the kerb. It was by another hydrant but the cars lining both sides of the street encroached so much on the hydrant's space there was barely room.

Sessions got out of the car and crossed the street. Lesgroe was lounging in a doorway opposite 221, smoking a cigarette and acting like a resident taking the cool night air but Sessions made him instantly. 'Lesgroe?' he said softly, going up to him.

Lesgroe's eyes narrowed. 'Who are you?'

'Sessions. Homicide.'

'Oh, O.K.' Lesgroe flicked the cigarette. 'I'm Lesgroe. With the three-four.' He shook hands. 'They're still in there unless they sneaked off while I was phoning. The subject and a blonde girl. I don't have any ID on her.'

'I do. Her name's Linda Glazzard. She's the daughter of the deceased.'

'The daughter?' Lesgroe jerked a thumb at the building. 'And him? They in it together?'

'Those who kill together sleep together. That's how I make it.' He turned to cross the street.

'You going to break in on them?'

A corner of Sessions' mouth tightened and he turned. 'The hell with them,' he said bitterly. 'Let them have their fun. They did enough to earn it. I just want to go see what names are listed in the vestibule.'

Lesgroe went with him and they mounted the steps to the high porch, brightly lighted by lamps on either side of the door. They went inside and Sessions ran his finger down the names alongside the buzzer buttons. It took him three seconds to spot Randy Benson's name in the slot for 4A. 'Jesus Christ,' he said and tried the door.

'What's the matter?'

'I think the son of a bitch ditched the mother to get the daughter and she doesn't know it. That's a different kind of a story.' He pressed several of the first-floor buttons and laughed with a certain relief. 'Let's pay them a visit after all and hear what she says when she finds she's being victimised.'

Linda climbed the stairs slowly. She didn't really want to go up on the roof and she couldn't understand Randy's insistence. Of course it would be nice out and the towering buildings, lighted and spotlighted, would be beautiful but what did that have to do with the scheme of things? They had, unexpectedly, another night together and presumably, since he called her, wined and dined her and brought her back to his humble abode, he wanted to finish it as he had before. This was what she was prepared for, what everything should be leading to, and yet, here he was stalling in the strangest manner. First a cup of coffee, now a visit to the roof for a look at the view. 'I didn't know you were such a lover of views,' she said as they reached the sixth-floor hall and went around to the special stairs that led to the roof.

He laughed lightly but it was really forced. It was a bad job. He hadn't been able to sell her on a trip to the roof at all. She was patiently waiting for him to take her in his arms and start the activities the whole evening had pointed toward, and she was not at all interested in rooftops. His excuses to drag her up there had been lame and awkward, and he'd be hard put trying to justify them afterward. But there wouldn't be any afterward and there wouldn't be any delay on the roof. He'd get her to the edge and over just as fast as he could.

She opened the door and stepped out onto the rough tarred surface. 'Look at that,' he said, following and gazing over at the white brick fourteen-floor and penthouse apartment beside them. He said it without a great deal of enthusiasm for there really were an awful lot of windows lighted and they threw an awful lot of light on the roof. To the left, however, was something he liked better. Beyond the masonry railing that divided his roof from the roof of the next apartment building was another doorway down. That was a good touch. After she went over the rail at the back, he could go down the stairs in the next building instead of his own. He could go down and out without ever having to return to his own room. He could leave by a different front door and never come back at all.

'Well,' Linda was saying, 'now you've shown me the roof. You got anything else?'

He was going to have to touch her. 'Come on,' he said, putting his arm around her waist. 'Don't be in such a hurry. Let's enjoy it up here.'

Damn it, he thought, I can't go down in the next building.

I'll have to go back to 4A. Her coat's there, my coat's there. Her purse is there. I'm going to need every cent she's got. To her, he said, 'Let's see what's down in the back yards.'

Frank Sessions and Jerry Lesgroe climbed the stairs slowly. Down on the first floor, people were opening doors, wondering who'd rung for them, but the detectives had already passed from view. They found 4A around the corner from the top of the stairs and Frank rapped sharply on the door. There was no response and he tried again. He turned the knob and the door swung in. Two coats, a woman's purse, and coffee things were there but no people. 'What the hell,' Sessions muttered. 'Did they hear us coming?' He checked the kitchenette and bath, throwing open the little bathroom window that looked out on the back court. There was nothing there for the fire-escape went down the front of the building. Frank and Lesgroe went out into the hall to the windows on the street but the dust there had not been disturbed. 'They didn't use the fire-escape,' he said. 'Suppose you try the cellar, Lesgroe, and I'll try the roof. They can't have gone far, they only just left.'

'No, I don't like the edge.'

'Don't be silly. Look how high the rail is, darling. It's perfectly safe. Come here.'

'I'm close enough. I can see very well.'

'Lean over so you can look straight down.'

'I don't want to look straight down. What should I want to look straight down for?'

'It's good for you.'

'To look down into an old back yard?'

'To do something you're afraid to do. I'll hold you. I'll hold you so tight nothing can happen.'

'I don't get it. Why is it so important?'

'Oh it's not,' he said, and his voice was offhand but in his heart he was fuming. The cussed perversity of women. She'd only get so close to that rail and no closer. She would not cross that last foot and press her body against the brick and masonry of the railing, she would not lean over it, and without these aids, how was he going to get her over the side? He could not wrestle with her for she would scream. Then strangle her? Or hit her. Knock her unconscious. He'd like to hit her, the recalcitrant, stubborn bitch.

Then Linda was saying, 'All right. If I look down once, will you be satisfied? Then can we leave?'

'Darling, of course.'

'You'll hold me?'

'Ever so tight.'

He took her arm in an iron grip. That would help catapult her. 'All right, darling.'

'Wait. I'm not ready. Randy, what are . . .'

That was the moment Sessions threw open the door. It made noise and the noise made Randy hesitate and in that moment he lost the initiative. 'Shhh,' he whispered to Linda. 'Somebody's up here.'

'Well I don't care if they are,' she whispered back angrily. 'What were you trying to do? I wasn't ready!'

'Shush,' he said and put a hand over her mouth. 'Get down.'

But there weren't any hiding places and Sessions had them spotted. 'Linda. What the hell are you doing up here?' he said and she straightened in wonder.

'And Robert Motley.'

Linda said, 'Who? What?'

'Your friend. Hour mother's friend too. And your mother's pin. Did he give it to you?'

She turned and said, 'Randy,' but he broke and ran. Sessions said, 'Stop!' and drew his gun.

He didn't stop. He vaulted the rail onto the next roof and ran to the doorway to the stairs. Sessions called, 'Halt or I'll shoot,' and let one go in the air. Linda said, 'No!'

The doorway in the other building was locked. He gave two

tugs, then turned and ran on. Linda pulled Sessions' arm. 'Don't kill him.'

'I won't kill him.' He jerked his arm away and fired another shot in the air.

The man didn't stop. He vaulted another railing.

But this time there was no roof on the other side—only six floors of space with a concrete bottom. His scream lasted two seconds and ended in a crunching thud.

WEDNESDAY 3:30–3:50 A.M.

It was half past three by the time Linda got to bed but despite the hour she knew she wasn't going to sleep. Too much had happened, too much that was horrible. Randy had really meant to kill her. Frank explained it to her. Randy—or was it Motley—or was it something else? Her lover. Her fiancé. Her mother's killer.

This was something she was going to have to live with, get used to, learn to endure. But she had loved him—or at least loved the man she thought he was. It was a man who didn't really exist. The man she gave herself to, trusted and believed in, was a monster instead. That was the tough part. And her on-again, off-again marriage plans went off for good and cancelled in a way and for reasons more horrible than any girl deserved. Maybe God was punishing her for her multitudinous sins. Maybe you never were forgiven for what you did, even if you did reform. But where did she get such thoughts? There wasn't any God. Monica wouldn't have Him around. Religion in all shapes and forms were screened from Linda's childhood and when she picked up words and thoughts on the subject from outside, Monica laid them low with acid logic.

No, Linda would have to struggle in an uncertain world

and when the uncertainties became too severe, she would have to turn for succour to her analyst. Gods were unreal but analysts were real indeed. And maybe she had better get back to one and find out where she should go now. A woman pushing thirty, very much in need of a husband.

She thought about Frank Sessions. Could she persuade a man like Frank to accept a halter? Hah, could she persuade him first ever to see her again? He had driven her home after all the statements had been taken and everything was over—well, he and three other detectives had driven her home—and he had told her he was going directly to his own place after that. Well, let him sit in his empty apartment and he'll think of how she filled it. Let him get into that bed and he'll remember when she was there.

Uptown, in his small Third Avenue walkup, a half-dressed Frank Sessions sat on his daybed staring gloomily at the television movie. A cigarette smouldered in the glass ashtray on the coverlet and he held a can of beer in both hands.

He smoked and sat and sipped the beer and watched the television and contemplated the two days off the lieutenant had given him and shifted restlessly. Finally he got up, shut off the set, went in to the phone and dialled a number. When a coarse-voiced man answered, he asked for Liz and said, 'Tell her it's Frank Sessions.'

After a bit a hearty voice said, 'Frankie, honey. What do you know?'

He was brighter now. He laughed. 'Nothing much, Sweetheart. Say, what time do you get through slinging hash?'

'In ten minutes. At four o'clock.' She laughed with rich, mirthful humour. 'Why? As if I didn't know.'

He laughed back. 'How about my coming by for you with a taxi and a toothbrush?'

'It's always a pleasure.'

He hung up, smoothed his hair, whistled a toneless tune and started to dress again.